First Edition: May 2019

Cover Design by Simon Avery

Library of Congress: 2019903828

ISBN: 978-1-7338620-0-4 (e-book)
ISBN: 978-1-7338620-1-1 (paperback)
ISBN: 978-1-9554760-0-3 (hardcover)

Published by Darn Pretty Books

Instagram: @darnprettybooks

i

PREFACE

The Red Rover. Origins.

A story that began as a dream. The Wanderers. Several visions of characters I had just met, yet somehow intimately knew, interacting with a world that felt enthralling, yet often times, unfamiliar.

I awoke with newfound energy, grabbing my behemoth of a laptop, typing what felt like a hundred words a minute; all in hopes of remembering those evocative snippets from my subconscious that feed my literary urges.

Of all the ideas, outlines, synopses, teleplays and screenplays, this one felt different. No, this one was different. It was not just a story. It was THE story. An epic saga that was yearning to be shared with anyone who would dare entertain it.

Orion Moore and his classmates represent the youthful exuberance in all of us; who still believe that there is more to life than what we've been told. That our destiny isn't pre-ordained. That the path to greatness or success or happiness is more than likely to be filled with obstacles. Adversity is par for the course. But adversity does not have to equal failure.

Humanity has proven time and time again, no matter what the circumstances, that they will overcome. They will adapt. They will improve. And most importantly, they will thrive. Despite their inexperience, the members of The Red Rover are cut from the same cloth. Their youth… is the key.

To be a great explorer, one cannot fear the unknown. For it is the unknown that truly makes this life worth living.

ACKNOWLEDGEMENTS

Special thanks to my mother, Deboran Patricia Whitaker and father, Charles Everett Whitaker Jr. for always encouraging my creative pursuits, even if the focus was primarily on improving my spelling and penmanship. I would like to think that I have improved. ☺

To my manager, Le'Ander M. Nicholson at Believeland Management. We met under less-than-ideal conditions, yet here we are, all these years later, taking giant leaps forward one small step at a time. Anyone would be lucky to have an advocate like you in their corner. And you're still short!

To the deceased, who mentored me; my lovely aunt Grenna Francine Whitaker, whose grace and intelligence continue to inspire me to be a better artist, but more importantly, a better human being; and my darling Susan Smith, my former employer, who gave me the tools [both professionally and economically] necessary to succeed in this often-frustrating business of Hollywood. She and I were kindred spirits in many ways.

Last, but most importantly, my best friend and favorite person in the whole world, Allritch C. Tessono Jr.

Junior was a genuine beautiful soul, who passed unexpectedly at the beginning of 2017, the same year I finished the manuscript for The Red Rover. What a bittersweet year that turned out to be. Your laugh was infectious, your humor was always sharp and your smile, could make even the surliest individual, brighten up. How could anyone ever forget those big pearly white teeth?

You were what our mutual friend Noel would appropriately describe as "a good dude." If you ever had the luxury of knowing Cool Breeze that is about the highest praise a person could receive.

Allritch was without question the best good dude I have ever had the pleasure of knowing. None of this happens without his support. It goes without saying that I continue to miss him every single day.

Wherever you are my brother, I sure hope I'm making you proud. I LOVE YOU!

CHAPTER ONE

A DESTINATION CANNOT EXIST WITHOUT A JOURNEY

Orion heard his own heartbeat thumping his eardrums as he sprinted through a winter wilderness. Those beats eventually consumed by the sounds of his huffing and puffing combined with the vibrating crunching melody that his footsteps produced over the snow-covered forest ground. His green eyes opened wide, struggling to focus through his foggy helmet shield: this wooded area, shrouded by snow-capped mountains, was unfamiliar territory to him.

The frozen forest was an environment the faint of heart dare not tread. The trees towered over Orion's head. As he looked skyward, it was clear that they were dizzyingly high. It was hard to tell where the trees stopped and the planet's sky began.

Orion kicked up fresh snow with each step as he trekked through the dark woodlands dressed in his black and chrome spacesuit. His suit protected him from the elements. He was keen to remain on his current path, guided by the several footprints left straight ahead of him. He had done his best to avoid the broken branches as well as the snow-covered holes and steep embankments.

1

Attached to his hip was a matching silver side-arm fusion weapon, the color blending with his spacesuit. The perfect firearm for an unsuspecting enemy. In skilled hands, the powerful tool could be used to diffuse even the most dangerous of situations. However, Orion was still a neophyte.

The perilous conditions, worsened both by the weather and the woefully uneven terrain, caused Orion to lose his balance, sending him sprawling towards the stump of a large tree. He reached out with his gloved hands fanned to break the fall as his side-arm was shaken loose from its magnetic holster, landing on the snowy embankment beside him.

Orion reached for his neck and popped off his chrome helmet, revealing his jet-black hair and baby face. He was a teenager with very youthful features. Whenever he met someone for the first time, they almost always assumed he was younger than his current age. Not that he ever understood the reason. He was thirteen. In some Earth cultures that meant he was already a man.

As his helmet rolled down the slope, he felt the shock of the freezing cold on his nose and ears. His warm breath formed steamy clouds in front of his flushed face. He would soon have frostbite if he didn't keep moving.

Orion took long, deep breaths as he tried to calm his nerves. He staggered to his feet as the guttural growl of an animal startled him.

He immediately crouched back down, staying out of sight. The elements were no longer his primary concern. He looked in the direction of the growl. Trees stretched as far as his eyes could see. He heard the growl again as his eyes searched frantically for the source. Soon, there were more growls in unison. Orion swallowed hard as he trained his eyes on the deep woods, watching for any movement.

"Orion! Where are you?"

Orion turned in the direction of the young female voice that echoed in the distance. That sounded like Rio, a member of his team. God only knew where they were. If they were still nearby, he couldn't see them.

He tried to stand, but his right leg buckled under the weight of his body. He probed his leg for any injuries and then, sensing only minimal pain, steadied himself against a nearby tree and rose to his feet.

He froze against the tree trunk as a pack of ravenous snow leopards emerged from the woods just a few yards away. The only way Orion could see the white spotless beasts was through their dark beady eyes and red gummed mouths filled with jagged teeth. Their growls became more animated as drool seeped from the corners of their jaws. It was feeding time, and Orion was their dinner.

More and more of the leopards came into his line of sight. Orion searched for the pack leader. The first rule in cosmic combat, according to his team's instructors, was to identify the head of a foreign faction before assessing a situation and acting accordingly. The pack leader stepped forward, salivating as the animal sniffed the air with its pointed wet snout.

Orion sharpened his gaze, never once taking his eyes off of them. He was severely outnumbered. He spat in their direction as they continued to growl and slowly stalk towards him. They were feeling him out—to show fear was certain death. He slowly leaned down, his eyes still trained on the predators.

Any sudden movement towards his sidearm could cause the animals to strike. He carefully reached for the weapon, but alas it was gone. He briefly looked at his hip, then the ground around him and back to the leopards.

A bead of sweat trickled down the side of his head. He was defenseless now. Panic bubbled inside him. The pack leader snarled, a showdown was inevitable. Orion inhaled deeply and, like a bolt of lightning, took off running—his injured leg be damned.

The leopards were tenacious in their pursuit. As he weaved through the trees, the leopards fanned out, running parallel in groups on either side. They were closing in.

Orion felt one of the larger leopards gaining on him from his right. He glanced briefly at the creature allowing a second unseen leopard on his left an opening to attack. The leopard leapt towards him as Orion felt the air shift around him. He ducked just in the nick of time as the leopard slammed head first into a tree, yelping as Orion didn't dare look back again. His mistake had only allowed them to catch up to him in the first place, there wouldn't be a second time.

He ran deeper into the thick forest, as the howls faded in his wake.

"Uh… guys, we're running out of woods here."

Rio removed her helmet and looked out at the wide expanse of the crystal blue lake roughly fifty feet below her. The cold air caused her freckled cheeks to tighten. She had reached the edge of the forest as the other five members in her group came running up.

Rio turned and looked at her team briefly before looking back at the calm, serene lake setting. Before she could address her group, one of them zipped by her, taking a flying leap off the cliff, flipping into a perfect swan dive: *Jovan.*

Rio watched stunned as gravity pulled Jovan towards the water like a missile. His body was rigid, his fingers balled up almost as if he were a superhero flying to save the day. Jovan cracked the lake with a whisper as the water rippled slightly in all directions.

The other four team members joined Rio at the edge of the precipice. They looked on, speechless, as Jovan swam towards the cavern shore.

"Show off!" Gordie said, shaking his head back and forth.

"Where's Orion?" Callista's voice bordering on panic.

The remaining five looked at one another. At some point during this mission they had lost their young comrade.

"I don't know, but I'm not waiting around to find out." Gordie declared as he followed Jovan's lead and jumped off the cliff. He slammed into the water with a great splash.

"Guys, we can't just leave him behind." Rio continually looked back to the forest, hoping Orion would reveal himself.

"Yeah, but we also can't fail the mission. Come on Drew." June said as she grabbed her adopted brother's arm and they leaped over the edge together.

Callista gave Rio and apologetic look. "Sorry Rio," she said before diving over the edge, leaving Rio standing alone on the cliff.

Rio watched her land in the water, sighing as she rested her head back against a tree. She was having a hard time reconciling that none of them were willing to look for Orion or even wait a few minutes to see if he showed up. June did have a point, though, regarding the mission. If Orion were lost, there was not much she could do about it without the rest of her team.

Rio took one final look back into the woods, still no sign of him. She put her helmet back on, securing it tightly, before reluctantly leaping off the cliff. She crashed into the frigid depths, resurfacing in seconds. She swam to the shore to join the rest of her team.

<>

Orion ran towards the cliff. Footprints all around, although his team was nowhere in sight. He turned back to the forest. The snow leopards had caught up with him once more and had gathered several feet away. Orion peered down the steep drop to the lake and saw his team gathered on the shoreline.

The growling grew louder behind him. Orion returned his attention to the snow leopards. He grabbed on a low tree branch and began to climb. He needed time to figure out his next move.

"Orion!" Jovan called out.

He looked back down towards the lake.

"You have to jump."

Orion clung tightly to the tree as the snow leopards began to stalk him in a crescent moon formation. He hadn't climbed so high that the leopards would give up hope.

They were closing in on him as Orion continued to sweat. It was becoming clear that his options boiled down to the lesser of two evils. He wasn't the best swimmer, but he no longer had his weapon.

Orion gulped. "Please God, don't let me die!"

He closed his eyes, launching himself from the tree toward the water below. One of the leopards sprang forward, swiping at him with one of its talons. It slashed through the left leg of his spacesuit. Orion felt the cold resistance of the wind as he plunged toward the icy lake, hitting the surface with a violent slap.

When Orion breached the surface, he looked up at the hungry leers of several leopards on the cliff. One of the animals lost its footing and fell over the side, crashing into the water only a few feet away.

Orion pushed himself back towards the surface as the leopard continued splashing nearby. The water became choppy in every direction, filling his spacesuit in the process. Without his helmet to prevent the water from seeping inside his suit, he was only becoming heavier.

He paddled his arms as fast as he could, but with the leopard now in the water he lost his concentration, pushing him back below the surface.

"Orion! Come on! You can make it!" He heard one of his friends' shout.

More and more water filled his suit. The shoreline and his awaiting team weren't getting any closer: he was caught in an undertow. Orion reached and pulled with every stroke, trying to break free of the water's grasp. He was growing breathless and his lungs ached as the waves slapped his face.

"Orion!"

Orion flailed for a few more moments before his arms became completely still. His head lowered as the last breaths of oxygen drained from his body.

He closed his eyes as he sank into the murky abyss and everything went dark.

<>

A red button began flashing on the command center console located at the front of a rectangular room filled with computers. Dr. Donovan Marius studied his students, who were in a room on the other side of a two-way mirror.

Marius had a reputation as a no-nonsense authority who wore a scowl as if it were a smile. Although he would never admit it, he did take the slightest bit of glee in exerting his dominance over his students—whenever the situation warranted it, of course. He would probably best describe it as "tough love."

A highly decorated member of this space community known as the Rover Base Alpha, Marius's decision never to have a family made him an obvious choice to run their introduction to cadet training and space exploration classes.

To the uninitiated, Marius's job was a simple one. He was to evaluate the strengths and weaknesses of every student, once they hit the pubescent ages of around thirteen or fourteen, to see which track they would be best suited for. Such career paths included construction, robotics, leadership, military tactics, education, aviation, healthcare, food services and domestic roles.

However, where Marius's position became complex was in how he specifically came to his decisions. For the vast majority of students who had come through his instruction, once they were placed on a specific career path, there was no deviating from it.

Marius was so strong in his convictions that the words "perfectionist" and "clairvoyant" had been used to describe him over the years. He was responsible for making life-altering decisions for teenagers who had by and large never even experienced their first kiss. It was a lot of pressure to put on one person's shoulders. But if there were anyone who could handle it in this community, it was him.

Marius removed his glasses, pinching the bridge of his nose. He was stressed, primarily because this particular group of students was making it their mission to fail his exercises, day in and day out. The red button stopped flashing when he flicked a switch before pushing back his chair and rising to his feet. He stared through the mirror at the immaculate and Spartan room where the seven students were strapped into angled virtual reality (VR) chairs, complete with VR helmets in a clean room.

The boys wore helmets with red shields while the girls wore yellow. Preparing the next generation for space travel always began in this room. Marius exhaled, limped slightly as he headed for the exit, the door sliding open as he approached.

Marius entered the simulation chamber. The students were in unconscious states, still connected to the simulator. He approached the podium, which was monitoring the physical health of the kids. He typed in a couple of codes, deactivating their VR helmets.

One by one, each of the students began to fidget in their chairs as the gas used in their helmets to put them into a dream-like state, started to wear off. They slowly removed their helmets, remaining in their chairs—all except for Orion, who was not moving at all. Although they were the same age, they all looked so different.

Marius always had a diverse set of students. Their entire community was diverse. It had to be. if it was going to survive. When they departed the Earth generations ago, their particular group selected families from all over the planet.

If humanity was going to survive an elongated space exploration, each group needed to possess diverse genetic material to help stave off disease and infection. If everyone was from the same place with the same physical limitations, they could be more susceptible to extinction.

Marius opened a hidden compartment below the podium, pulling out a handheld prod that contained adrenaline. Every now and then, VR training gave a user emotional trauma that could make it difficult to wake them. Thus, the exploration simulators were forbidden to be used by anyone unless there were trained professionals around to supervise, safety was always paramount.

Marius closed the compartment and approached Orion. He unlatched his helmet, pushing it off of his head. With his free hand, he touched Orion's right wrist, making sure he had a steady pulse. "Orion. Orion. Orion, can you hear me?" Marius asked in a low voice.

Marius did a silent count of three. Just as he was about to use the prod, Orion's eyes opened. "Yes."

"What happened out there?"

Orion swallowed. "I… I don't know, I just—"

"Failed! That's what you did." Marius took a cursory glance around the room to make sure he had the rest of the class's undivided attention as well. "In fact, you all did."

Marius shut off the adrenaline prod and stuck it in his pocket as he walked around his still strapped-in students. He couldn't even bear to look at them as he searched for the right words. "I'm beginning to sound like a redundant fool. How many times do I have to express that exploration is not a zero-sum game? When one of us loses, we all lose."

"Yeah, Jovan!" June sarcastically remarked.

"It's not just him. That goes for everyone." Marius put both hands over his face. Their constant penchant for failure was exhausting his patience. He sighed.

"The fact that none of you felt any impetus to jump back into that water and help your struggling classmate, says a lot, don't you think?"

Some of his students were listening intently while others dropped their heads in shame, knowing that he was exactly right. When the going got tough, they all left Orion behind to fend for himself.

Marius went on. "The universe is filled with wonders we can't even begin to imagine, but it's also filled with danger and try as we might, we don't know much about it." He looked around one more time to make sure he still had their undivided attention. "But here's what we do know: we are a collective. We work for the greater good. Of each other. Because there's not that many of us left... At some point, you all are going to have to work together." Marius took a moment and exhaled. "So, I want you all back here tomorrow..."

"On our day off?!"

Marius shot Gordie a fiery look. "Don't ever interrupt me again." Gordie dropped his head instantly, secretly pointing to Andrew, like Marius wouldn't know that he was the one who said it.

"We will continue to work every day until I am pleased. No ifs, ands, or buts. Is that understood?"

"Yes, Dr. Marius," his students uttered meekly.

"I didn't hear you."

"Yes, Dr. Marius!" They shouted in unison.

Marius nodded his head several times. "Good. Dismissed."

<>

Orion was in the shower rinsing himself. It had been a long day. His was the lone shower running amongst the dozen-divided showers, giving everyone their privacy. He banged his hand repeatedly against the wet tile wall.

He was frustrated. What happened to him earlier in the day was becoming a regular occurrence. Every time he put on that VR helmet, he never knew what would happen next. His confidence in his abilities was at an all-time low.

It was possible he had the yips and just didn't realize it. Whenever the focus shifted to him, he was never able to get comfortable and perform. Whatever it was, all Orion knew was that he and the simulator weren't mixing lately, and that needed to change. He was tired of getting yelled at by Marius. Especially considering Marius was a long-time friend of his father. Not that he could ever tell by the way he treated Orion. If this was Marius's definition of special treatment, he would rather not receive it.

Orion reached out, turning off both the hot and cold faucets. He grabbed his towel and began drying his hair. Laughter came from the adjacent locker room. The voices of his classmates bounced off the tile walls and the acoustics were such that Orion could easily hear them talking.

Orion could see some of his six classmates still in the locker room ahead of him having already showered, they were changing back into their civilian uniforms.

"So how long do you think it will take until Orion causes all of us to fail Dr. Marius's class? I'm guessing we've got about three more screw ups before he finally goes nuclear on us." Gordie asked.

Orion stopped cold, hiding behind a wall, still able to see them. If they were going to ridicule him, he would be best served remaining in the shadows.

"Then we'd all probably end up working in the commissary like Rio's family." Gordie tossed his backpack over his shoulder, snickering as Rio shook her head, unamused at his mean-spirited jokes. She ignored him, continuing to put on her shoes.

Gordie loved making snide comments whenever someone made a mistake. The irony being that, whenever he messed up, he was always quick to say that it wasn't funny. He could dish it out, but he sure could never take it.

Gordie was just lucky no one else in their class was as immature as he was—except for June. She was a brat. And a princess. And a Daddy's girl. Her father was a major on the leadership council, so she rarely listened to anyone, even Marius. She also made fun of Rio a lot, probably because Rio was from the servant class.

"Don't you have somewhere to be Gordie? You barely broke a sweat… as usual." Callista said, untying her hair, freeing her bushy locks.

"That's because I sweat internally. My grandpa says to never let them see you sweat, so that's what I'm doing."

"Well, see you guys tomorrow. Drew and I have to get home. Dad's cooking tonight and if we know what's good for us, we'll eat something before he gets home. Come on Drew." June headed for the exit as Andrew quietly followed her out the door.

The others left the locker room one by one, except for Rio. She was usually the last one to leave. For some reason she dreaded going home, although she never said why. It probably had something to do with what Gordie had said about her family. She violently kicked her locker as Orion flinched. She grabbed her backpack, exited the locker room.

With the room finally cleared, Orion entered with the towel wrapped around his waist. He walked down the row of metal lockers, all emblazoned with his teammates' names: "Rio Venkatsamy"; "Jovan Llenas"; "Andrew Le Roux"; "Callista Guimaraes"; "Gordie Kishore"; and "June Shimizu".

He stopped at his locker which revealed his full name: "Orion Moore". He was relieved to be alone with his thoughts, away from the criticisms of his so-called team mates. For some reason, they seemed to enjoy smacking him around. Frankly, he was sick of it.

He pounded his fist against his locker several times. It was cathartic. A single tear escaped his left eye as Orion wiped it away. He aggressively opened his locker. It was time to get dressed and put this day behind him. He looked at himself in the mirror inside his locker, he was disappointed in what he saw. Constant failure. He rested his head against his locker door.

If only I could know what it felt like to win... just once.

CHAPTER TWO

HOME...
AN UNCOMFORTABLE PLACE TO FEEL

Orion peered through the telescope on the observation deck. The planet Cnaeus came into a sharper focus: it had an atmosphere, but more impressive was the asteroid ring that floated around it. It reminded Orion of pictures he had seen of the planet Saturn in his astronomy class.

The Rover Base Alpha rested in the middle of a solar system containing fifteen planets—along with several dwarf planets—all revolving around a neon yellowish-green star named Galicia. This hyper-star was roughly ten times the size of a normal sun star, according to Orion's father.

From the moment they had arrived in this star system, the leadership had kept the Rover Base at a significant distance away from Galicia, due to its erratic displays of energy. It was an active star that burned radiantly as volcanic eruptions on the surface were heard periodically even at their current position. Every attempt to examine the celestial body had been met with failure thus far.

On the fourth level of the Rover Base where Orion was at the moment, there were several observation decks along a series of corridors, that allowed members of the community to take a seat, relax, and see just exactly what their immediate universe had to offer. Not being able to simply open a window and breathe in the fresh air, could induce claustrophobia among some of the inhabitants, so the observation decks were built as a happy medium.

The Rover Base was a tremendous achievement in human engineering. The space station was massive, with six separate levels. Once, his father had arranged for a private tour of the space station and only then was Orion able to comprehend its expanse. It was literally a floating city.

The Rover Base was originally designed to act as a mass evacuation transport, one of the ten that were ultimately built, as a fail-safe should a cataclysmic event ever happen on the planet Earth. Over a century since its original creation, it remained a vertical marvel of technology. The Rover Base's apex housed the starboard command center, which was the brain of the circular monstrosity. The second and third levels were built to function as living quarters for those on board.

The higher of the two levels housed the families of the leadership council like Orion's family, as well as other families deemed vital to the well-being and survival of the community at large. Of all the families living on the second level of the Rover Base, only Orion's had more than two children. The third level, on the other hand, housed the families of those with more common abilities. There definitely was a class divide, although Orion wasn't exactly sure why. He never felt any better off, that was for sure.

The fourth, fifth and six levels were used primarily to preserve the quality of life for the space community. Some of the other amenities, besides the observation decks included an engineering and robotics lab, commissary, education center, hospital, greenhouse and loading bay. These and other critical facilities were central in keeping everyone in line and under control. The morale of the community was always teetering on the edge, which was probably why the words "order", "routine", and "discipline" were repeated *ad nauseam* to the children since the time they were infants.

Orion continued fine tuning the telescope, he had been examining every inch of Cnaeus' asteroid ring. He never understood how they continued to float around the planet without them flying every which way. The gravitational pull of the planet must be incredibly powerful. He had always hoped he would get to find out for himself one day.

If he could just get over his struggles in Marius' simulator, Orion and his classmates would eventually be sent to Cnaeus to put everything they had learned into practice. It was on Cnaeus where the adolescents came of age. It was a rite of passage where they separated the weak from the strong, the cowardly from the brave, the leaders from the servants.

Orion smiled as he imagined his place in the hierarchy of their community. It would be during his generation when the Rover Base discovered a new home planet and he would play a pivotal role in that coming to fruition. If he ever told anyone this, they would probably laugh at him, but to Orion, this wasn't an impossible dream. Having his father for a role model showed him every day what he could achieve. If he really wanted to be a leader, there was nothing stopping him from making it happen—provided he could stop self-sabotaging himself.

Orion detested the fact that he cared so much about what other people thought about him. If his classmates teased him for being weak at something, he would go into a funk taking their criticism as fact rather than opinion. He possessed an insane desire to be liked and respected, and no one would respect him or listen to him just because he asked them to. He had to prove himself, as did everyone else in this community.

On the Rover Base, no one gave a damn about who you *wished* you were. What mattered was what you did and how important you were to the overall community. Even being the son of a member of the leadership council didn't earn Orion any extra kudos. His older sister possessed tremendous talent—she was the type of athlete Orion wished he could be. She was the one who took after their father, not him. Orion wasn't simply fighting against himself, he was fighting against his family's reputation. Greatness was expected of them, but nothing he did ever came naturally. If he didn't work for it, he usually failed.

Why does everything have to be so hard? Just once, why couldn't I have it easy?

Orion felt a vibration against his left arm. He pulled back from the telescope. He wore an arm band that could send and receive text messages. There was a message from his mother that read: *"Orion, where are you? Your dinner is getting cold."*

Orion pushed a button on the band displaying a mini-keyboard. He typed "on my way" and hit the send button as the keyboard disappeared.

He grabbed his backpack from between his legs and draped it over his shoulder, before taking one more look at the planets through the transparent plexiglass. Without the telescope's ability to cover long distances, they looked like nothing more than twinkling stars. Galicia, however, could be seen just fine. That's how vast this star system was and how big and powerful Galicia was.

Orion began his trek back for home, passing an elderly couple who were sitting on a bench admiring the view. He did a double take, looking back at them for a moment. He always wondered how someone so old felt about living in these conditions for decades.

Are they not bored with life? Surely at some point living this way had to get old. Is it possible that they are just resigned to their fate and no longer see a need to dream of anything better anymore? Mom was probably half their age and she acted exactly like that."

Orion shook his head, walking briskly towards the elevators. He needed to get home soon before his parents came looking for him. That would have been a bad look. He was becoming too old to have his parents coming to get him.

Orion turned the handle to the Moore family quarters and slipped inside, mentally preparing himself for the tongue-lashing he was sure to receive from his parents for coming home so late.

"As Mom is my witness, I swear I'm telling the truth!" Orion's older sister, Delly, was already in the middle of another one of her arrogant tirades.

Orion sighed, carefully closing the door behind him. *Here we go...*

<>

Delly's auburn hair with its blonde highlights swayed ever so gently as she was holding court in the family's kitchen,

20

surrounded by her seven-year-old brother, Pharaoh, and their parents, Derrick and Carolyn.

Like everything else it seemed on the Rover Base, the kitchen was of the quaint variety: just enough room for the five of them, around a tiny circular table with barely enough distance between the sink and the stove. This bit of luxury was afforded to them mainly because their father was an officer on the Rover Base leadership council. Otherwise, the alternative for them would be even smaller.

"Coach B said that in the ten-plus years he's been teaching, he's never had anyone score as well as me over the course of a semester. You know what that means, don't you?" Delly gleefully looked around the table awaiting a response from her parents that never came.

"What Delly?" Pharaoh's hands were under his chin, beaming at her, hanging on her every word.

Delly turned to her precious little brother. "It means that one day… I'll be handed the reins to my own space mission." She revealed a toothy grin, while nodding ever so smugly. "Major Delly Moore, Explorer to the Stars. It's got a nice little ring to it, don't you think?"

Their father rose from his chair, taking both his and their mother's bowls to the sink. Their mother was fiddling with her ponytail, which she only seemed to wear at dinner time— probably to keep her hair out of their food. It was pretty long, after all. Still, the ponytail was a good look for her—it made her look younger.

"You're getting a little ahead of yourself, don't you think, sweetie?" Her father had his back to them as he turned on the faucet to rinse the dishes.

"Dad, seriously? I'm eighteen years old, I'm top of my class in both field and administrative training exercises, my loving father is a Captain, so I'm a legacy…" Delly playfully pointed finger guns as her mother scoffed. She had to make sure her family understood that this was her future, whether they wanted to believe it or not. She was speaking it into existence. "And, I've got this super awesome personality to boot!"

"Yeah, you're like super incredibly humble. Who wouldn't want to take orders from somebody like you?" Orion said as he entered the kitchen. He made his way around the table to take a seat as all eyes turned to him. It was easy to tell that they were siblings considering they looked so much alike. Plus, they were practically the same height, even though Delly was five years older.

"Well, well, well! Look who decided to grace us with his presence. Did mean ole' Doc Marius keep you guys after class again? You know, so you could finally learn how to tie your boots while you're in the simulator?" Delly reached out, tugging on her brother's sleeve as he batted her hand away.

"You do realize none of that stuff is real, don't you?" Delly went on, giving Pharaoh a playful wink. Her youngest brother covered his mouth to hide his laughter.

"That's enough, Delly." Her mother said. She always said that she hated seeing her children picking on each other, which really meant she was talking to Delly. "Do me a favor and help your brother get ready for bed."

"Aww…" Pharaoh moaned.

Their mother snapped her fingers, which in this family meant "no back talk". She was the disciplinarian of the household, and the kids feared her remonstrations way more than they did their father's.

"Come on, squirt. Time to get you a bath. You need one." Delly held her nose as she rose from the table and moved toward the exit. Pharaoh followed her. As she passed Orion, she raised her hand, pretending like she was going to smack him. Orion flinched.

"Delly!" Her mother shouted.

"What?" Delly put her hands up, trying to look innocent.

"Go!" Her mother pointed angrily.

Delly punched Orion in the shoulder before dashing out of the room.

<>

Orion wanted desperately to chase after Delly and pop her one good, but he was stuck. He leaned his chair back against the wall and stared at the floor. There was no way he would be able to leave the room without speaking to his parents first.

"Are you hungry?" His mother asked.

He continued looking at the floor. He wasn't sure what he wanted in that moment. Not today. Not after what his friends had to say about him when he wasn't around.

"Orion? Is something wrong?"

His father stopped washing dishes and turned to him. He was a broad-chested man with light eyes. He also was incredibly polished and rarely ever smiled. He and Marius seemed to suffer from the same affliction. They were always so serious, which was more annoying than anything else.

"I believe your mother asked you a question, son."

Orion looked up at them, letting his backpack slide to the floor. "I'm not hungry."

23

His mother raised her eyebrows. "Well you can't honestly expect me to send my child to bed without supper, can you?"

Orion shrugged.

His mother turned to his father as Orion just wanted them to yell at him and be done with it. He was not in the mood. "I'm gonna make you a plate." His father said.

Orion's mother rose from her chair, moving towards the sink. She whispered something inaudible in his father's ear, before crossing the room to Orion. She wrapped her arms around him and kissed him on the back of his head. Orion didn't flinch as she squeezed him tightly, "I love you."

Orion gently patted her arms. "I love you too, Mom."

His mother released her bear hug and walked out of the kitchen.

His father came to the table with a bowl of potato soup and a piece of wheat bread on the side. He set it down in front of Orion. "

What's this supposed to be? I thought you were making a plate…" Orion pointed. This is a bowl."

His father took a step back. From the looks in his eyes, it was clear that he didn't think Orion had any kind of future as a comedian in their community. Their relationship was of the 'yes sir, no sir' variety. The jokes in this household were saved for the children when amongst themselves, not him.

"I'm sorry, are you being smart? Because for a minute there, I believe you forgot who you were talking to." His father waved at him. "Hey, hi Orion, it's me, Dad, remember me, the person you get your good looks from. The person who worked his butt off to make sure that you and your siblings have comfortable accommodations. The person who has zero tolerance for a bratty teenager who speaks with no respect for his parents. That guy."

Orion looked away, staring at his food.

"Now I don't know what's gotten into you tonight, but honestly, I'm really not in the mood to find out. So if you want to mope around and be miserable, please go right ahead. You certainly wouldn't be the first or the last person to do it here on the Rover Base."

His father rose to his feet. He was about to step away from the table, when he felt compelled to give Orion one final warning. "But I'd advise you, to watch how you speak to your mother and I. Puberty is not an excuse to be a jerk. Fix your attitude… or I'll fix it for you. And I know you don't want me to do that." His father exited the kitchen.

Orion shook his head, waiting a moment just in case his father returned to give him more of a tongue-lashing. When that didn't happen, he got up from the table to get a spoon from the cupboard. He walked back to the table and sat down. He slurped his soup. It was the same as it always was. Bland, predictable. Everything was so damn predictable. Nothing ever changed. He noticed he hadn't closed the cupboard, so he kicked it closed. He was pouting.

At some point things had to change, didn't they?

Orion exited the adjoining bathroom wearing his pajamas. He approached his stasis pod bed. One of the reasons humans had been able to survive on the Rover Base for as long as they had, could be traced to the stasis pods, which placed them in a suspended animation-like state for five to eight hours every night. The idea behind their design was to prolong human life for as long as possible.

As Orion climbed into his pod, he looked over to see his mother sitting at the side of Pharaoh's bed. Orion hated sharing a room with his little brother. To add insult to his frustration, he also shared the exact same bedtime as Pharaoh, who was half his age. And they wondered why he was always frustrated.

Their room was sterile, white, and cold—like a hospital room. The environment did nothing to foster creativity or imagination in him. In a way, that had become the hidden tragedy of their survival after all these years on the Rover Base. There was rarely any room for the unimaginable. Everything was always a matter of life and death, and everyone was always so serious. It was exhausting, especially to a child. Orion pulled his pod cover closed, sealing himself inside. At least he could still find purpose in his dreams.

"Mommy?

"Yes, babe." Carolyn Moore answered her youngest as she sat at his bedside.

"Do you think Delly will really be in command of her own ship one day?"

Carolyn couldn't help but smile at Pharaoh's angelic face. He was so young, yet so inquisitive—she adored her baby boy. She rubbed his head as she searched for the right words to best put his mind at ease, but also to best describe her feelings to his question.

"I think if Delly really wants it, she'll make it happen. She has a knack for overcoming obstacles. Lord knows where she got it from, because it certainly wasn't me."

Carolyn looked down to see her baby boy hanging on her every word, even though he was getting sleepy. "Is that what you think too?"

Pharaoh nodded, fighting off a yawn.

"I think it's about that time. Let's get you nice and comfy." Carolyn moved a blanket up to his shoulders, tucking him in. "Hush, little baby, don't say a word, Mama's gonna buy you a mockingbird. And if that mockingbird don't sing, Mama's gonna buy you a diamond ring." Pharaoh closed his eyes, nestling his head deeper into his pillow.

"And if that diamond ring turns brass, Mama's gonna buy you a looking glass. And if that looking glass is broke, Mama's gonna buy you a Billy goat. And if that Billy goat won't pull, Mama's gonna buy you a cart and a bull. And if that cart and bull turn over, Mama's gonna buy you a dog named Rover. And if that dog named Rover won't bark, Mama's gonna buy you a horse and a cart. And if that horse and cart fall down, you'll still be the sweetest little baby in town."

Carolyn kissed Pharaoh on his forehead and rose to her feet, grabbing the top of the stasis pod. She pulled it down, securing him inside. She could still see Pharaoh resting peacefully as she beamed.

"Okay, Orion, bed time, let's go." The room was silent as she waited for a response from him. "Orion?"

Carolyn looked to his pod, noticing that it was already closed. She approached, looking over the top of it. Orion was sound asleep as well. She paused a moment. This was the first time he had ever closed his pod cover without exchanging a single word with her. She was at a loss for what could possibly be going on with him.

At the very least, she could always count on a 'goodnight mom' from him before bed, even if he refused to let her kiss and hug all over him, like she used to do when he was Pharaoh's age. Could he be angry with her? Was he suffering from middle-child syndrome and she had been too scatterbrained to pick up on it? This turn of events was alarming, if for no other reason than in this household, there was routine. That's just the way things worked and that's the way they liked it.

Carolyn shook her head and headed for the exit. She slightly bumped her bare foot against the base of Orion's pod.

"Ouch." She hobbled to the door, turning off the ceiling light. She exited, holding the door for a moment almost waiting to see if Orion would open his pod. A few moments passed as she finally closed the door.

CHAPTER THREE

A ROCK AND A HARD PLACE

The neon, yellowish-green radiance emanating from Galicia shined above the dark clouds of the planet Prisca. Prisca's clouds were so thick in appearance, they looked as though they could be walked on. The sky was solid pink in daylight.

The shuttle cast a massive shadow against the clouds as it entered the planet's lower atmosphere. The long, horizontal, charcoal-colored shuttle, known as the Grey Rover, was distinguished by two solid light grey stripes that ran parallel across the surface of it on both sides. The other Rovers were differentiated by color as well. An I-ching emblem of the letter "E"—also light gray in color—near the bottom of the ship symbolized "Earth" or "Earthling". These emblems also doubled as the Rover's homing beacon should they ever become lost.

Inside the cockpit, sat the seasoned pilot, Webb, biting on a plastic chew stick to keep his nerves in check. His co-pilot, Etsitty, sat next to him. Etsitty was a good "number two" primarily because he knew when to talk and when to listen. Their navigator, Janis, was seated behind them at his own work station, making sure that they were traveling in the right direction. He was the new guy, having replaced their old navigator who had become violently ill from a malfunction in his oxygen supply. They all were given new spacesuits at the start of every week after that mishap.

Webb and company braced themselves as the Grey Rover entered the cloud cover below. The ship's front dual hydro-beams illuminated, on each side, lighting their path through the dangerous conditions. The turbulence was ferocious, shaking this powerful piece of manmade machinery like only Mother Nature could. As big as this ship was, this was always the scariest part of their journey. Each time they traveled through the clouds they were putting their lives at risk.

Webb kept the Grey Rover steady as particles pounded the ship's outer shell. During the week, at the end of every day, the ship received routine maintenance to make sure it remained in excellent condition. Their mission on Prisca depended on it, so the Rover Base leadership took no chances.

The Grey Rover was one of two transports used by the Rover Base to shuttle precious rare minerals from Prisca back to the community. It was through these minerals that the Rover Base was able to sustain itself technologically, considering how much energy the space-station consumed just to remain functional.

The ship was also used to transport members of the mining crew home every other Friday evening, so they could spend time with their families over the weekend. The miners were separated into A and B groups. A's traveled home on the first and third weekends of a given month, while B's traveled on the second and fourth. As long as they were to remain in the Galicia star system, the work these men did was paramount to the Rover Base's continued survival.

Through the ship's reinforced windshield, the cockpit crew watched as the paths of their hydro-beams only revealed more darkness. Their only saving grace was the ship's navigational computer, which told them just how much farther they needed to go until they reached the surface.

The Grey Rover finally exited beneath the cloud cover. Prisca's surface was bathed in perpetual nighttime due to the clouds. As Webb leveled off the ship, Etsitty repositioned the hydro-beams to light their path to their destination.

"Chalk another one up for the good guys," Webb said.

"You always say that. But I've been meaning to ask you, who are the bad guys in this scenario? The clouds?" Etsitty slightly turned to him, making sure to keep his eye on what was in front of them.

"It's just a superstition. I mean we haven't had a crash since I've been saying it. But I can stop if you want."

Etsitty nodded. "Good point. Forget I said anything."

Webb smirked as he continued to fly the ship. Prisca had zero forms of life or vegetation due to the lack of sunlight. However, what it did have were dangerous mountain ranges that were not always visible in the darkness. The Grey Rover had to lose air speed as those mountains would sometimes appear out of nowhere. This was why the hydro-beams were so important. The hilly terrain twinkled with its numerous deposits of precious metals and minerals that had yet to be mined. The planet itself was one massive quarry.

A digital map on the onboard console showed them just how far they were from Base Camp with a static black dot.

Theirs was a flashing white dot currently on approach, with an estimated time of arrival being under an hour.

Like the members of the Rover mining crews, it took a certain type of person to do this kind of work daily. This was no walk in the park.

<>

Huge flood lights, connected to steel beams that were bolted to the ground—a precaution due to the constant whipping winds—surrounded the outer perimeter of the Mining Base Camp. Without them, the crews would be in a constant state of perpetual darkness. The lights revealed a large crater caused by long-term, extensive excavations. They have been working at the site for many years.

One of the two camp foremen, Matthys Venkatsamy, sat on a bench in a fitted spacesuit complete with transparent helmet. His helmet glowed, eliminating the need for a headlamp. He waited for the Grey Rover in front of a gigantic sealed metal tent—the camp's commissary. There were military-style barracks on both sides of it.

Six huge oxygen tanks located behind the structures pumped a steady supply of O_2 as the planet offered none of its own. As such, both the barracks and the commissary were each supported by a clean room. In this room, once everyone was securely inside, the dangerous toxins were sucked out, replacing them with clear air so the miners could lie down, relax, have some coffee or a hot meal without fear of suffocation.

Another scarce resource on Prisca was water. Matthys' men were given a maximum of five minutes to shower each night. This had caused a few problems at the camp as it was unwise to be the first one to shower, because it could take some time for the water to warm up. They initially tried an honor system, but no one could be trusted, so they instituted a token system instead. Every night, the miners were given one token, which they could use to shower for five minutes.

An unintentional consequence to the long days and nights spent working on Prisca, was that some of the men had taken to gambling via card games, using their tokens as chips. One thing was for certain, being around the losers after a game could make for an uncomfortable night for one's nostrils.

Across the camp, away from the barracks was a cave entrance, where they did most of the excavation. The heaviest pieces were often saved for the robot miners, who assisted the humans, saving them from the most dangerous work. While the humans slept and ate, the robots were grinding away on that rock. As a result, the robots were in constant need of repair.

There was a landing zone on the far side of the camp closest to the cave. Its lights activated automatically, revealing the emblem of the Rover Base as the Grey Rover came into view just beyond the base camp. The Grey Rover soared over head, slowing to a crawl over the landing zone.

Brackets extended from the bottom of the spacecraft to the ground, allowing the ship to gently land. The power from this ship caused the ground to rumble around it, like a mini-earthquake. Matthys rose to his feet and stretched his arms. He started walking towards the ship.

<>

Major Ananke "Dream Crusher" Thayer, a raven-haired genius, sat behind her desk in an office that only a hoarder could love. She was approaching middle-age, yet unmarried. She was instead betrothed to her work, to the point of obsession. As the Rover Base's chief technology expert, Thayer was never afraid to speak her mind on any occasion. Some of that had to do with her unmatched scientific knowledge.

Her office, located on the starboard level, was one of the larger ones on the Rover Base, although it was hard to tell due to the many files and boxes lying about. There also was a pull-out cot in one corner so she never had to worry about taking her work home.

In Thayer's mind, when she was at work, she *was* home. Even with the sheer volume of files she possessed, everything was organized. Her three primary workflow piles, labeled "Prisca", "Project Pioneer", and "RBA" (Rover Base Alpha) were practically stacked to the ceiling.

Thayer gazed at the triple computer monitor setup on her desk, deeply engrossed by what she saw. The telescope lens located inside of a transparent reinforced bubble turned ever so slightly, bringing Galicia into sharper focus. The lens itself was attached to a small pod, large enough for an adult to ride on. It was made entirely of titanium alloy, complete with jet propulsion on its top and bottom to move it along.

These pods, codenamed "Trailblazers" were remotely controlled Mini-Rovers used by the leadership as data collection for their research into the cosmos. The Trailblazers also possessed some artificial intelligence based off mission protocols. Simply put, when they were sent on an assignment, they had the ability to override a mission if the danger superseded their ability to gather information. This had been enacted almost immediately after the Sonain disaster, where the Le Roux family had been tragically lost.

Thayer's middle screen showed her the view of Galicia from the Rover Base telescope. This also provided her with visual confirmation of the Trailblazer's journey as it could be seen as well. Meanwhile, the left screen displayed the pertinent stats of the Trailblazer itself like battery life, current distance from the Rover Base and temperature. The pod was created to withstand heat in excess of four thousand degrees centigrade.

Her right screen was currently loading. As the Trailblazer moved it would need to be refocused on Galicia. It was still too far away from it to scan the surface and uncover exactly what elements combined could have possibly made such a humongous sun star.

Thayer moved her right hand across a keyboard that was built into her desk, typing on a few buttons. Galicia was moving closer, albeit slowly.

"Unbelievable," she muttered to herself, shaking her head as she marveled at what technology allowed her to do every day. "Okay, baby. Let's see how much closer you can get." Thayer pushed the "up" arrow on her keyboard. The distance from the Rover Base was currently reading 292,000 miles and rising.

The Trailblazer propulsion rockets activated, moving it much faster than it had been traveling up to now. The closer it got, the bubble protecting the telescope lens began to show signs of cracking, tiny at first, but growing larger by the second. Undeterred, Thayer continued to have the Trailblazer proceed. Eventually the bubble popped and the Trailblazer exploded on the middle screen as she jumped back in her seat.

"Goddamnit!" Her right screen went dark.

Thayer heaved a sigh. This was what she got for getting her hopes up. She turned her attention to the left screen, the Trailblazer's final statistics before its destruction showed that it had only made it 297,423 miles away from the Rover Base. The temperature gauge had spiked to over nine thousand degrees centigrade.

Thayer agitatedly tapped the desk with both hands as she sat back in her chair. Her desk actually had divots where she would rest her hands—and those divots were not built-in. She needed a place to channel her compulsive behavior.

Thayer rose to her feet and began a controlled manic pace around, always careful never to knock over her life's work. She plopped down on the cot. She stared at the ceiling, double-tapping her forehead in frustration. At some point she was going to crack this nut. She just had to go back to the drawing board.

"Bollocks."

<>

The noise coming from heavy drilling echoed from inside the cave as Matthys exited his barracks. The sound of the titanium bit hitting the iron ore was ear piercing, even when outside.

Matthys' primary responsibility was to make sure his workers continued to practice the highest safety standards possible as they could not afford to lose anyone—human or robot. His other more understated function was monitoring the mental health of his men, some of whom were eighteen, fresh out of completing their secondary education, and now working for the greater good of the Rover Base. These young men needed the most attention as it was a culture shock for them to have to spend the majority of their time away from their families, save for a couple of weekends each month.

Matthys was headed for the cave to effectively call it a night when he saw his shift supervisor emerge from the hole in the earth and head towards the Grey Rover.

"How we doing?" he asked.

"Doing great. They're almost loaded up."

"Well, hurry up, we have a schedule to keep here."

"Yes sir."

The two men went their separate ways as Matthys approached the cave.

Inside the hollowed-out cavern, the drilling machine continued to punish the walls made of iron ore. As it dug deeper into the rock, huge portions broke off and crashed to the ground. Several of the miners were covered head to toe in black dirt. When the dirt became too much, they would bend over, dusting their helmets so they could still see.

There were several carts of already mined iron ore sitting nearby. The miners shoveled much of the smaller pieces into them. For the larger pieces, they relied on the robot miners to handle them and place them in the empty carts. Matthys appeared behind his crew. No one seemed to notice his presence as they continued working feverishly.

With the drill still going they would never hear him. Matthys pulled an air horn from his hip, closing his eyes as he sounded it. The crew stopped what they were doing immediately. Lord knows they hated when he used that thing even if that meant the work day was over.

"Alright guys, that's it for today. Let's pack it up before the sun goes down."

"What difference does it make? We can't see the sun anyway," one of the crew scoffed.

Pockets of laughter echoed through the cave as Matthys shrugged. At least the men still had their senses of humor. His crew began setting down their equipment, turning off the drilling machines. As they headed for the exit, the cave began to tremble violently as rubble fell and dust clouds grew. Some of the crew hugged the walls of the cavern, while others curled up in the fetal position. There really was nowhere to hide if they couldn't get outside. After a couple of tense moments, the trembling dissipated. Matthys got back to his feet.

"Son of a... you would think those idiots would wait for us to get out of here before taking off." A miner groused.

"Yeah, well, apparently common sense isn't all that common. Let's pick up the pace gentlemen." Matthys led his crew out of the cave. When they emerged, they stopped dead in their tracks.

"What in the world?"

Matthys exchanged worried looks with his men. The Grey Rover was still docked in the landing zone. Whatever the tremors were, they had to have come from the planet itself. Matthys and his men had never experienced anything like this before. It would definitely have to be reported.

Thayer was sound asleep on her cot when a chime went off. She blinked rapidly as she tried to focus. What moron dared disturb her much needed slumber? The annoying sound repeated, and she sighed loudly. "Yes."

The door to her office slid open and in walked Thayer's apprentice, Toni Apostolos. Toni was a six-foot plus, breathtakingly beautiful technical savant. When Thayer first met her, she initially wanted to dismiss her right then and there, but Toni's acumen was too great to ignore—her beauty was secondary to her ability.

Toni took three short steps, keeping her distance. She brushed away a wisp of blonde hair that had come loose from her tightly-wound bun. "Are you busy?"

"I don't remember sending for you. What do you want?" Thayer tapped her forehead once more—why was Toni still talking to her?

"I figured you'd want to see this." Toni held out her hand, revealing three miniature digital hard drives.

"Pfft!" Thayer responded with an eye-roll as she turned on her side away from Toni. She had no intention of playing a game of twenty questions with her assistant. Undeterred Toni walked to the cot and stood over her.

"Look, I get it. You're a giant, but you don't have to be annoying too." Thayer sucked her teeth as Toni continued to cast a shadow over her. She turned back to see Toni brandishing the three hard drives up close and personal. She looked back up at Toni. "And what's that supposed to be?"

"Project Pioneer."

Toni smiled widely as Thayer sat up in the cot as if she were a mummy rising from the dead. "You're so full of it."

Toni shook her head no. "I had a feeling that would perk you up." Toni placed the drives in Thayer's hands.

Thayer looked at them as if she had just discovered fire or invented refrigeration. "Welp... I'll get out of your hair now and leave you to it." Toni turned to exit as Thayer remained enthralled.

"Stop right there!"

Toni stopped cold just before reaching the door. She turned back to Thayer.

"I need your help." Thayer was now crossing back to her desk as Toni's shoulders slumped. She was mere steps away from exiting.

"Major, there's over a year's worth of data we have to look at, this will take us weeks to sift through at a minimum."

Thayer thought for a moment, before unearthing a jagged smile, revealing her crooked teeth. "I know, so I'd advise you to put on several pots of coffee. We've got a lot of work to do. This could be a game-changer for us." Thayer clapped her hands. "Aren't you excited?"

She took a seat at her desk as Toni nodded, revealing a tight-lipped lifeless smile. This was going to be their lives for the next couple of weeks, maybe even months.

A card game of War had broken out on one side of the barracks. Seven members of Matthys' crew were playing cards, going around in a circle. On the other end of the barracks, two miners were engaged in a quiet game of chess. Matthys sat on his cot nearby, thumbing through a digital book filled with pictures of mountains, rivers and grasslands. Nature in all its majestic glory.

He rested the book on his chest as he reached behind his pillow and felt around. He produced a photograph of his much younger self, along with his beautiful wife Riana and their daughters, Cazimira, Susara, and Rio—*the little pipsqueak.*

Matthys uncorked a smile: the photo was an excellent reminder of why he worked so hard and what he had sworn he would always protect. He yearned for his family to be part of the first generation to find a new home.

"For the love of God, will you please make a move already?"

Matthys snapped out of his haze to see one of the chess players, Kaushik, becoming irritated during the game.

"Patience is a virtue friend. Chess isn't just about making a move; it's about making the right move." His opponent, Pennesi, gently held his knight in preparation for his pending move.

"Okay, how do you like that one?" Kaushik swept his hairy arm across the board, knocking several pieces to the floor.

Pennesi leaned back, looking at the ruined board game. He looked up at Kaushik who was defiantly smirking at him, he could careless that he cleared the board. "Funny, you're a funny guy." Pennesi casually flipped the knight onto the board, sprung from his seat, grabbing Kaushik by his collar. "How 'bout this, you find this funny?"

The two men began wrestling, slamming each other against the wall and the nearby cots as Matthys hopped off the cot to intercede. The others watched from a distance, finding their entire exchange funny. The cerebral chess players were brawling like clowns while the card players were civil. The irony of it all.

41

"Hey, hey, hey…" Matthys stepped in between them. Kaushik and Pennesi were both huffing and puffing, not giving an inch. "You guys know the rules. You got enough energy to fight, you got enough to get back out there and work. So I suggest you figure out how to get along or don't play chess anymore. Alright?!"

The two men nodded their heads, realizing their mistake, primarily because they really didn't want to go back outside and work. They reluctantly shook hands as Matthys watched them for a moment. He rubbed his forehead walking back to his bed, not totally believing what he had just witnessed.

And here I thought chess was a game for the smart guys. This place is gonna be the death of us.

<>

The Rover Base Library was dark for the most part, save for a single light all the way in back, past the rows and rows of well-preserved paperback books. Seated at a desk under the small light, with her computer open, was Rio Venkatsamy. She was wearing headphones so she wouldn't be disturbed, but also so she wouldn't disturb anyone else, even if she was the only one still in the library.

A thick encyclopedia-like book lay beside her computer. Rio was looking through photographs of Ancient Rome on the computer. She turned a page on the book and her eyes flashed. A picture of Queen Zenobia, the third-century queen of the Palmyrene Empire, in what would later be known as Syria, appeared before her. Rio ran her finger across the book. Zenobia was legendary for having led her armies into battle on numerous occasions against the Romans.

Rio stopped reading and turned back to her computer. She typed Zenobia into the Library's digital database. One of the first things she saw was a black and white sketch photograph of an armored warrior queen, with a sword on her hip, leading her troops into battle as a city burned in ruins in the background. She closed her eyes for a moment, imagining she was that warrior queen. What an exhilarating feeling it must have been for Zenobia to defend her people against an oppressive regime.

Even if such situations made for traumatic or gut-wrenching memories, in many respects a person could be at least somewhat in control of their destiny—unlike what they had come to expect on the Rover Base. Nothing ever changed. "Order", "routine" and "discipline" were words that had been embedded into her brain since birth.

Rio heard a buzzing sound and opened her eyes. Someone was messaging her on her computer. She tapped a button on it as a hologram of her father popped up.

"Pip, what are you doing up? Where's your mother?" Matthys asked.

"Probably sleeping, I'd imagine."

Matthys frowned. "Where are you? Are you at home?"

"No… I'm in the library." Rio's attention wavered as she ran her finger across the encyclopedia page, still reading more about Zenobia.

"So you're doing homework."

"Not exactly." She shrugged. "Just reading, that's all."

"About?"

"The early Roman Empire. You know… the time back when people actually experienced things. Not just being forced to live in this floating prison." Matthys put his hand to his forehead, sighed. He stared at her, pausing several times as she continued reading, paying him no attention.

"Alright, I think I've heard enough. Look at me, Pip." Rio stopped reading, turning to the hologram of her father. "You're not the first person nor will you be the last I'm sure, to express your displeasure about having to live on the Rover Base, but let me tell you something Missy. I'm the one down here, busting my hump every single day, with little to no sleep, low oxygen, garbage flying all over the place and God knows what else."

Matthys coughed several times, clearing his throat. His skin was very pale. He also looked like he had lost weight since she last saw him in person. He went on. "But you know what? I suck it up and do my job. Because it's not just about me. And my feelings. Too many people depend on me, yourself included. Your sisters. Your mother. Everyone on board. The work we do down here, keeps that 'Floating Prison' as you so eloquently put it… functional. And if it didn't, none of us would be here. Would you prefer it, if that were the case?"

Rio sat quietly, ashamed. There was nothing she could say that wouldn't make her seem like an entitled brat, even if she and her family were nowhere close to being viewed in that way. They were the servant class in this community. And as much as they hated it, that was their position and they had to make the best of it.

"While I applaud your desire to learn, you learning Earth's history, is a pointless endeavor, because it literally has no bearing on what our circumstances are right now. I need you to be in the present Pip, not the ancient past."

Matthys was exasperated at this point, his eyes were beginning to shed tears. "If I've said it once, I'll say it again… you are our future. It's up to you to be better, way, way… better than us. That's the only way we're ever gonna get off this godforsaken rock and you up there. Don't you get it?' He wiped away his tears.

Rio took off her headphones. He had made his point as her eyes were becoming a little watery themselves. "I'm sorry Daddy."

She sat there for a moment, in silence, staring at his hologram image as her father did the same opposite her. Try as she might to free herself from their current existence, that was a fool's errand. At this very moment, this was their plight.

CHAPTER FOUR

HOPE: THREE STAR SYSTEMS AWAY

The freshly pungent odor of human sweat was everywhere inside the Rover Base Gymnasium. Delly and her classmates, a group of ten in total and all between the ages of seventeen and eighteen, were doing diamond pushups under the watchful eye of their instructor, Pete Biancuzzo.

Coach B, as he was affectionately known to his students was a bold man with an infectious smile. He was in his fifties, yet he remained a fit athlete. His arms were ripped, even at his age. He also was balding something fierce as the follicles on the sides of his head were almost totally gone and noticeably gray. It never made sense why he didn't just shave them off.

He paced back and forth, watching the students' form and technique. A whistle dangled around his neck. Coach B wasn't too dissimilar from Marius in his tough-minded approach, possibly with the exception that he had dealt with a more mature group of teenagers than his colleague. When it came to education of the Rover Base youth, discipline and accountability were the constants. It was frustrating for the young people no doubt, but such was life.

Coach B continued to watch the group—at present they showed no signs of fatigue. His students were well-oiled machines. He stopped pacing, pressed the whistle up against his lips and blew. Instantly, his students jumped to their feet. "Well done… Now we climb."

He gestured to the rope climb area at the far end of the gym where three ropes hung from the ceiling over some thin floor mats that offered little to no protection at all. If anyone ever fell, they would spend many days in the infirmary. Delly led the others as they hustled over to the mats. The students all stood by the ropes, waiting for Coach B, separated into two groups of five. They left the middle rope free for their instructor.

Coach B filled the space, removing his whistle. "Hold this for me."

He handed the whistle to Delly's boyfriend and Jovan's older brother, Kristian. A few months' shy of his eighteenth birthday, Kristian was not the athlete his younger brother was, but he held his own all the same. He made up for whatever he lacked in physical prowess by outworking the competition. He also was great with his hands. Delly had experienced that up close and personal.

Coach B grabbed the middle rope. His hands were hardened and full of callouses, yet they were strong. Coach B closed his eyes, engaging in a silent count of two and in an instant, began climbing the rope. His students cheered him on as he reached the top, tapping it twice while keeping himself perfectly balanced at the apex. He then smoothly slid back down the rope, landing on the floor like a cat. He did that which such ease. Delly always wondered how he never got rope burn.

"Ah, woo. That was good. I told you the old guy still has it… a bit." He was breathing a little heavy, but still fired up all the same. He looked at his students who were ready to compete against one another—this was the environment he had fostered. Iron sharpening iron. "Alright cadets, first group, you're up."

Coach B stuck out his hand as Kristian passed him his whistle. He stepped aside as three of his students, including Delly, stepped forward. The other two were boys as was per usual in Coach B's class. Other than one girl named Shaw, whom he taught well over a decade ago, Coach B's classes were always filled with teenage boys. Delly was literally breaking all the rules.

Delly and her classmates were ready, focused and hungry to win the approval of their intense instructor. "You don't stop until you hear the whistle, am I clear?"

Silence from his students. There was no time for talk. It was time to win.

"Alright, in five, four, three, two…" The whistle blew as the teens hit the rope, climbing as fast as they could. At first, Delly trailed the two boys, but it didn't take long for her to make up ground. She reached the top just split seconds behind them. She tapped the ceiling and began her descent breathing down their necks.

They were not allowed to slide down the rope as Coach B had done. They always went down as they came up, one full body length at a time. Delly reached the ground first as she was shorter than the boys. Her movements were more crisp and compact.

She immediately began to re-climb the rope as the two boys reached the floor split seconds later. They turned to Coach B with confused looks.

Coach B shrugged, "Did you hear a whistle?"

Back up they went, now trying to catch up to Delly, who had built a sizable lead on them. Coach B smiled. It was nice having someone like her in the group. She pushed them to compete harder.

General William Aresco brought the steaming hot cup of tea to his lips. The current leader of the Rover Base, Aresco was a forthright man with leathery skin. Like his predecessors before him, he was worn down mostly by the prolonged search for a new home. When he assumed the position, there was chatter of how much things would change under his stewardship and yet here he was, old, drained, standing in exactly the same place he was when he was first given this tremendous responsibility.

Aresco gave a gentle blow to the cup to cool it off. His accommodations were the finest on the Rover Base. The walls of his sitting room were reinforced transparent plexiglass, allowing him to watch the stars every night before bed. A plush couch stood nearby, good for a nap or entertaining, albeit he hadn't done much of the latter for quite some time. He was content to remain here, alone in his thoughts, slowly waiting for the end to come. *Perhaps there will be someone else in the leadership ranks who will one-day step forward to do what I wasn't able to do.*

A fleeting thought, as Aresco had no intention of willingly giving up the leadership. If someone wanted his job or this view, they would have to wait until he died, as far as he was concerned. He stood next to the window, cup in hand. From his perch, he could see the Grey Rover on approach towards the Rover Base. He took a sip, smiling fondly—it had been years since he traveled in one of those. An alert on his computer pinged as Aresco turned to his workstation. He approached his desk, setting the cup down.

He touched the monitor display to wake it up. A group notification had been sent out to all members of the leadership council: "Urgent. War Room. One Hour. Respectfully, Major Thayer." Aresco rubbed his chin, his mind racing in all directions. Considering who sent the message, this could be any number of scenarios.

The corridor was uncomfortably warm, Galicia's rays were hitting the tall plexiglass windows, turning it into a hot box. Aresco had begun to sweat around his head and neck, even on the short trek from his quarters to the War Room. No matter how much they turned up their air conditioning to counteract the heat, it was still hot.

Aresco was escorted by two baby-faced base officers. They looked barely old enough to drink, let alone do their jobs protecting the leadership council and their families just in case the unthinkable were to happen and there was a mutiny. Luckily or unluckily, depending on which way someone might look at it, the community at large didn't have the stomach to fight for a regime change anyway. Not everyone was built to lead and many had become understandably world weary.

Aresco reached the door, stopped and waited. The officer to his left stepped forward, putting his left handprint up against a control panel. The panel scanned the print. His identification was a match. The officer to his right did the exact same thing only with his right hand. A moment later, the war room door slid open.

"Wait here." Aresco's officers nodded as he disappeared into the war room.

Standing around a long glass conference table were the other eight members of the Rover Base's leadership council led by Aresco's second-in-command, Major Fawn Hurley. Hurley had several moles on her face, her skin was almost as weathered as Aresco's. Time had not been kind to her. She always held a pen in her hand, constantly rolling it against her fingertips. No matter where they were or what the situation called for, she never appeared comfortable—which was exactly why Aresco made her his number two. She wasn't a legitimate threat to his leadership.

The rest of his council also included Thayer, Captain Derrick Moore, and Major Ian Shimizu. Shimizu was a duplicitous individual who most certainly could never be trusted, but more importantly, he was fiercely loyal to Aresco and that was all that mattered. He currently ran logistics out of Prisca for the Rover Base.

Thayer's apprentice, Toni, stood behind her. Although she attempted to be inconspicuous, hovering in the background, her height made it a futile exercise. She was a sight to behold, dwarfing several of the men in the room.

Aresco scanned the table. Everyone, other than Thayer, had looks of inquiry on their faces. They seemed just as in the dark as he was.

"Okay Ananke, the floor is yours." Aresco took a seat, while the rest of the council sans Thayer, followed his lead. Toni sat as well.

"Thank you sir." Thayer cleared her throat, activating the table which turned into a visual hologram of the Galicia star system, the Rover Base and lastly, three other unknown star systems, each with their own grouping of planets. Aresco and a few others of the leadership council perked up—this wasn't what they were expecting at all.

"As many of you are aware, about a year ago, we sent remote Rovers to the following neighboring star systems, which we have since named. Marilia, Ogun and Heru."

As she named them, the stars displayed their physical distance from the current position of the Rover Base. They immediately stood out as different from Galicia in that they were much smaller in size, being more akin to the size of the earth's Sun.

"Codenamed Project Pioneer, there was little reason to believe that they would actually find a suitable planet for human colonization."

Shimizu rolled his eyes to the ceiling. "Here we go. DC in full effect. Didn't even make it a full minute before you threw water all over it."

Aresco shot him a look of displeasure and Shimizu looked away, turning his attention back to Thayer.

Thayer appeared to shake off the ridicule and went on with her presentation. She moved from the diagrams to a collage of pictures taken in the newly discovered star systems. The photos revealed at least thirty planets, all in different colors, vibrant and bright.

"Now, the images our rovers have sent back, as you can imagine, are awe inspiring. Within those three systems, exists, what we believe may be seven different planets suitable for human life."

"I'm sorry, did you just say seven?" Hurley asked.

The council members shifted in their seats as they whispered among themselves. They all seemed to be trying to wrap their heads around that specific number. Had she said one or two, that would be one thing, but seven planets would be beyond a miracle. If she were right, they could build an empire. However, it did begin to call into question the validity of Thayer's research.

"Yes, although that's just at first glance."

Thayer scrolled through more photos, isolating the seven planets on the display. From the images, many of them resembled the Earth, three of which appeared larger in size, while the remaining four were roughly the same. "Unfortunately, our remotes are only capable of flybys, not actual exploration, which is why..." Thayer turned to Aresco, "it is my recommendation that we put together an expedition, actual human-led Rover teams to explore these three-star systems and those seven planets specifically."

Thayer's proposal caused an immediate shockwave. More murmuring around the table ensued as Aresco processed the information. *Who would be sent out on these expeditions? Who would be tasked with leading one? What did that mean for the families here on board the Rover Base?* As the leader of the community, these were questions he would have to answer.

Shimizu leaned forward. "Do we even have the manpower for such an operation? You're talking about them traveling millions of miles in space without the Rover Base. Something we haven't done in a generation."

"I'm aware of that Major. And to answer your question, yes, we do have the manpower—if we send some of our cadets."

Captain Moore spoke up. "Our cadets? The vast majority of whom can't even drink? And you want to send them out to some unknown system of planets? That's ludicrous Ananke! And no one in this room knows that better than I do. They don't belong out there."

Thayer glared across the table. "That's Major Thayer, Captain Moore."

The captain held up his hand in a gesture of apology as Thayer looked around the room.

"And pardon my tone, but what else do you all propose? Us just sitting up here forever, floating around, waiting for the end to come? What was the point of training them for exploration if they never explore anything? Just to give them something to do? Cause I can assure you, there are a lot of people up here who are bored and would kill for something new and exciting."

Aresco's hands were clasped in front of him as he contemplated Thayer's observations. Her points were almost too valid to ignore.

"The fact remains, we have to look for a new home and this particular system, doesn't have enough freshwater to sustain any type of colony. Nothing long-term anyway."

"That's not the point Major. You're talking about our children here. It's different. You don't have any, so how would you know?" Captain Moore was once again unable to control his emotions on the matter.

"Enough." A forceful tenor from Aresco before Thayer had a chance to defend herself against the accurate yet hurtful comments. Everyone turned their attention to the head of the table as Aresco leaned forward. He took a look around the table at his council, gauging their eyes and body language. From what he saw, there wasn't a consensus here. Some were ready to attempt something new, while others preferred the status quo, primarily because they were afraid for what Thayer's plan would do to their families no doubt. This was a risk not everyone was so eager to take, especially when it hit this close to home.

Aresco unclasped his hands. "Perhaps, it would be best for all of us if we table this discussion for the time being and move on to other things. Agreed?"

Silence abounded as they all knew this was more of an order than a request. Thayer took a seat, frustrated, turning off the hologram display.

Aresco turned his attention to Shimizu. "Alright then, where are we on the mining?"

Shimizu stuck out his chin, smiling broadly. "Smooth sailing on that front, sir. The Grey Rover just returned from Prisca and the mining crews seem to be in good health across the board. While that planet may not be suitable for habitation, it's natural resources have proven to be a godsend."

"Excellent. Keep us updated Ian." Shimizu nodded and then shot a wink in Thayer's direction. Aresco chose to ignore it.

<>

The aroma of potatoes, with just a hint of pepper, filled the air. A pot of stew was boiling on the electric stove as Orion's mother put on a pair of oven mitts. She opened the oven, pulling out a tray of fluffy, golden brown homemade biscuits.

She placed the biscuits on the counter behind her next to a big salad bowl, before turning her attention back to the stove. In the adjoining family room, a table had been set. This table was just a little bit larger than the one in the kitchen. Their mother tended to make them sit here for special occasions, although none of the children were quite sure what was so special about tonight.

Orion was seated at the table, off in his own world, thinking, almost as if he were talking to himself. Delly entered the room. She quizzically looked at him for a few moments. She checked to make sure their mother wasn't watching before she punched him in the shoulder and ran. Orion sprang to his feet, chasing after her.

He caught up to her in the next room. "Sorry, sorry, sorry, sorry." Delly put her hands in the prayer position, turning around to face him. Every time he was going to retaliate for her hitting him, she did that. She had built up hundreds of punches through the years and he always caved as soon as she said sorry. He had never gotten her back once. All he needed was one good crack and he knew she would stop once and for all.

Orion turned to see Pharaoh standing in front of the wall with his back to them, wearing a VR helmet. He was making all kinds of physical moves. He must be playing a video game.

"Did you guys wash your hands?" Their mother's voice called from the next room.

"Yes."

"No." Delly tried drowning out Orion's voice as he shot her a menacing look. She gleaned over her shoulder returned a smirk while she approached Pharaoh, reaching over top of him to remove his headset.

"Hey!"

"Sorry squirt. It's dinner time." Delly took his headset, setting it down. She then tickled their baby brother as he hurried to the table to grab a seat and get away. Their mother entered the room pushing a rolling cart with their dinner neatly prepared on it. Her presentation was lovely as she began putting the food on the table.

"What are we having?" Delly unfurled a napkin to rest in her lap.

"Potato soup, salad and biscuits."

"Oh my God, Mom. Again?!" To say that Delly was ready for some variety in her diet would be an understatement. Orion shared her sentiments. Pharaoh reached for a biscuit. Their mother gently tapped his hand, causing him to pull it back. Soup and salad first, she didn't want him filling up on bread.

"You act like I make potato soup all the time." Their mother was fixing Pharaoh's bowl, using a ladle to pour some soup in it. If she had the ability to make other types of meals, Orion was sure she probably would, but she could only work with what she had been given on the Rover Base.

Delly threw her hands up, "that's because we're always eating it."

"Well, last I checked, your legs still work, so if you wanna go in there and whip us up some dinner, I'd be delighted."

"Bet." Delly tapped the table, she was beginning to hover.

"Sit down." Their mother pointed as Delly parked her butt right back down.

Orion puts some salad on his plate, was surprisingly enjoying watching the two of them go at it. Delly was becoming more and more independent with each passing day. He chose to remain quiet instead, continuing his recent pattern of flying under the radar. Maybe if they never noticed him, they wouldn't keep asking him how he was feeling.

Delly continued making a mockery of dinner, by over-exaggerating her blowing of the hot soup. Their mother was watching her with a frown. She was about six seconds from giving Delly a piece of her mind.

"Mommy, where's Daddy?" Pharaoh had stopped eating as Orion and his sister looked at one another. It was rare for them to have dinner without their father present.

"He's in a meeting sweetie." Their mother pointed at Pharaoh's soup bowl with her spoon, then to her mouth, while rubbing her belly. This was her attempt to re-focus him on the task at hand, finishing his dinner.

"Yeah, didn't you hear Pharaoh? Word going around the base is that they just discovered some new planets." Delly smiled with her mouth full of biscuit.

"Really?" Pharaoh gleamed.

"Uh huh. And chances are they're gonna need some of us to go check it out." Delly revealed a wide devilish grin, just saying those words her eyes lit up. She was downright giddy.

"I wanna go."

Delly turned to Pharaoh, looking him square in the eyes. "Aww, sorry kiddo, you're way too young for that, but I on the other hand, am top of my class. So you just know they gotta take me. We all know it's my destiny to be an explorer."

Orion rolled his eyes. No one loved Delly more than Delly loved Delly. "That's not fair." Pharaoh sucked his teeth and began to pout.

"I know, that's why it's so important to do well in school little man, so you can do all the fun stuff too." Delly playfully rubbed his head.

Their mother was staring at her so hard now. She really was making a mockery of their family dinner, yet their mother still wasn't doing or saying anything. She was showing Delly preferential treatment, which she always told Orion didn't exist in their family.

"Delly, while I appreciate your interest in your brother's education, I'd prefer you not filling his head up with nonsense, so please stop talking and eat your food."

Their mother was clearly fed up with Delly, yet for some reason she remained calm. Orion waited patiently for her to yell at Delly and yet that was all she would say. This was so disappointing. Delly was being a pain in the ass and there would be no repercussions. She always got away with murder in this house.

Maybe their mother knew something the rest of the family didn't. Was that why Dad hadn't come home yet? Could he be leaving them to explore these unknown planets?

"Anything for you mother dearest." Delly dug her spoon into the soup, lifting some out, blowing on it way too many times before finally slurping it. She looked at Pharaoh, gesturing for him to join in her tomfoolery. Pharaoh lifted his spoon, began copying her.

Their mother sighed, shaking her head. She snatched the spoon out of Pharaoh's hand, slamming it down on the table which surprised the three children. She immediately got up from the table, left the room to her bedroom. Orion resumed eating his dinner, this was not his fight. The mood was no longer playful as Pharaoh and Delly just sat there, they were still in shock. For as mature as Delly liked to believe she was, she most certainly had the ability to be even more juvenile than Pharaoh on his worst day.

Orion and Pharaoh stood side by side in front of the bathroom mirror in their pajamas. Their mouths closed yet contorted, the blue glow emanating from it would be a dead giveaway. Orion opened his mouth revealing a black self-cleaning electric mouthguard covering both the top and bottom teeth. Disposal toothbrushes were a thing of the past.

Orion removed the mouthguard, it was drenched in saliva and cleaning solution, gross. Pharaoh watched him as he spit out the cleaning solution. The automatic faucet sensor turned on, rinsing out the sink. He placed the mouthguard under the water for a few seconds getting all of the solution off before returning it to its holder.

"Alright boys, time for bed." Their mother called out as Orion turned to see her waiting just outside the door. Pharaoh removed his mouthguard, it was even more disgusting than Orion's as he admired it for a moment, holding it up to see his saliva and solution slowly descend into the sink.

"Ugh, don't do that." A grossed-out Orion, nudging Pharaoh with his hips. Pharaoh got the message, began rinsing off his mouthguard as Orion had done moments before.

Orion entered their room to see their mother standing near Pharaoh's pod. She looked at him giving him a warm inviting smile.

"Look Mom, I'm all clean." Pharaoh raced into the room next, running straight for her, giving her the biggest hug around her waist.

"I can see that Ro." She returned his affection with a deep embrace and a kiss on the top of his head. "Ready for bed?"

"Yup." He released his embrace before hopping into his pod. She put a blanket over him. "Mommy, are we gonna find a new home soon? I mean a planet."

Their mother paused a moment, such a direct question from Pharaoh out of nowhere. He was absorbing information so quickly. She gave Pharaoh a glowing smile as she massaged his head. She bent down, kissing him again, this time on his forehead. "Yes, I believe we will."

"Cool. I can't wait to actually go outside."

"Me too sweetheart. Me too." She grabbed the top of his stasis pod. "Now you sleep tight. Don't let the bed bugs bite."

"I won't." Pharaoh yawned as their mother chuckled. If only she could bottle these moments forever, while forgetting about this evening's dinner. She closed his pod, locking it for the night. She checked the timer on his pod, which read 7:25am when he was to awake. She looked up from Pharaoh's pod, noticing Orion's was still open, he was in bed just staring up at the ceiling.

"I figured you didn't need my help anymore."

"I don't. I can do it myself." Orion remained focused on the ceiling. Their mother walked around Pharaoh's pod to where he could see her.

"Is everything alright?" You barely said a word at dinner. This is becoming a habit with you." She seemed to take a lot of pride in being worried all the time, like she had forgotten what it was like to be a kid.

"Kind of hard to speak when Delly does all the talking." She smiled, almost laughed, but she always refused to engage in any ridicule of her children, even if Orion hoped she would laugh just once. "But I'm fine, seriously. Just another long day in the simulator, that's all."

She nodded. It was doubtful that she totally believed Orion, but if he said he's fine, then she had to take him at his word. "Okay. Well, if you ever wanna talk about it, I'm always around."

"I know. Good night Mom." Orion half-smiled, he was ready to be left alone. She got the hint, headed for the exit. She shut off the lights on her way out. Orion watched as she closed the door. The night lights turned on as he sat there alone, in mostly darkness.

<>

Derrick sat exhausted on the couch in the family room. He loosened the top button on his uniform and leaned his head back. Carolyn entered the room with two mugs of coffee. She set a mug down in front of him. He grabbed it, bringing it to his nose, soaking in the aroma. It was black, just the way he liked it.

"So which way do you think he's leaning?" Carolyn sat with her mug, adjacent to him.

"I haven't the slightest idea. But it doesn't take a genius to realize that we can't stay out here, in the middle of nowhere, forever. At some point, we're gonna have to find a home. If for nothing else, for our children."

He took a sip of coffee and looked into his wife's eyes. It was nice having something to take the edge off.

Orion was curled up on the floor in the hallway, just outside his bedroom. He was eavesdropping on his parents' conversation. He quietly rocked back and forth, not wanting to make a sound.

"You know Delly's just chomping at the bit to be on one of those Rover teams." His mother said.

"That doesn't surprise me in the least."

"Cause she takes after you?"

"Cause… if Aresco gives a greenlight, she's more than likely gonna be on one of those ships, whether we like it or not. And as much as I worry about that happening, for all intents and purposes, she's an adult now. It's not our decision to make." Orion's father swallowed. He was choosing his words carefully. "All I could do in that scenario is be supportive of her. And be her dad."

Orion heard his mother emit a long sigh. "Yeah. Well, I guess we'll just have to cross that bridge when we come to it."

"Exactly."

Orion remained seated on the floor just outside his room. He began wiping away tears of his own. Even though he understood that this was potentially the greatest news they ever could have received, all he could think about in this moment was how would he cope with the knowledge that his big sister, the one who lived to torment him, might no longer be around to give him grief and laughs. He would really miss the laughs. At least for the foreseeable future.

He sobbed in silence as this was a reality he was not yet ready to face.

CHAPTER FIVE

CHANGE IS IN THE AIR

Grunting reverberated throughout the gymnasium as Orion and his classmates trained with aluminum quarterstaffs under the watchful eye of their instructor, Shaw. She was a lean woman, muscles on muscles who wore a head wrap with an eye patch attached that covered her left eye. While many of the students often speculated on how she lost her eye, the patch was actually a device that allowed her to monitor how technically proficient they were at using the quarterstaffs.

With every dodge, thrust and defensive stance executed by her enthusiastic students, Shaw received real time information on whether her instruction was being absorbed properly. In her eyes, their moves needed to be smooth and precise. True mastery could only be achieved when the moves were instinctual, effortless. No wonder she was the first woman on the Rover Base to excel at the cadet training, at least before Delly came along.

Shaw continued to move about, her own quarterstaff in hand, stepping directly into their sight lines. She bypassed Callista, stopping in front of Andrew, who thrusted forward with his quarterstaff, mere inches away from her face. Shaw did not flinch. Andrew did, however as she had just broken his concentration.

"And stop!"

The students gave her their full attention as they held their quarterstaffs vertical in their dominant hands at their sides.

"I see progress, but I also see tentativeness. A hesitance to believe in your ability."

Shaw and Orion locked eyes for a moment before she moved on. "When facing an opponent, the most important attribute you possess is not your weapon of choice, but the belief that you can defeat them." Shaw banged her quarterstaff against the floor as all eyes remained focused on her. "For you see, even when on the offensive, one must think defensively and vice versa."

Shaw drew her staff out in front of her, spinning it several times with masterful control. Once she finished, she brought the quarterstaff back to its resting vertical position. "The line between victory and defeat is miniscule, at best, so your approach... and your attitude may in fact be the difference between winning and losing. Or life and death." Shaw looked around, Orion and the others were still engaged, paying close attention.

"Let's go again!"

The students resumed their training exercises while Shaw paced around them observing their progress.

Improvement would not always be linear—sometimes, things just clicked.

<>

An asteroid, around the size of three airships combined, could be seen screaming through space by Warzecha, the lead technician of the Rover Base starboard. The massive rock increased in velocity, crushing the smaller floating fragments of celestial shrapnel in its wake. Its trajectory putting it right in line with Galicia. Impact between the two at this stage was imminent.

Warzecha sat amongst a group of eleven other technicians, whose primary function was to monitor activity on and around the space station and the solar system at large. Their entire command center was surrounded by reinforced plexiglass, giving them a panoramic view of the immediate universe. It was an amazing sight to behold.

Warzecha noshed on a celery stick, dipping it in a food paste. He never knew what the paste was made of. All he knew was that he enjoyed it. "So did I tell you?" He took another bite of his celery.

"Tell me what?" His colleague Tinsley blew his nose into a handkerchief as he remained focused on the console.

"Wife wants to have another kid." Warzecha was disgustingly picking his teeth trying to remove some celery from in-between them. Tinsley laughed. He stopped working, turning to him. Warzecha was not laughing.

"Wait... are you serious?" Warzecha nodded, this was no joke. Tinsley took a moment, processing this information. "Wow. So what are you gonna do?"

"I don't know, but we already have two and she really wants a girl, so... I just, trying to kick that can down the road for as long as possible, you know?" Warzecha sighed. "Maybe if we didn't lose Annabelle the way we did, things would've been different." He was getting a little choked up.

"That's nonsense and you know it. You guys did what you had to do. Okay?" Tinsley grabbed Warzecha's shoulder in an attempt to console him. "Lord knows what I'd do if faced with the same decision, but raising a disabled child up here? With no end game in sight? It's hard enough for us now as is and we're able bodied."

Warzecha tapped Tinsley's hand, appreciating his comforting yet sobering candor. No matter what he did for the rest of his life, nothing would ever allow him to forget having to get rid of his child simply because it didn't meet the health pre-requisites for life on board. Both men re-focused their attention on their work, the mood was definitely no longer jovial.

"Hey guys, check it out." The two men turned to see the rest of the technicians gathered around the window with the best view of Galicia. They rose from their seats, hurrying over to join their colleagues. Everyone stood in awe as the asteroid was mere seconds away from hitting Galicia.

As it moved closer to the hyper star, the asteroid composition began to change, dissolving it like an ice cube in a glass of boiling water. It dissolved almost until it was barely a boulder.

"Holy mother of God, does that thing have a force-field or something that I don't know about?" Warzecha was speaking more to himself than the group at-large.

"Seriously?" Tinsley answered. "That's just pure kinetic energy my friend. If only we could bottle it for ourselves. We would've left this system ages ago." Their attention, along with everyone else's, remained firmly on Galicia. The sun was totally unaffected as the asteroid had been reduced to dust particles like it had never existed.

<>

"Gordie watch your back."

"I see 'em. Thanks Callista." Gordie was strapped in his chair, wearing his VR helmet. Orion, Rio, June, Andrew and Jovan were also strapped in as the group were currently in the middle of another simulation.

Marius was seated at his console watching them through the two-way mirror. His demeanor a sharp contrast from when he first began working with them, this was probably as close to being pleased as he had ever been. Marius was still as hard as they come, but the kids were beginning to acclimate to his tough love approach. They were making a concerted effort to work together without having to be scolded into doing it. He was seeing their improvement in real time which pleased him.

Marius monitored their vitals on the computer. They seemed to be around their normal health levels, the time was coming to eventually increase the danger factor. Just a little test to see how much they had really learned over the past few months. Marius preferred seeing them sweat, although maybe he would save it for their next session.

The control room door slid open as Marius turned to see Aresco standing before him. He quickly rose to his feet and saluted.

"General."

Aresco gestured for him to stand down as he approached. "Donovan. You look tired." The two men shook hands.

"Well, considering what I'm dealing with in this batch, you shouldn't be surprised." Marius smirked, half-joking, half-serious as Aresco maintained his usual poker face. He was such an impossible man to read.

"So are you telling me they're not ready for Cnaeus?"

"That depends on your definition of ready." Marius half-smiled again, still nothing from Aresco. "I mean possibly, if they ever stop failing the simulator. I still haven't taken them beyond the intermediate level. It could be another six months before they complete this, maybe longer."

Marius stopped; he was nervous. He didn't want to make it seem like he was throwing his students under the bus. If they were struggling, that was just as much of an indictment on his teaching as it was on their performance. "But they are improving. I will tell you that."

Aresco nodded. "I need you to push up the timeline."

"Do you mind if I ask why?"

"In due time. But... in the meantime, get them ready for Cnaeus. That's an order!"

"Yes sir."

Marius saluted as Aresco turned and headed for the exit without returning the gesture. Marius turned his attention back to the two-way mirror, taking a step closer. He slowly shook his head.

They aren't ready.

<>

Stars twinkled in the distance from the lowest levels of the Rover Base. It was anyone's guessed what lurked in and beyond them. Delly could see Kristian was staring out into the nothingness of space as she quietly crept up from behind.

Kristian was a very sweet young man. Some might consider him average, but that was just part of his charm. He was cute and he made Delly feel like she was the most important person in the universe. His hands were in a triangle form covering his nose and mouth area as he breathed in and out. *Maybe he was meditating.* Delly thought.

"What are you doing?" Kristian turned around; boy was she a sight for sore eyes.

"I thought you weren't going to come."

"Well, here I am. So you wanna tell me what we're doing here now?" Her hands were on her hips. She never liked having her time wasted. Kristian gestured to the closed door to his right as Delly turned to it. It said "Authorized Personnel Only." He approached the control panel, typing in the password before using his right thumb and pinky fingerprints to activate it. The door slid open as he turned to Delly.

Delly hesitated. "Are you sure about this?"

"What happened to all of your typical bravado? This isn't the Delly I grew up with."

"Fine. Let's go." Delly entered first as Kristian smirked, following in after her. Motion lights turned on as Delly stopped in her tracks. They were in the Loading Bay.

Before them rested the seven Rover space shuttles: Grey, Black, Green, Yellow, Blue, Purple and Red. The Rovers were distinguished by the two solid-colored stripes running across their exteriors and the I-ching emblems.

She turned back to him, "I don't understand Kristian, what is this?"

"Well... I figured you'd be excited to go in one of the Rovers to see the improvements they've made." Kristian smiled. "Thus the perks of my weekend job. Even the Rovers need maintenance from time to time."

Delly scoffed. She couldn't believe what she was hearing. Kristian looked at her with loving eyes. "So are we gonna go in one or do you want to just stay here looking at them from afar?" Delly had the biggest grin, still in disbelief at what he had done for her. Kristian reached out his hand as she took it. He then led her towards the nearest Rover.

The cockpit door of a Rover opened as Delly entered first with Kristian right behind her. She passed the Navigator post, stopping at the raised Captain's seat, which was located about six feet behind the two pilot's seats in between them. Without hesitation, she climbed up into the seat, getting nice and comfy. This was where she had always dreamed of sitting since she was a little girl.

"How's it feel?" Kristian already knew the answer, he just wanted her to say it.

"Like heaven." Delly was soaking it all in.

"You know it occurred to me, when the day comes that you're captain of your own Rover, what better way for us to remain together, then me being able to fix all this." Delly looked down at him as Kristian shrugged. He knew his limitations. "Not much of a fighter Dear. Definitely more a lover."

Delly suppressed a laugh. She nodded her head several times before jumping out of the seat. She approached Kristian, stopping once they were face to face.

"It's a good plan, no?" Kristian smiled.

Delly reached out with both hands, pulling his face to hers, laying a passionate kiss on him. Kristian was a bit startled at first, but it didn't take long for him to figure out what to do next. He wrapped his arms around her waist, if only they could have this moment forever. Delly pulled her face back, still in his embrace. "You're a pretty good boyfriend Kristian Llenas, you know that?" Delly gave him two more soft pecks on the lips.

"So I hear. But when do I get to tell our parents that we're in love?" Kristian looked into her eyes, which unfortunately sucked all the romance out of the room like a vacuum. Delly wanted no parts of answering that question. She slowly removed his hands from around her waist, turning away from him while rubbing her forehead.

Kristian was at a loss, his hands fanning out. "What did I say that was so wrong? Don't you love me too?"

Delly sighed, this was a conversation she never wanted to have. "Of course I love you. But… I'm not ready for that. We're still in school."

"For a couple more months and then what?" Kristian was getting upset. "Don't you see, if you get sent away, it's easier for us to stay together if I'm your husband as opposed to your boyfriend." Kristian reached out, taking one of her hands, caressing it. "I think your father would understand that."

"Kristian, this has nothing to do with my father." Delly pulled her hand back from him. "I'm not ready to consider the rest of my life at eighteen like you seem willing to. I mean, if the opportunity to traverse the universe is really something that exists for me, then I owe it to myself to make that happen." Kristian stood there, silent, her strong words coming down on him like a hammer. "And if you can't understand the way I feel, then maybe we're not as right for each other as you seem to think we are."

Kristian took a step back. He turned away from her, screaming loudly to the space in front of him as she flinched. He had never reacted that way in front of her before. That was intense. He rubbed his face, his body still slightly turned away from her. "I have been in love with you for as long as I can remember." He sighed. "I don't know why I didn't see it sooner..."

"Kristian." Delly wanted to comfort him, but he gestured to her not to approach.

He turned to her, taking a moment. His eyes were getting watery. "You care more about space travel than you do about me and it doesn't seem like that's gonna change. Right?"

Delly looked at him, she felt terrible but she couldn't hide her truth to spare his feelings. That was never going to work. "I'm sorry Kristian." Delly headed for the exit as Kristian covered his face to hide his tears. Although, she didn't technically break up with him, their relationship at least as far as she was concerned, was definitely over.

"Good evening, members of the Rover Base Alpha."

Aresco stood at a podium in the community's press room with Hurley and Shimizu flanking him on both sides. The rest of the leadership council listened closely. He looked into a camera that digitally fed monitors throughout the Rover Base. Everyone would be listening today.

"I'm sure many of you have heard the rumors milling about regarding the discovery of new planets in our neighboring star systems and let me be clear... they are true."

Aresco briefly looked down at his handwritten speech. He was a traditionalist. "After careful consideration with the leadership council, we agreed that the time for action had come."

Aresco cleared his throat. "The time has come for us to send some of our best and brightest... out into the universe to secure our new world. Let me be clear, I am under no false illusions that everyone will be one hundred percent for this plan, but I owe it to the members of this community to think of the greater good for us all."

Aresco hesitated, this was more difficult than he anticipated. "Which is finding a home for our children, our children's children and the future generations beyond. Man was not meant to float around in space forever. Now is the time for us to do something about it."

The leadership council applauded as Aresco raised a hand, he was not finished. "And to further elaborate on the actual mission, I'd like to ask Major Fawn Hurley to step forward at this time. Major." Aresco stepped aside as Hurley stepped to the podium.

"Thank you, General. Good evening, ladies and gentlemen. I will attempt to make this as brief as possible as we would like to give you all the opportunity to process our ever-changing circumstances. For this important mission, we will be sending out three Rovers. Each of which, have been outfitted with homing beacons, that shall be dropped every half-million miles, thus leaving us a trail to follow."

Hurley gestured for Thayer to join her at the podium. "Over the coming days, Major Thayer and I will be working together to assemble the members of these Rover teams. Our goal is quite simple. Within the next year, we expect to have found our new home."

The leadership council applauded once more as Hurley nodded her head. Everyone knew the risks. This decision had to work.

<>

Orion and his family were seated around the dinner table, awaiting their father, who had not yet returned home. While the meal remained the same for the umpteenth time, the energy in the room was different. How could it not after hearing the big news?

The front door slammed shut as Pharaoh sprang to life, "Daddy's home." He began sliding out of his seat.

"Uh uh, you keep your butt right where it is mister. Finish your dinner," their mother said.

A moment later, their father entered. Delly fidgeted in her seat, barely able to contain her excitement as Orion kept his eyes on their father. His face was pale and he looked tired as he gazed around the table. "I take it you all saw the General's press conference?"

"We did."

"So am I going?" Delly interjected, her energy bursting out all over the dinner table. Their father looked at their mother, who immediately dropped her head. The day she had been dreading was finally upon them. Their father turned his attention to Delly, who waited with bated breath.

"Yes... you will be on the Yellow Rover team. Unofficially, as of now."

"Oh my God. Daddy, are you serious?" Delly rocked in her seat, she looked like she was going to burst into flames she was so happy. Their father slowly nodded; it was true. Delly jumped out of her chair, rushing to him. He could only accept her warm embrace and numerous wet kisses on his cheek. "Oh thank you, thank you, thank you Daddy. I love you so much."

"I love you too sweetheart." He patted her back, trying to let Delly have her moment, even if the uncomfortableness had not totally left the room. Delly released her embrace, turning back to the rest of the family at the table.

"Oh my God, this is gonna be so amazing. I can't wait." Delly pumped her fist in celebration as everyone watched her. Their father waited for her to get back into her seat before dropping another bombshell on the family.

"Yeah and you're not the only one who's going." All eyes were on him now as their mother couldn't believe she was receiving more bad news. She shook her head over and over, waiting for the other shoe to drop.

"You're going too?" Delly was beginning to realize the ramifications if their father had to leave the family as well. This new mission was going to completely alter their family's lives.

Their father shook his head, "No. Orion's going to Cnaeus."

"He's *what?*" Their mother was angrier than the kids had ever seen her as she was staring a hole through their father's soul.

"Aresco wants him and his classmates to go through the live-training exercises before we leave the solar system." He explained, knowing that it wouldn't make much of a

77

difference to her. She was too furious to care about the reasons.

"So we just send our only daughter on a mission to the unknown and our younger son is also leaving? And you're okay with this?" Their mother was trying to understand why he wasn't fighting harder for the family to stay intact.

"Carolyn, I don't have a choice."

"You always have a choice Derrick. You just don't let your voice be heard. That's probably why you're still a Captain." She hit their father where it hurt. He was trying to keep his cool in front of the children, but she was pushing him.

"Listen. You know the drill. When Orion turned thirteen, it was only a matter of time before he had to go, just like Delly before him. The only difference here, is that everything is time sensitive. So... he's going and that's the last time we're going to discuss this. The end." Their father put his foot down in front of everyone. This had never happened before.

Their mother glared at their father with a mixture of disgust and pain. She looked crestfallen. She got up from the table, leaving the family behind.

Their father threw his hands up in frustration. This was probably not the way it was supposed to go down, yet unavoidable. There was never going to be a good way to deliver this news. He looked around the table. "Finish your dinner guys."

Their father exited as Orion and Delly looked at one another. They would never get used to seeing their parents argue. The children resumed eating in silence. "Hey Delly?" Pharaoh stopped eating, breaking the silence.

"Yeah squirt."

"Why is Mommy upset?" Pharaoh seemed genuinely curious; this moment was still a little too mature for him to comprehend. Delly put her hand on his head, looking at him, it finally dawned on her that she wouldn't be seeing his angelic face for much longer. It almost choked her up.

"Just finish your food Pharaoh." Orion interjected as Delly turned to him. He reached out, tapping her hand. He gave her a reassuring smile and nod. He was proud of her.

Delly pulled her hand away, making a fist. They bumped fists together as she looked at him for a moment as well. She was going to miss Orion too. They returned to their dinner. Tonight had unleashed a whirlwind of emotions.

Carolyn sat on the floor, curled up in a ball. Their room was identical to Orion and Pharaoh's, with the exception that their stasis pods were built to house adult bodies. She could hear Derrick's footsteps as she sobbed. He slowly entered the room, albeit hesitant.

"Babe." Derrick softly called out.

She couldn't bring herself to face him as she wiped away tears that seemingly wouldn't end. This was hitting her like a ton of bricks. "This isn't right Derrick. This isn't right and you know it." She was an emotional wreck at this point. Derrick leaned against the wall, smartly giving her space.

"Sending three different Rover teams out to three different galaxies." Carolyn turned to him, with a half-laugh, half-cry. "I don't know, maybe I'm dumb, but this clearly looks like someone hedging their bets that at least one of those Rovers isn't coming back. And what if that's the one that Delly's on, huh? What then?"

Derrick didn't respond, he understood that she needed to release all of her anger and frustration. Carolyn shook her head over and over. "But what I can't understand, is how you're so okay with all this?" She was becoming angry all over again.

"I'm not, Carolyn! I'm not okay with any of it. But it's also not my decision." He felt compelled to approach her, to comfort her, even if all she wanted to do was hit him for not doing more. "Delly is eighteen years old, she can do whatever the hell she wants. She can even decline-"

"We both know that's never gonna happen." Carolyn interrupted, still shaking her head over and over.

"So what do you wanna do? Break her legs? Poison her? Tell me, so you can stop blaming me and we can move past this." Derrick put his hand over his face, it was clear he was hurting just as much as she was.

Carolyn turned to him, struggling to find the words. "I don't wanna lose my family Derrick. They're all I've got left. I don't wanna lose them." She was sincere in her defeat.

He couldn't stand it any longer as he bent down beside her. "I know honey, I know." He put both hands on her shoulders as she clutched his left hand. Carolyn began to sob as Derrick stayed with her, giving her the comfort she desperately needed.

CHAPTER SIX

THE LONG GOODBYE

Departure Day, or D-Day as it had come to be known on the Rover Base, had arrived. Weeks had passed since the general's announcement. Now that the day of reckoning had arrived, mixed emotions ran rampant among the community at large. This was a day that would irrevocably alter the lives of many families for good or for bad.

Five of the seven Rovers were docked, ready to be boarded here in the Loading Bay. The Grey and Black Rovers were noticeably absent as they traveled to and from Prisca. Even on an important day such as this one, there was still important work being done on that planet.

Aresco stood on a raised platform, overlooking the hundred and fifty or so people awaiting his last-minute words of encouragement. The members of the Rover teams, distinguished by their silver and black chrome spacesuits, stood out amongst the civilians of the Rover Base.

There was an equal mix of young men and women who were in spacesuits. Twenty-seven men, twenty-seven women. This was no ordinary exploration. Should any of the Rover teams find a new home, a colony would have to be established. It was the only way life could go on.

Aresco took another look at his notes, this moment calling for the speech of a lifetime. He was sending his teams of would-be explorers out into the great unknown and whether he liked it or not, history would judge him based on what they accomplished. Aresco cleared his throat in the microphone as the conversations ended, all eyes were now on him. He looked over the crowd once more, what an incredible day this was.

"Good afternoon, members of the Rover Base Alpha." Aresco's voice bellowed as the sound reverberated all around them in the cavernous space. It was like he was Moses come down from the mountain to talk to the Israelites. That was something Orion had recently learned in his ancient history class.

"Good afternoon." The community responded with great enthusiasm.

"I stand before you all, a very proud man by what I see here today. The faces I see, your faces, are ones of strength, bravery... and passion." Delly stood between their parents with their arms interlocked, proudly taking it all in. For her, this was essentially her graduation day. The time had come for her to stand on her own two feet.

Aresco dug his hands into the podium. "Whether you are truly aware of the gravity of this juncture, please understand that you all are following in the footsteps of some of humanity's greatest pioneers. And I don't believe that I overstate this when I say that your mission is probably the most important of all time. For you see, the only way humanity can continue to exist, you... must... succeed." Aresco pointed in three different directions at the crowd.

Some of the members of the Rover teams swallowed, to hear it put in those terms, really drove home just how important this exploration really was. Mankind's survival depended on them.

"When we find our new home, it will be because of your ability to sacrifice for the greater good of us all." Aresco paused, the silence around them was eerie, you could hear a pin drop. "As far as I'm concerned, this isn't goodbye, this is hello... to new possibilities as you write the next chapter in humankind's glorious history."

Orion's mother sported a skeptical expression as he briefly looked at her, before turning back to the general. "I'd wish you good luck, but then I remember, you're all highly trained, motivated and equally up to the task at hand. Make no mistake, you were born to do this. Everything you've experienced thus far has led you to this very moment. I know you'll make us proud."

Aresco saluted. The members of the Rover teams along with members of the leadership council returned his gesture. Little Pharaoh saluted as well, wanting so desperately to be like their father and Delly. Aresco held his salute for a few moments, almost like a moment of silence. He wanted them to understand just how important they all were to everyone here on the Rover Base. He lowered his salute. It was officially time for them to depart.

<>

The large crowd that had gathered for Aresco's speech was now splintered into three smaller groupings in front of the Blue, Green and Yellow Rovers respectively. Shaw, Orion's self-defense instructor, stood at the top of the side ramp of the Green Rover, gesturing for the members of her team to come aboard. She also had been selected to command one of these rovers. It seemed like everyone who was anyone on the Rover Base was being sent away. Orion wondered would anyone be left to train the next generation. All of the teachers were leaving it seemed like. Except for Marius, of course. Orion wasn't that lucky.

Near the Yellow Rover, their mother was hugging Delly tightly, doing her best to hold back tears. "Now don't be a stranger. You hear me Delilah? Drop us a couple of video logs when you can." It was rare for her to use Delly's birth name. That usually only happened when Delly had done something to make her angry. Mom brought Delly's head to her lips, kissing her several times. Although she was her first born, she still was her baby.

"Will do Mom." Delly held their embrace longer than she normally would.

"I love you sweetie."

"I love you too." She gently tapped her head back against their mother. This was just as hard for her as it was for everyone else. Delly released her embrace, noticed Pharaoh wiping away tears. It was finally hitting him that big sis was leaving, for God only knows how long. He didn't understand that this could possibly be the last time he ever saw her. There was no telling if or when she would be back. That's tough for anyone, let alone a seven-year-old.

Delly moved towards him, bending down so she was at his eye level. "Hey, hey, what's all this? Come on Ro, look at me." Pharaoh kept his head down, if he looked at her, that would only make it real. "Pharaoh, look at me." Delly put her hand under his chin as Pharaoh begrudgingly raised it.

"I don't want you to go." Pharaoh was devastated. His little heart was breaking.

"I know squirt, but I have to. This is what I was born to do, remember?" Delly put her hands on his shoulders. "But we're gonna see each other again, real soon, okay? Promise." Pharaoh nodded. He still didn't understand, but he always wanted her to be happy. "I love you."

Pharaoh unexpectedly hugged Delly, almost causing her to fall backwards. He wrapped her up tight, not wanting to let go. Orion had never seen Pharaoh that upset. He noticed that Delly was surprised as well. Delly returned his gesture as their mother covered her mouth. This was becoming too much. Delly kissed Pharaoh on the side of his head before releasing their embrace. Pharaoh finally let go as well.

Delly rose back to her feet. "Now you be good, okay? And don't give Mom too much grief. She gets enough of that from me and O."

"I won't." Pharaoh sniffled, holding back his tears. Delly nodded, smiled, before turning her attention to Orion, as her smile subsided.

"Alright, looks like you finally get your chance to shine." Delly was as sarcastic as ever. When it came to Orion, she just could never be serious with him.

"Oh please."

"I thought you might like that." Delly extended her arms. They shared a warm embrace. She leaned closer to his ear, whispering. "Listen, I know you think I don't like you and you'd be right. I love you, that's why I'm always giving you shit."

"Should I thank you for that?"

Delly nearly chuckled, but she was able to suppress it. "You're a funny guy when you wanna be. But seriously, I want you to kick so much ass out there. I know you got it in you. You just need to stop being so hard on yourself and let it flow. Remember, you have my DNA in you." She got Orion to chuckle instead.

"Thanks Delly. You too." The two siblings released their embrace. Orion reared back, punching Delly as hard as he could in her shoulder. Delly couldn't believe it as a big smile came over her face.

"Orion have you lost your mind? What are you doing?"

"No, it's cool mom. He owed me." Delly laughed as Orion did too. Their mother shook her head, she had no idea what was going on. Orion had finally got her back for all those years. Delly extended her hand as the two siblings bumped fist. She was proud of him.

Delly turned to see their father, who was holding her space helmet at his side. He pretended like he didn't see what Orion had just done. "Cadet." His goodbye was a sharp contrast to the rest of the way the family said theirs to her.

"Captain." Delly saluted as he returned the gesture. "I promise I'll make you proud."

He unearthed a smile. "Too late for that I'm afraid." He extended his arms as Delly disappeared in his bear hug; it was the biggest hug of them all. In this instant, it was like all the memories from her birth to now had come flooding back to the forefront of their minds. The family was literally changing overnight.

"Thank you, daddy. For everything. You made me who I am today and I'll never be able to repay you for it, but you better believe I'm gonna try my hardest. I know how difficult this has been for you." Delly let it all hang out. This wasn't the time for her to mince words.

"More than you know."

The side ramp of the Yellow Rover began to move as some of the families moved out of the way. As the ramp touched down, Coach B appeared in the entrance.

"Alright Yellow Rovers, the time has come to get this show on the road. We have a job to do." The other seventeen members of the Yellow Rover finished their goodbyes before beginning the boarding process.

Delly released her embrace with their father. "I guess that's me." She grabbed her backpack and duffel bag before turning back to the rest of the family. Their father extended the helmet to her, Delly accepting it with her free hand. She waved goodbye before following after the others walking up the ramp to the Yellow Rover.

Their mother blew kisses to her oldest, while their father watched Delly for a moment, before turning back to the family. "Come on guys, we can watch them from the deck upstairs." Pulling a resistant Pharaoh along, the Moore family began heading for an exit. Orion lingered for a moment, watching his sister walk up the ramp. He swallowed hard.

Be safe, Delly…We love you.

The Loading Bay had been cleared of all human activity as the Blue, Green and Yellow Rovers were now operational. A siren went off, alerting members of the Rover Base that the Loading Bay doors were about to open. The Loading Bay doors were massive. They had to be to fit these giant transport shuttles inside so easily. The doors activated, opening as air was immediately sucked out into space. Anything not secure would surely be jettisoned.

One by one, the brackets keeping the Rovers in-place disengaged. With the air no longer inside, the rovers were now floating. The doors fully opened as the ships departed the Rover Base, beginning with the Blue, then the Green and finally, the Yellow. The Rovers were flying away in a triangular alignment, Blue on the left flank, Green in the center, and Yellow on the right.

Orion and his family were perched on the observation deck watching the three ships head out towards the great unknown. They were surrounded by many more in their space community.

"Think we'll ever see her again?" Orion covered his mouth; he hadn't meant to say that out loud. Their mother shot him a look of incredulousness. They had just left Delly and Orion was already putting that kind of negative energy out in the universe.

"Of course we'll see her again. What would possess you to say something like that?" She didn't want to hear that kind of talk ever. Orion recoiled, realizing his mistake. There was no malicious intent on his part, he was simply curious.

"Delly's tough. She can take care of herself, Mom." Pharaoh chimed in as their mother looked down at his smiling face. His innocence, not to mention his confidence in Delly, was cute, if not reassuring.

"She sure can sweetie. She sure can." Their mother rubbed his head as they watched the Rovers until they disappeared from view. Delly was really gone.

<>

"I can't believe we have to keep doing this. I'm guessing it's because Orion can't handle the simulator. This is idiotic." June led her five classmates through the corridor, presumably for another date with the dreaded simulator.

"Speaking of Orion, where is he?" Rio asked.

June shrugged. "Who cares? We've got more important things to worry about, like what Marius is gonna complain about next. That guy is seriously wound-up way too tight. I swear he's gonna pass out one day and when he does, we'll probably still be in the simulator, getting our asses kicked."

"Well, however Orion is, I'm pretty sure it can't be much worse than my brother, that's for sure." Jovan added.

"What's wrong with Kristian?" Callista wondered.

"What isn't? Ever since Orion's sister left, he's just been moping around, not eating, crying like a baby, telling everybody he doesn't wanna live anymore."

"That sounds kind of funny." Gordie chuckled.

"What's so funny about that? That sounds really sad. Is he gonna be alright? Rio said as Callista nodded in agreement.

"I don't know. Maybe. My dad keeps trying to console him. I don't think it's working." Jovan shook his head. "But if that's what love is all about, who needs it?"

"You don't think that's a little harsh, Jovan?" Rio seemed genuinely surprised by his bluntness.

Jovan shrugged. "No. I mean how good could it have been? She still left him." It was hard to argue with his logic. "Anyway, we have more important things to worry about, like which one of you guys is gonna finish second to me in the simulation today."

"Yeah, totally. I mean if it wasn't for the simulator, how else would we know about Jovan's greatness? Oh yeah, he would tell us." Callista rolled her eyes as everyone laughed.

"Nice." Gordie gestured for Callista to give him a fist bump which never came. The group reached the simulation chamber door which opened automatically and revealed Marius standing next to Orion.

Marius paced around them as they all stood at attention inside the chamber. "The next few months will be the most challenging of your lives. Only in this case, the penalty for failure, could be the loss of life."

Marius paused to look at them. If he didn't have their attention before, he definitely had it now. "So it goes without saying, that I need each and every one of you to check your egos right now, because in my eyes, you aren't cadets, not even close. You are neophytes, who have yet to earn my respect. As far as you're concerned, I'm no longer Dr. Marius. My name is Sir and only Sir. Any question you have for me, every time you reply to me, you end with sir." Marius smirked. "Do we understand each other?"

"Yes sir." The group answered in unison.

"Excellent. We ship out in two days. I'd advise you to say your goodbyes and get some rest before then. Dismissed." Marius gestured for them to leave as the teens headed for the exit.

The group exited the chamber looking rather lost at one another. It was unusual that they would no longer be using the simulator, which was both exciting and scary at the same time.

<>

Orion felt the cold stethoscope move across his back. He hunched over, embarrassed by his undeveloped chest as Dr. Marsilio Llenas, Jovan and Kristian's father, examined him. If there was one thing Orion detested more than anything else, it was feeling vulnerable.

"Breathe in. Then breathe out." Dr. Llenas continued moving the stethoscope around. Orion did as he was told. His mother observed the examination from a chair in the corner. Orion was seated on a raised exam table as Dr. Llenas tapped him on his back. Orion sat up straight. "Have you ever had any trouble breathing?"

"No." Dr. Llenas turned to his mother, neither one was totally buying it. He turned back to Orion.

"Are you sure?"

"Yes, I'm sure." Orion's eyes bugged out a bit. There was no need to keep asking him the same question. Dr. Llenas nodded, putting the stethoscope around his neck.

"Okay, but the reason I'm asking is because the oxygen levels on Cnaeus are about eighty-five percent of what we have here on the Rover Base, and that's at the surface level, so how well you breathe is very important Orion."

"I don't have problems breathing." Orion was becoming defensive, but was still trying to keep a respectful tone. He anxiously clicked his feet together. This needed to be over soon.

"If he says he doesn't, then he doesn't." Orion and his mother exchanged glances. She winked at him.

"Uh, okay." Dr. Llenas grabbed his chart. "Looks like you've got yourself a clean bill. Good luck out there, soldier." The doctor began making notes on his medical chart while Orion put his shirt back on. His mother rose to her feet as Orion hopped down off the exam table. She opened the door for him as Orion exited without saying goodbye.

On his way out of the main office, Orion noticed Callista sitting alone. Her big hair was always a dead giveaway. The two briefly made eye contact as Orion awkwardly waved. "Hey."

"Hey." She replied as Orion's mother hurried to catch up with him before he disappeared into the corridor.

<>

"Callista?" Dr. Llenas was standing just outside his office door. She rose to her feet, approaching the office door. He was holding her medical chart.

"Hey Doc."

The doctor stepped out of the way as she entered his office. He looked out into the hall once before shutting the door behind them.

"Hey. Where's your mom?"

Callista was uneasy, rolling her tongue around her mouth. "Oh, she wasn't feeling well today, so she told me to just come by myself. You know my Dad would come, but he's working on the planet." Dr. Llenas looked at her carefully, she seemed somewhat nervous, although that wasn't unusual for his adolescent patients.

"I understand. It's not a problem. However, as far as your Mom's concerned, do I need to go see her?"

"No, I don't think so. I figured she was just tired, that's all. She was fine yesterday." Callista shrugged her shoulders. This wasn't a big deal.

Dr. Llenas tapped his medical chart. He wanted to make sure there wasn't more here than she had let on. He wouldn't be doing his due diligence if he didn't offer his services. "Okay. Well take a seat, let's get you checked out." Dr. Llenas gestured for Callista to hop on the exam table.

Callista did so as he put his chart down, turned back to her. "I'm gonna need you to take your shirt off."

"Can't I do the check up with it on?" Dr. Llenas paused as it was obvious that Callista was uncomfortable. This was why parental consent and supervision was so important.

"Uh, yeah, that's fine. No problem." Dr. Llenas took the stethoscope from around his neck. He put his hand on Callista's shoulder as she shivered. He instantly recoiled. "Too cold? Did I hurt you?"

"No... it's fine. Go ahead." Dr. Llenas paused, this was becoming uncomfortable for him as well. He placed the stethoscope on her back over her clothes as she slightly shuttered again.

Callista closed her eyes. The sooner this was over, the better.

<>

Gordie's little brother Ham reached for the shiny green apple. It hung from the lowest branch of a tree here in the Rover Base's greenhouse. The bright environment, incubated totally in artificial light, was where the members of the community received their fresh produce. Ham continued tugging on the apple until Gordie came over and snatched it from the branch. He handed it to Ham.

Gordie's entire family—mother, father, two sets of grandparents and three younger brothers—were all together. They were the largest clan on the Rover Base. They were browsing the greenhouse produce, searching for all the right ingredients for a proper departure meal for the Kishore's oldest child. Considering how Gordie had performed in school, they were never sure if this day would ever come.

"So Gordie, have you decided what it is you would like to eat for dinner tonight?"

Gordie picked up a cucumber from a bin. "You say that like I have much of a choice. How many ways can you guys dress up a cucumber and tell us it is something other than a cucumber?" Gordie answered honestly, not a hint of humor nor snippiness detected.

"Gordon. That's no way to talk to your father." Gordie's mother held his baby brother Emil in her arms. "You should be appreciative of the time you have to spend with your family. You're going to be away from us for the next couple of months and that's gonna be very hard for you, trust me."

Gordie chuckled. "Yeah, no offense Mom, but I think I'll be okay." Seeing how big his family was and where he fit in the pecking order, he was a lot more open to leaving the nest than she realized. Gordie always had more fun when he was with his classmates than when he was at home. He was just itching to spread his wings outside of this huge family where he was always being told what to do. Sure Marius told him and the others what to do, but that was only one person, not six.

"We'll see mister smart man. We'll see," his mother said.

<>

The smell of cheese filled the home as Orion's mother went all out for dinner. He couldn't believe that she actually made them pizza. Orion and Pharaoh scarfed it down, vaguely remembering the last time she made that for the family. Sure the pizza was covered with way too many vegetables and the cheese didn't look how it looked on the computer, but hey, pizza was pizza.

Their parents watched as Orion and Pharaoh devoured their meal, just enjoying the moment as this was the last one they would have together as a family, at least for the foreseeable future while Orion was on Cnaeus.

His father took a sip of juice, honing in on Orion. His mother noticed as well. It was almost like he was waiting for Orion to acknowledge him. Orion looked up from the pizza, the faux cheese dangling from his mouth. "What? What are you looking at?" Orion's mouth was full. He wondered if he had done something wrong.

"I know it's been hard, for you... being the middle child. I get it. You never get the attention you feel you deserve, nor the love, nor the Atta boy's. The way to go son." Orion wondered where his father was going with this. While he definitely was spot on in his assessment of how Orion had always felt, he wasn't sure if he was intentionally trying to ruin his dinner by bringing it up in this particular setting.

His father continued, "But that all changes now. Because you my son, are about to embark on a journey to adulthood.

95

Some of us become men and women sooner than others. Not me, I like to believe that I was a bit of a late bloomer, but... I just wanted to say, that I believe in you son, we all do."

Orion looked at his mother, who gave him a reassuring nod. His father was telling the truth for both of them.

"You're special." He pointed as Orion turned back to him. "Now that doesn't mean you're perfect, you've definitely got some growing to do, but if you bust your rump and really give it your best, then you my son, can do anything."

Orion struggled to contain his smile. His father had never spoken to him in this manner before. These kinds of talks were always reserved for Delly, not him. "And that's what you need to remember the most when you get out there. That you belong. Just as much as anyone else in your class or those that came before you."

His father tapped his heart. "It's all in here." Then he tapped his forehead temple next. "And here. Now that's all I got to say on the subject because I really don't feel like crying tonight." His father winked, before picking up a slice of pizza from his plate and taking a bite.

Orion soaked in his words of encouragement, really trying to comprehend what his father was telling him. "Thanks Dad." Orion smiled, that was the confidence boost he never knew he needed.

"Alright." His father gestured with his slice for Orion to finish eating. He had said enough for one evening. His mother continued to beam proudly as they enjoyed their last meal with Orion.

CHAPTER SEVEN

THE RED ROVER

The Loading Bay space seemed even larger than normal, with only the Red and Purple Rovers remaining. Orion and his six classmates were dressed in their spacesuits and wearing their backpacks. They held their helmets at their sides as they walked toward the Red Rover.

For this expedition, there would be no goodbyes, grand speeches nor festivities. Since they had been in the Galicia star system, this training mission to Cnaeus was a rite of passage. One that every member of the Rover Base must endure once they reached the age of thirteen, sometimes fourteen, if there weren't enough kids in a specific grouping.

The seven teenagers stood below the Red Rover side entrance. The ramp was nowhere to be found.

"So are we early or something? Cause I don't see anybody around here." Gordie said as he looked around.

They continued to wait as Orion thought what a cruel joke it would be if after all their preparation they weren't actually going anywhere. Suddenly, the side ramp to the Red Rover began to extend. Once lowered, Marius appeared with a slight smile on his face.

"Neophytes. You're on time for once. I like it."

June and Jovan attempted to board the ramp as the others followed their lead. Marius put his hand out. "Hold on, I don't remember granting you permission to board, did I?"

Everyone stopped as Marius' smile broadened as he called out over his shoulder. "Dee-Dee, Ozone."

Within seconds two silver and black chrome android robots named revealed themselves to the surprised neophytes. They were nothing like the other robots they had encountered on the Rover Base. These aero-dynamic metalloids possessed artificial intelligence, while their movements and body types were humanlike. Bright teal lights flashed in their eyes and across their torso's indicating their life-force. Dee-Dee sported a wild white headpiece that looked like a punk-rock hairdo. Ozone on the other hand, appeared as if he could be Dee-Dee's android sibling, albeit bald, no headpiece necessary. His exterior was sleek and athletic.

"Dee-Dee and Ozone will be assisting us during your training. I expect that you all will treat them with the utmost respect. They are an extension of myself."

"Yes sir." The group responded in unison.

Marius grinned. "Excellent. Your permission to board has been granted."

The seven neophytes began boarding, passing Marius on the way. Once they had all entered, Marius looked up towards a control room window above. Orion followed his gaze to see his father and Shimizu standing next to one another, overlooking their departure. This wasn't too surprising considering they were both on the leadership council.

Marius saluted before nudging Orion further inside the Red Rover. A moment later, the side ramp retracted and the door closed.

<>

Derrick watched the Red Rover's preparation for departure along with Shimizu. This moment was bittersweet. On the one hand, he was a proud parent of what his two children were accomplishing. But on the other, he was a concerned father and husband. He turned to Shimizu. "So how are you dealing with them going away?"

"Dealing?" Shimizu sported a look of confusion before he burst out laughing. "This is the first bit of peace I'll be getting in years. Believe it or not, I'm relishing every moment of this Captain."

Derrick was taken aback by his candor.

"But in all seriousness, I have no doubt that Andrew will be fine out there. He's experienced more hardship than any one of us and yet he's still here. As for June... I'm just hopeful Marius beats the princess out of her. Lord knows her mother and I haven't been able to and frankly, I'm not up for the job." Shimizu paused and looked at him thoughtfully before he added, "Full disclosure, if my kids were like yours, I'd probably be devastated they were leaving."

Shimizu turned back to the window as Derrick processed his words for a moment. It was interesting to hear another father's perspective on this situation. Derrick dropped his head, engaging in a silent prayer.

God please watch over my kids. Please keep them safe, healthy and strong.

<>

The neophytes filed into the main cabin of the Red Rover, each trying to find a place to get comfortable. Unlike the Yellow Rover or any of the adult Rovers, the seats were small, definitely not designed for adult passengers. It was evident that the Red Rover was only used for neophyte training.

Gordie hurried towards the front of the cabin and hopped into a seat in the first row, while everyone else began removing their backpacks.

Callista stared at her space helmet, feeling a sense of accomplishment. "This is gonna be so cool. I can't believe we're finally getting to leave the base."

"Yeah, considering how much Orion sucks at the simulator, I was starting to think it would never happen." Gordie chided.

Orion shook his head. Even outside of class, the jokes just kept on coming. The only way he would ever shut them up was by showing and proving, so there was no point in getting into an argument.

Rio stepped forward. "Hey, lay off Orion already. It's getting old. Besides, it's not like you're much better, Gordie."

"We're talking about Orion, not me." Gordie became defensive as usual even though he was the one who started it.

"I didn't say anything about Orion. Okay!" Callista put her hands up, she did not want to be dragged into this conversation any further.

"What gives Rio? You're like always defending Orion. Do you like him or something?" June was making strange kissy faces at the two of them.

Rio and Orion exchanged embarrassed flushed looks. She would have been better off not getting involved.

"I bet it's because they both got Rio in their names." June continued.

"Oh my God, how am I just noticing that now?"

"Cause you're a clown maybe?" Callista said.

"That's not funny." Gordie was becoming very serious. That was one joke at his expense too many. He was so thin-skinned.

"Alright neophytes, find your seats." Marius entered. The tomfoolery ended right then and there. "We're going to be up here awhile." Marius approached the front of the cabin as the teens got comfortable, strapping themselves in.

Marius entered the cockpit as Dee-Dee and Ozone were seated in the pilot and co-pilot's seats preparing the Red Rover for take-off. "Systems good?"

"Almost complete sir. Estimated time of departure, under five minutes."

"You guys are the best. Lord knows what I would do without you." Marius climbed into the raised captain's seat behind them.

The Loading Bay doors opened as Dee-Dee and Ozone awaited his instructions. "Whenever you are ready sir."

Marius took a deep breath, so began another journey with a crop of neophytes. "I'm ready." Dee-Dee turned to Ozone. All of the instruments had been checked, they were ready to take off.

The brackets released from the base of the Red Rover as the ship's booster rockets activated. Dee-Dee began carefully piloting the ship out of the Loading Bay into the blackness of space that enveloped them. Almost instantaneously, the Red

Rover's interior lighting activated to keep the ship from becoming pitch black.

With the Red Rover now fully disembarked from the Rover Base, the Loading Bay doors retracted, their journey to Cnaeus had begun.

<>

Orion stared in awe out of his cabin window as the Red Rover continued soaring through space. The shuttle passed the colorful moons of a giant gaseous planet their community didn't know much about. Several attempts had been made to explore the planet, named Sonain, but were ultimately thwarted by its chaotic atmosphere. Wind gusts had been recorded to travel in excess of six thousand miles per hour.

The Rover Base had yet to develop technology capable of breaching Sonain beyond its outer atmosphere. It's treasures, secrets and dangers remained a mystery, even with its relative proximity to the Rover Base. Sonain's five moons revolved around the planet, ranging in size, no two moons sharing the same dimensions. These moons did possess a common trait however, they all lacked atmospheres; thus they could never be used for colonization.

The other neophytes were also pressed against the windows, observing as much as they could. They were finally getting the chance to see what they had been deprived of their entire lives up close. It was even better than they could've ever imagined. The observation decks were good for what they were, but nothing compared to what they were seeing now.

Orion sat in a solitary mood, soaking in everything as best he could. He was filled with mixed emotions. Their family was extremely close and until now, he had never spent any time away from them. He could probably count the number of times he didn't sleep in his own bed on both hands in his thirteen years of life.

Orion exhaled, no matter how difficult this was for him, he needed to suck it up and make the best of it. There was no way he was coming home without completing this. That was the only way he was going to make his parents proud of him. He closed his eyes as his mother's voice began to sing a familiar tune in his head.

"Hush, little baby, don't say a word, Mama's gonna buy you a mockingbird. And if that mockingbird don't sing, Mama's gonna buy you a diamond ring."

<>

An elevator door opened as Derrick stepped off. A long walk down the corridor to his family's quarters awaited him. "And if that diamond ring turns brass, Mama's gonna buy you a looking glass."

Carolyn was seated on the couch, stroking Pharaoh's head, which rested comfortably in her lap. "And if that looking glass is broke, Mama's gonna buy you a Billy goat. And if that Billy goat won't pull, Mama's gonna buy you a cart and a bull."

The front door opened as Derrick quietly entered. He shut the door behind him, slightly banging his head against it. It was difficult seeing two of his children leave so close together. "And if that cart and bull turn over, Mama's gonna buy you a dog named Rover."

Derrick entered the family room as Carolyn could hear his footsteps, turning back. "And if that dog named Rover won't bark, Mama's gonna buy you a horse and a cart." Derrick nodded; it was official. Their middle child was gone as well. Carolyn sighed, dropping her head a bit. She wiped away tears with her free arm. "And if that horse and cart fall down, you'll still be the sweetest little baby in town."

Pharaoh had fallen asleep as Carolyn put her hands over her face, she was trying so hard to keep it together but it was impossible. She whimpered in silence as tears fell down her cheeks, some landing on Pharaoh.

Derrick approached the couch, wrapping his arms around her, just holding her in an embrace. This was difficult no doubt, but they were going to get through it… as a family.

Marius entered the Red Rover main cabin. The neophytes were resting for the night. He stifled a yawn: this had been an eighteen-hour journey thus far and they still hadn't reached Cnaeus. As he made his way towards the front of the ship, he spied Gordie's backpack on a chair in the front row. The backpack had the initials "GK" on it. He grabbed it and stowed it in a compartment beneath the seats.

Marius went to the cockpit. Dee-Dee and Ozone were piloting the spacecraft in silence. That was the difference between the androids and humans: no need for idle chatter. When Marius entered, Ozone turned to him.

"Dr. Marius, you're awake. Is everything alright?"

"Yeah, everything's fine." Marius closed the door behind him and it secured itself automatically. "Seeing how this is our final mission together before we leave the solar system, I realized I've never had the pleasure of seeing planetary entry before." Marius chuckled, "So I'm knocking it off my bucket list."

"Very good, sir." Ozone nodded.

"We should be landing within the hour sir." Dee-Dee said.

"Right on schedule. I love it." Marius climbed into the captain's seat, strapping himself in.

The Red Rover was now mere miles away from the planetary rings which protected Cnaeus. The closer the Rover got to the rings, the more amazing they truly were. Huge fragments of rock floated in perfect symmetry around the planet's gravitational field. If Cnaeus were to disappear, many of these rocks would probably be considered asteroids—they were that big.

Dee-Dee and Ozone were unfazed by the beauty that was before them while Marius sat wide-eyed, captivated by the view. It was almost like he was a kid again. It was one thing to see this environment in a photograph, but it was a whole different ballgame when a person was able to see it through their own eyes up close and personal. Marius undid his straps and climbed out of his seat. He came up behind the two androids, still looking out the dashboard window.

Ozone turned to him. "Dr. Marius, I would advise that you please get back into your seat and secure yourself immediately. We're about to enter the planet's atmosphere; this is very dangerous." The android was mindful of its tone as Marius was still its superior.

"I know, I know, but look at that." Marius waved his hand. He would not be denied this opportunity, not now. Asteroids were flying all around them. The Red Rover was like a guppy swimming through a pod of whales. "This is incredible. Sometimes it's easy to forget just how lucky I am to be alive."

There was a loud thud and the cockpit jostled, nearly knocking Marius to the floor. Dee-Dee and Ozone turned their attention back to piloting the ship, checking if the Red Rover took any damage. One of Cnaeus' rocks banged against the ship's exterior. Marius that big of distraction to the androids.

"What was that?"

"I implore you to please be seated sir. Ozone and I must focus on landing the Rover safely." Dee-Dee remained focused on piloting the ship.

"Okay, okay, you've made your point." Marius nodded, hurrying back to his seat as another thud was heard against the ship, which almost brought him to the ground again. He used his left hand to break his fall. Marius hopped back into the captain's seat, strapping himself in. This could be a bumpy ride.

The Red Rover flew through the asteroid ring. Even though the asteroids remained within the gravitational pull of Cnaeus these huge rocks were in constant motion, making the journey through them that much more difficult. Some of the smaller fragments bounced off the ship's exterior.

It was easy to forget that, despite the Red Rover's size and capabilities, flying through this rocky maze unscathed was a difficult task, even for an expert pilot. With some slick maneuvering by Dee-Dee, the Red Rover dodged the majority of the giant fragments while busting through the smaller ones. It eventually passed through the ring and entered the planet's atmosphere.

The skies were dark, yet illuminated. The stars, along with the planets closest to Cnaeus, could visibly be seen in the night sky as there wasn't a cloud in sight. This was Galicia's effect as a hyper-star.

Dee-Dee flew the Red Rover over a mountainous desert region. Its landscape was similar to that of the Grand Canyon. Flat, arid conditions, albeit the dirt was a greyish color. It was also deserted. Not a soul or living thing in sight.

The android steered the Red Rover for a few more miles, searching for a proper place to land. It eventually came upon a spot between two mini-mountains. Its landing gears extended as the booster rockets underneath activated, giving the ship the energy needed to make a smooth and safe touch down.

Grey dirt spewed out in every direction as the Red Rover continued its descent. As the dust was blown away, the Rover Base emblem was uncovered underneath the ship. This was their training ground. The spaceship landed with a loud boom, sending shockwaves across the landscape.

Marius loosened his seatbelt. Getting here was the fun part. Now it was time to get down to business.

CHAPTER EIGHT

THE BEGINNING OF CHILDHOOD'S END

The Red Rover engines powered down as Dee-Dee flipped switches to conserve the ship's energy. Now that they were too far from the Rover Base to use it as a resource, every move they made must be precise and calculated. The Rovers by and large had a finite power supply. However, their exteriors possessed solar technology which helped them replenish primary and auxiliary power while the ship remained in an idle state, provided sunlight was available.

Marius climbed down from the captain's seat. He cracked his neck in two places, that was a rougher landing than he anticipated. "You two check for any hull or system damage while I wake the neophytes."

"Yes sir." Ozone plugged himself into the ship's mainframe. This allowed the android to perform a full diagnostic of the ship interior, the same way someone might defrag a computer to fix system bugs. Marius headed towards the main cabin of the Red Rover.

Marius stood at the entrance as the seven neophytes rested peacefully in stasis pods that slid comfortably into the walls on both sides of the habitation chamber. These stasis pods were designed to protect passengers in the event of turbulent conditions. The pods were also capable of being jettisoned from the Rovers during an evacuation if need be—which would have been considered a worst-case scenario.

A solid blue light emanated from every occupied pod. Should a pod malfunction or be unoccupied, the light above them would be red. There were ladders furthest away from the door attached to the pod walls extending from the floor to the ceiling on both sides. Like bunk beds, these ladders allowed the passengers to climb in and out of a stasis pod without disturbing anyone else.

Marius moved towards the pods as the ship's auxiliary lights activated detecting his body movement. He took a look at both sides of the room. There were three blue lights to his left and four to his right. His seven neophytes were right where they should be. Marius quietly pointed at all of the illuminated pods.

This was his version of "Eeny Meeny Miny Mo." He pointed at one of the pods to the right, was higher than his eye level. He stepped on a ladder and peeked inside: *Gordie*. Marius shook his head, he had to try again.

He remained on the ladder, pointing at all the pods, excluding Gordie's. He stopped at the pod on the floor across from him. He climbed down the ladder, approaching the pod. Inside he found Rio. There was a small box underneath the blue light that Marius opened.

Inside it was a qwerty keyboard, the same style as would be found on a computer. He typed in her name backwards, hit enter. He hurriedly closed the box on her pod before moving out of the way as Rio's pod slid open, making a hissing sound.

Rio remained asleep as Marius watched her. It was only a matter of time before the cool air of the Red Rover would wake her now that she was no longer in stasis. Rio slowly opened her eyes to see Marius standing over her.

"Ahhhhh." Rio screamed, startled by his face being the first thing she saw when she awoke. He smiled at her. "Dr. Marius… Sir, what are you doing?"

Marius leaned closer. "Nap time is over Rio. Time to get up."

He pulled back from her as Rio sat up in her pod. Although his neophytes had only been in these pods for a few hours, sleeping in them always made it easy to lose track of time. Years could feel like minutes regardless of if they found themselves in on the Rover Base or the Red Rover. However, the amenities and conditions on this spaceship would pale in comparison to what they were accustomed to on the Rover Base.

"Are we here already?"

"We are indeed, so I need you to wake the others and meet me outside in ten minutes. Is that a problem?"

"No, no problem."

"Good, then you can start now." Marius headed for the exit. Just as he was about to leave, he stopped, turning back to her. "Oh. I'd also advise that you all have your helmets and your backpacks. You're gonna need them."

"Yes sir." Rio saluted. Marius exited the room without returning her gesture.

<>

Rio rolled out of her pod, she was still trying to get her bearings as so many questions ran in and out of her head. *Who*

110

do I wake up first? Where is our gear? And why did she tell him that she could do this in ten minutes? She needed to hurry.

"Ah crap, think Rio, think."

Rio looked at the higher pods. Due to the timeline given to her by Marius, it made more sense to let them out first, because they would cover the ones below them. Rio climbed the ladder on the same side she slept on. Near the top she found June inside. She opened the small box on June's pod, typing in her name. Nothing happened. She did it again. Still nothing happened.

"Oh my God, what the hell?" Rio was becoming frustrated, banging her head with her fists. She almost lost her balance on the ladder, grabbing on it. "Aww, of course."

Rio typed June's name backwards. She leaned back as June's pod slid open, making a hissing sound. June didn't immediately wake so Rio reached out, touching her shoulder. "June, June, wake up."

"Ahhh. What?" June looked up, startled by her face. "Rio, oh, are you insane? Go away."

"Get up June. We don't have much time." Rio hopped over to the other ladder as June rolled over on her side, not wanting to be bothered.

"Oh my God. Why are you acting like an idiot?" June was trying to go back to sleep.

"Because Dr. Marius said we have ten minutes to get outside." Rio opened the small box to Gordie's pod. She was typing his name in backwards as June rolled back over towards her.

"What? Why didn't you say that when you first let me out?" A befuddled look adorned June's face. She sat up in her

111

pod as Rio finally got Gordie's pod to open before descending the ladder to wake the others.

"I don't know, maybe because I was trying to get you all out at the same time." Rio was unsure of who to let out next. June had climbed from her pod to the ladder.

"Well we're never gonna make it at this pace." She watched as June jumped down to the floor.

"That's why you should be helping me." Rio was shaking. If she didn't calm down, she was going to have a panic-attack.

"Why are you guys yelling?" Gordie wiped the cold out of his eyes as he stretched his arms. He was moving even slower than June had a moment earlier.

Shut up Gordie." Both girls yelled back. Gordie put his hands up indicating he didn't want any trouble. He watched as the two girls were desperately trying to wake the others, opening the small boxes to the still occupied pods.

Gordie waved them off, choosing to lie back down in his pod. He was no longer visible to either of the girls. "Get out of the pod Gordie." Rio shouted. He quickly rose back up.

"I'm up. I'm up. Jeez."

A beautiful twilight appeared in the night sky as the rings of Cnaeus could be seen from the ground, the view breathtakingly clear. Marius stood just outside the Rover's side air lock in his spacesuit along with Dee-Dee and Ozone. The universe's beauty held no interest to him now that they had finally arrived. Here on Cnaeus, he was all business. The business of whipping these neophytes into shape.

He breathed into his helmet, his shield's color was black, which was standard for all the commanding officers when they found themselves away from the Rover Base. It fogged up a bit, he was growing more and more impatient by the millisecond. Marius checked his left arm band, the ten-minute countdown he gave Rio had already elapsed. They were now at negative seven minutes, twenty-four seconds and counting.

He turned to his android helpers, "I would say I'm surprised, but then again, that would be a lie." Ozone and Dee-Dee looked at one another.

This training mission was already off to an inauspicious start.

Pandemonium took place just outside the airlock as the seven neophytes were putting on their backpacks and securing their helmets. Rio put her helmet on last. "Are we good?" The click from her helmet fastening could be heard.

"I can't find my backpack." Gordie looked around as everyone's shoulders slumped. They knew they couldn't move forward until everyone was ready.

"Oh Gordie, where did you last leave it?" June sighed.

"I don't remember. Marius made us go to sleep and I… the cabin!"

"What?" Callista was perplexed.

"It's in the cabin. Just wait one second, I'll be right back." Gordie stormed off back towards the front as the other six remained.

"So are we really going to just let Gordie look for it all by himself?" Orion asked.

No one answered as they all sort of just looked at each other. One by one they followed after Gordie to help him find his backpack. If they didn't help him, lord only knows how long they would have been waiting.

Gordie opened every overhead compartment. They were all empty. The other neophytes entered. "Gordie, did you find it?"

"No. I don't know where it is. I put it right on that chair." Gordie pointed to an empty seat in the front row. "I checked all the compartments, it's not here."

"Did you look under the seat?" Andrew said, not a hint of sarcasm detected.

Gordie smiled. "I did not." He got down on his knees, looking under the seat of the front row. He dug in, pulling out his backpack. "I found it. Someone must've put it there." Everyone groaned as he put it on. Marius was going to be so angry.

"Can we go please? June pleaded. We are so screwed." One by one the neophytes hurried out of the main cabin.

They returned to the side air lock as Jovan approached the control panel. "Is everybody ready?" His fingers were eager to push those buttons so they could finally get their training started.

"Ready!" They all responded in unison.

"Okay, here we go." He keyed the "Air" button on the control panel. The air was vacuumed out of the airlock and recycled back into the rest of the ship. Jovan then hit another button that said "Ramp." A door opened as the ramp began to move.

The ramp lowered to the ground, revealing an irritated Marius with his arms folded, flanked by Dee-Dee and Ozone. The two androids were holding six long metallic rods apiece, three in each hand. The neophytes reluctantly came down the ramp. They weren't officially outside until they were off the Red Rover completely. Gordie was the last one off. "Well, well, well... seems you neophytes finally decided to join us after all. How long did it take them, Dee-Dee?"

"Twenty-nine minutes and thirty-four seconds, sir."

Marius shook his head. "Twenty-nine minutes and thirty-four seconds. Wow. Now I distinctly remember telling Rio, that you had exactly ten minutes to get out here. Anyone care to explain why that didn't happen?"

The neophytes stood at attention, no one would dare speak unless he pointed a question directly at a specific person. Marius attempted to make eye contact with each of them. Surely one of them would crack under the pressure and blame Rio for wasting too much time or them having to wait for Gordie to find his backpack.

"Okay, fair enough." Marius nodded. He turned to Dee-Dee and Ozone, who were still standing at attention while holding the metallic rods. "Drop 'em." He pointed as Ozone and Dee-Dee dropped their rods. They clanged against each other. The neophytes watched, not totally sure what was going on. "Now, can anyone tell me what these are?" Marius turned back to his students.

The group looked at them for a second, everyone still seemed hesitant to speak. "Are they our training batons?" Gordie said, taking a shot in the dark. Marius laughed, that must not have been that bad of a guess. The kids relaxed a bit, this may be the first time they've ever heard Marius laugh, let alone smile. For once he was not mad at them or so they would think.

Marius's face immediately turned sour. "No. Not even close. And since you obviously don't know and would rather guess than simply admit that you haven't a clue, I want you to pick 'em up." Gordie didn't move, not totally sure if Marius was talking only to him or to all of them. He looked directly at Gordie. "I gave you an order neophyte."

"Yes sir."

Gordie saluted, hurrying towards the beams. He bent down, attempting to lift one. He struggled, having underestimated just how heavy one of them was. While he continued to struggle, Andrew went over to help him. The others soon joined them, helping Gordie get the first rod upright. One by one the neophytes got the rods upright, with everyone holding two with the exception of Orion and June, who were each holding one. Marius walked around them.

"Okay. Now I want each of these rods secured in the ground around the Red Rover. But, they must be of equal distance apart, so it would behoove you all to work together, unless you would prefer to still be doing this when the sun rises."

The group huddled together dragging the rods with them as Marius watched.

"How the heck does he expect us to measure the exact distance between these things? None of us has a ruler." June whispered.

"There's gotta be a way. He wouldn't have us do this if there wasn't." Rio said.

"You sure about that?"

Everyone turned to Jovan. Even though no one had brought it up earlier, how Marius expected them to exit the

Red Rover within ten minutes knowing they had been asleep and that they still needed their full gear, was a mystery. He had given them an assignment that was damn near impossible to complete.

"Neophytes, the sun is going to rise. Every second you waste is another you lose of sleep." The group continued to huddle as Marius sighed.

"Is it possible to have the robots help us, sir?" Callista asked.

"The robots?"

"I mean, uh… Dee-Dee and Ozone."

Marius turned to the androids who were standing by, awaiting his instruction.

"Sure, I don't see why not. Dee-Dee. Ozone." Dee-Dee and Ozone approached the neophytes to help them secure the rods.

<>

Ozone slammed a rod into the grey dirt as Andrew and Jovan were on their knees filling the hole around it with dirt. They packed it tightly and tamped it down further with their boots.

"Is it in tight?" June asked.

Andrew attempted to shake it; the rod didn't move. "Yup, it's secure."

"How many do we have left?" Jovan approached June, who watched the others working on another rod. Judging by her position, it seemed like she spent more time supervising this exercise than helping.

"That's the last one." June pointed.

"Uh, thank God." Jovan pumped his fist.

117

Dee-Dee jammed a rod into the ground as Rio and Callista packed the dirt in tight around it. "Okay, that's all of them." Rio said.

The two androids immediately began walking around the front of the Red Rover to the other side where the ramp was. The neophytes followed after them. Marius was sitting on the ramp waiting for them, possibly deep in thought, possibly asleep, it was hard to tell from the distance. The Red Rover was a long spaceship across when walking around it.

Marius noticed them approaching, yawned, "Are we all set?"

"We are sir." Jovan said.

"Okay then." Marius stood turning sideways as Dee-Dee and Ozone continued to the Rover, walking up the ramp without breaking stride. "We'll see you neophytes in the morning." Marius walked up the ramp after them.

Everyone looked confused, first at him, then at each other. "Sir? You expect us to sleep out here?" Callista asked.

Marius stopped, turning back to them. "Of course I do. It's your first night at camp, that means you all sleep under the stars. Luckily for you, they're pretty bright this evening. Good night neophytes." Marius entered the Red Rover as they watched him. It was hard to tell if he was serious right now. A moment later, the ramp retracted as the side air lock closed. If they didn't believe him before, now they did.

"Well, I guess we better find somewhere to sleep." June rolled her eyes.

"I don't know what you're complaining about. We've been cooped up on that base forever and now you're mad that we're actually outside? This is awesome." Andrew said, taking it all in.

"Sure we're outside, I'll give you that, but we don't even have any pillows. When's the last time you slept without a pillow, huh? I can tell you the last time I slept without one. Never." June was not feeling this at all. Before anyone could respond to her, the tops of the metallic rods all around the Red Rover began to glow, startling them.

The neophytes wondered what was going on as a blueish ion force-field materialized around the entire spaceship, with each rod sending energy to an antenna, which had extended from the roof of the Red Rover.

"Holy crap!" June exclaimed.

The force-field was visible, but it was also somewhat transparent allowing them to see through it. Jovan foolishly approached the force-field, reaching out to touch it. He was zapped by it, blasting him backwards to the ground.

"Oh my gosh. Jovan, are you okay?" Callista screamed as everyone rushed to his aid.

"Uh yeah. Just remind me never to do that again." Jovan struggled to sit up as Gordie laughed.

"I guess that means we just learned our first lesson on Cnaeus, huh? Good job Jovan." Gordie continued laughing as some of the others joined him. Even Jovan couldn't help but laugh. That was a good one, even if it did hurt a little more than his ego.

Rio was the only one not laughing. She dropped her head; something was really bothering her. "Hey guys?" The others turned to her. "Is there any reason why you guys didn't blame me when Marius asked us what took so long to get out here?" The others kind of looked at each other.

"Rio… it wasn't your fault. I mean, look how much stuff we had to do. Remember Gordie's backpack? If we would've blamed you, then we'd all be in trouble. And I think that's kind of the point of this." Callista shrugged.

"And there was no way to get us all out of that room in ten minutes. I refuse to believe that it's possible. He knew we were gonna fail." June said.

"Duh, that's Marius for you. He's nuts." Gordie smirked.

"Yup… and like it or not, we're a team now. So we might as well start acting like it." Said Andrew.

Rio smiled; it was comforting to know that they did have her back. Maybe things really would be different here for them.

"Wow, that was really touching guys, like seriously, my eyes are dripping… but that's just because I'm very sleepy. According to Marius the sun's gonna come up soon, so can you please try to keep it down?" Gordie sidled up next to the Rover, using it as a buttress with his backpack as his pillow.

"Good idea Gordie." Jovan hurried over to him, plopping down right beside. He wanted to get in nice and tight.

"Oh come on now. Look how long this ship is. At least gimme some room. Ugh, jeez, it's like I never left the Rover Base over here." Gordie pushed back, but to no avail. He was visibly frustrated, not only by his lack of sleep, but by his mates dogpiling on him.

"We love you Gordie." Orion joked.

"Oh, shut up."

The seven neophytes eventually got comfortable as the force-field protected them from the rocky landscape of Cnaeus. The twilight still showcasing the beautiful ring protector of the planet. They had truly arrived.

CHAPTER NINE

STRENGTH IN NUMBERS

Orion and his classmates remained huddled together, still asleep as the force-field dissolved. Not only had it protected them for the night, it also served as a sun-blocker. Orion was awakened by the daylight as loose particles of dirt dissolved in it. Galicia rose in the east in the white sky.

Even at Cnaeus' great distance from the sun, the ultra-violet rays of the hyper-star still held a powerful effect over the planet. As far as the Rover Base knew, there had never been signs of life on this planet. Their scientists always believed that Galicia was the culprit.

The neophytes were jostled unexpectedly by the lowering side ramp. It hit the ground with a thud and Marius emerged from the Red Rover, wearing his officer's uniform instead of his spacesuit and looking refreshed. Dee-Dee and Ozone were behind him.

"Neophytes. Good morning. Are we ready to begin?" Marius turned to them, his effervescent smile shining just as brightly as Galicia. This was twice in two days they would have seen him smile. That would be a record. He cast a shadow over a few of them as the neophytes slowly began getting back to their feet.

"Sir, you don't need your helmet?" Orion asked.

Marius laughed. "Well, it's obvious that none of you have begun to understand what we're even doing out here. You don't know what your helmets can do, none of your backpacks are open, so I'd wager that you have no idea what kind of supplies are inside."

Marius tapped his chest before jumping down from the ramp. "I need you all to understand that some of the planets in this solar system, when Galicia sets, the temperature drops hundreds of degrees below zero. Your suits are only capable of keeping you alive in minus fifty-degree temperatures centigrade, which could be worse if there is inclement weather. So it behooves you to know what's in your kit. For God sakes, that's what it's for."

Orion was fidgeted but didn't dare look away for fear of being singled out by Marius.

"This is not a summer camp, neophytes. This place is where you learn how to survive. Because the universe is nowhere near as kind as I am. It's a million times meaner if you can believe that. And if I have to tell you that, then you've already failed. And by extension... so have I."

Marius shook his head as he paced back and forth. "Now, there are three basic tenets that you must abide by if you want to survive in the unknown. The essentials are self-reliance, self-confidence and teamwork. And these are things I cannot teach you." Marius stopped pacing, turning back to them. "But... there are other things that I can teach you... so let's get to work."

Marius took a deep breath, exhaled. He clapped his hands multiple times at the neophytes—the time had come for them to get down and dirty for real.

<>

The neophytes shot out their grappling hooks as they latched onto the rocks above. Orion tugged on his line, making sure it was secure. This was a new experience for all of them. They were on the ground, roughly thirty feet below the rock's apex. Their grappling hooks were affixed to their forearms via armbands. Gordie was left-handed, so he wore his on his right arm, while everyone else wore theirs on their left.

Marius watched, flanked by Dee-Dee and Ozone. They tugged on their lines several times, but no one had the courage to climb yet. "While we're young, neophytes. Let's go." Marius clapped at them. It was time to stop stalling.

Jovan scaled the rock easily, at least when compared to everyone else. Rio and Andrew were about three-quarters of the way before they were forced to rest, clinging to the rock. June and Callista didn't even make it that far before coming back down to the ground.

Orion and Gordie dug their boots into the rock, but could barely pull themselves up beyond a few feet. Their lack of upper body strength was glaring amongst the group. Marius covered his face, shaking his head, they had such a long way to go. He urged them to keep going, just because they struggled, that didn't mean they got to stop.

On the next exercise, Marius had them doing push-ups while in their spacesuits, helmets and backpacks. The more exhausted they were, the better, it was the only way he could learn their limits. Ozone and Dee-Dee paced around the neophytes, helping them with their form, picking them up when it looked like they wanted to quit. Although they were not human, these two androids knew what teamwork was all about. This wasn't their first go-around working on Cnaeus with Marius.

"See you in three hours." Marius stated pointing at a ridge well beyond their training grounds.

The neophytes looked at one another, thus began a long trek to God knows where, while still being fully suited. The terrain itself wasn't too difficult to maneuver, but the hot sun, coupled with all of their equipment, did make for an uncomfortable experience.

Jovan was way out front again, leading the group as Orion tried to keep up with him. The lesser athletes brought up the rear. "Oh my God, my feet are killing me." June complained.

"Yeah guys, think we can take a break… please?" Orion found a nearby rock to sit on. He removed his backpack. Everyone stopped as Jovan turned around, walking back to the group.

"Marius said we have to be back in three hours. We have to keep going." Andrew said, standing in place while moving his legs up and down, not wanting to break his rhythm. Orion watched him, began doing the same thing while sitting on the rock. If their bodies went into rest mode, there was no telling how long it might take for them to get motivated again.

"Why? He's not out here. How would he know if we stopped early? It's not like he can see us. Look how far we are from the Rover." Gordie removed his helmet. "Seriously, what do you guys think?" A moment of silence fell over them as there seemed to be mixed interest in them not continuing.

"I think we should keep going. If we stop now, we're definitely not gonna want to start again." Callista said.

"I agree. We should move." Jovan agreed.

"Aww man." The others began walking as Gordie whined, putting his helmet back on. Orion slid off the rock as he hurried to catch up with them.

Dusk had arrived as Galicia was now setting in the West. Orion and his classmates were gathered on one end of a circular training field. They were tired, out of their suits, no helmets, no backpacks, standing side by side. Lying on the ground before them were fourteen black sticks. Across the field awaited Marius, standing in between Dee-Dee and Ozone. The two androids were also holding two black sticks each.

"Before we put a cap on another exciting day here, I have one more mission for you neophytes." Marius barked. From the looks in their eyes, it was clear as day that they were all exhausted. Even Jovan. It had been non-stop training since they've arrived on Cnaeus. "Your task is a simple one. I want you to disarm Dee-Dee and Ozone. Two against seven. The odds are in your favor."

The neophytes looked at one another, there was definitely fear in the air. Marius really expected them to fight these androids and win, especially in their current conditions. They did not forget that they needed Dee-Dee and Ozone to help them put the force-field rods in the ground. Now he expected them to fight these two and somehow defeat them. He was insane. This could have been another one of his psychological tests, where he knew they had no chance of succeeding, but he wanted to see them fight anyway. Nothing else made sense. "Your weapons are in front of you. I'd advise you to get them."

The seven neophytes turned their attention to the sticks, each grabbing two. Marius turned to the two androids. "They're all yours." He left the training field as Dee-Dee and Ozone slowly stalked their way across it. As they approached, they both flick their wrists in a downward motion, which extended the sticks out with three silver pieces turning it into one long baton.

The neophytes stood with their mouths agape. These androids were about to seriously give them a beating. "Aww man." Gordie slumped his shoulders, somewhat resigned to the beating he was about to endure.

As fear continued to permeate the neophytes' eyes, Jovan stepped forward. "Come on guys, don't be afraid. We can take 'em." Jovan dropped his wrists in the same manner Dee-Dee and Ozone did, extending his batons. He rushed towards them like a true warrior as the others had no choice but to follow his example, extending their batons and joining the fray.

Jovan brought the fight right to Dee-Dee and Ozone, but these two androids had years of experience training and had mastered the art of disabling the young neophytes while exerting the least amount of energy. Being that the neophytes had never fought in a group before, there was no strategy, no intelligence, so all they did was wildly attack, sometimes almost hitting each other. Dee-Dee and Ozone easily thwarted their attacks, before delivering punishing blows back onto them.

Jovan swung as Ozone dodged him, cracking him across his cheek. This sent him sprawling to the ground. He dropped both batons, grabbing his cheek. That was painful. Rio appeared next, thinking she had the drop on the android. She leapt into the air with a double baton attack. Ozone blocked it, kicking her backwards, causing her to lose one of her batons as she went flying.

Dee-Dee blocked the attack of June and Orion, ultimately using her strength to brush them back. They reattacked, but Dee-Dee swept their legs, crashing them to the ground. June realized she was in over her head as she dropped her batons and humorously rolled off of the training field. She was bowing out of this exercise. Apparently, she was too tired to fight anymore.

Orion stepped forward, but he was no match for Dee-Dee. With the exception of June, the neophytes didn't seem to have any quit in them as they continued to challenge the androids. Dee-Dee and Ozone were done playing with them as their batons illuminated, like they were electrified.

"Uh guys, what did they just do?" Andrew asked.

Playtime was really over now as the androids resumed their attack, this time making quick work of the neophytes.

Marius watched the battle with glee, although he was impressed. While he was certain they would lose to Dee-Dee and Ozone on their first go-round, the fact that they continued to pick themselves up after getting knocked down so many times said an awful lot about their character, both individually and as a group.

Except for June, of course. He knew better than to expect miracles. In the end, baby steps were still steps. This was something they could build off of.

<>

Night had set in as the aroma of the unflavored oatmeal filled the air. While the food was bland as bland could get, it sure beat the taste of potato soup. At last, some variety had entered their lives.

Orion and his mates sat in the Red Rover commissary on two aluminum picnic benches that were bolted to the floor. The area was not very big, but enough for the seven of them to eat as there was a sink, stove-top oven and cabinets. What it lacked in leg room or walking space, it made up for in charm.

It had been another long day on the training fields with Marius so seeing them smile and joke with one another was a welcomed sight. Some of their faces were battered and bruised as Andrew had stitches above his left eye, while there was an area of Jovan's right cheek that was reddish purple. Being forced to go blow for blow with Dee-Dee and Ozone on a daily basis was beginning to show on their bodies.

"I don't know about you guys, but while I love being out here, I'm kind of still missing my bed at the moment." Said June as she ate some more food.

"Here, here." Orion agreed.

Rio stopped eating, staring at Orion and June. "I'm confused. Don't you guys sleep in stasis pods on the Rover Base or do you get something better because your parents are officers?" Rio was genuinely curious, not trying to start an argument.

"Rio, you don't have to be jealous. Sure, what we 'technically' sleep in is a stasis pod, but there is no comparison whatsoever to the Rover Base. Here, it's like we're sleeping in a box."

"Or a coffin."

Everyone groaned, that would be the last thing they would ever want to compare the pods to. Gordie still hadn't learned how to read a room. He could be inappropriate with his sense of humor at times. "What? What I say?" Some of the others shook their heads, there were a lot of days where they wished Gordie would learned to keep his outside voice inside.

"Well one thing's for sure, I don't get any relief from being in those pods. I don't know how my sister enjoyed doing this. My body feels like it's on fire." Orion resumed eating, trying to steer the conversation back on track.

"That's because your sister's a badass. You know, my brother always said she was the best one in their class." Jovan emphasized his point using his spoon. "When she wasn't breaking his heart, she was kicking his ass. Ha-ha-ha. It's really not a surprise she was on a Rover team. It's actually super cool. Although, please don't tell Kristian I said that. He would just get all whiny and depressed, complaining to my dad that I'm making fun of him and then my dad would be mad at me, it's just… stupid."

The neophytes laughed at Jovan's impersonation of his older brother. "Honestly, it must suck to be you Orion. I mean, having a sister who makes you look soft in comparison." June said.

"We didn't need Delly for that. All we had to do is see Orion in the simulator, remember?" Gordie was always good for a dogpile provided he wasn't the one on the bottom. He and June laughed as Orion sat there for a moment with a look of disgust. Even after being on the field with them day in and day out working just as hard as they were, they still continued to make fun of him. He pushed his food away, abruptly getting up from the table. He walked to the exit.

<>

The room became eerily silent as the other neophytes save for Orion turned their attention to June and Gordie, who acted innocent as if they didn't know why everyone was looking at them.

"Great job guys. That's exactly the kind of stuff we're not supposed to be doing down here. It's okay if you keep your jerky comments to yourself. Seriously, it won't kill ya."

Andrew was the next to get up from the table. He had lost his appetite. Gordie and June were speechless as everyone else resumed eating their dinner. Their evening was ruined, so hopefully tomorrow would be a better day.

<>

Aresco sat perfectly still on his couch staring out the window at the stars. He tended to do that from time to time when he was alone. Even at his age, he still had a need for daydreaming. These last couple of weeks had been as tough on him as they had been on everyone else it seemed.

Not a moment went by that he didn't ask himself a series of questions: Was he too old for the position? Would the community be better off with someone who looked at their situation differently than he did? Was sending the three Rovers out to unknown star systems without the Rover Base in proximity a prudent decision? Would he have made the same decision if he also had children of his own?

The latter two questions haunted him the most because no matter where he went on the Rover Base, someone would invariably ask him if the Rovers had reached their destination or if their loved ones were safe. Knowing that he was never going to have the perfect answer to pacify them, Aresco had taken to holding himself hostage in his quarters, at least until he had something to say beyond "It's too soon to tell."

"Sir."

Aresco snapped out of his funk. He turned to see Thayer standing in the entrance way, alone. "I have the information you requested." Aresco turned back to the window, grabbing a remote control. He clicked a button, which lowered a shade, reducing the outside light.

Thayer crossed to a smaller version of the glass conference table from the war room as Aresco rose to his feet, meeting her there. "As of now, all three Rovers have completed the first legs of their journey."

"The beacons?" He asked.

Thayer connected her digital storage device to his table as a digital hologram activated, showing the Rover Base and three blinking dots that formed a triangle. The three beacons had been left half-a-million miles away from the Rover Base.

"All functioning. Once we begin the exodus, we should be able to pinpoint their exact locations in the respective star systems." Aresco looked at the hologram for a moment—this was good news.

"Good. Seems like everything's going according to plan."
He was relieved—he knew their community could use a win
for morale.

"Yes... although, there is another issue that I believe needs
your attention." Aresco gestured for her to continue. "Galicia.
Her composition is becoming highly unstable. Volcanic
activity all over the surface, let alone what's happening in its
interior, which unfortunately we have no tangible way of
measuring."

"Ananke, it's a sun. Isn't that what it does?"

"Yes, this is true. But, it is my belief, that we should end
the mining operations and begin our exodus immediately."

"Stop the mining? Don't be ridiculous." Aresco defiantly
shook his head. "We're still only at sixty-five percent in terms
of replenishing our auxiliary minerals and that's with two
teams working around the clock."

"Understood sir, but—"

"Once they are finished, we will be ready to depart this
solar system and not a moment before." He exhaled. "In case
you've forgotten, some of that ore will be necessary in
powering the station once we're no longer around Galicia.
The fact remains, we have no idea what any of those star
systems have to offer us as far as natural resources go. Aside
from that, you telling me that Galicia is unstable means what
exactly when you don't have the ability to prove what you're
saying?"

Thayer dropped her head. He wasn't technically wrong,
but looking at her, she clearly didn't believe he was right. "I
cannot in good conscience send us on that kind of journey
before we are ready without some form of information

beyond your gut feelings Ananke. When you have that information, we'll revisit this issue. Until then, we will stay the course. Is that clear?"

"Yes sir." Thayer nodded, understanding he was done with this conversation. She removed the digital device as the hologram dissolved. She headed for the exit as Aresco watched her. Once she exited, he put his hand to his mouth, rubbing his chin. He needed another potential crisis like he needed a hole in the head. Maybe retirement wasn't such a bad option after all.

Rio lay awake inside her pod, staring at the pod ceiling that was less than two feet from her face. She had just completed another grueling day of training with Marius and his androids. Her arms were battered and bruised. Her pod was about twenty-three inches wide, or roughly the size of a coffin. This was one of the primary reasons why nutrition and diet was such a huge aspect of the Rover community. Their technology was honed specifically to suit people of a certain height and weight ratio, be they children or adults.

Anyone who existed outside of their ideal had to be accommodated for, which only diverted time and resources. So the leadership council in previous generations wrote into law that any persons who didn't fit within their cultural parameters could be subject to removal, for the good of the Rover community at large.

Rio thought of Toni Apostolos. Her height alone would make her a prime target. Her saving grace was her genius level intelligence in mechanical engineering and robotics that kept her from joining the unlucky few. As with everything in life it seemed, exceptions could and would be made for the exceptional or the well-connected.

Rio's stomach gurgled. She was still hungry. This was the most physical activity she ever had to endure over a prolonged period of time and as such, the rations her and her classmates were given while training was barely enough to sustain her. She tried closing her eyes again, but it wasn't working. Her stomach rumbled again. She needed food and she needed it now. She noticed the keypad above her, typed her name in backwards as the stasis pod slid out to the familiar hissing sound.

Rio looked around, hoping she didn't wake anyone else. She sat up in the pod, before rolling out and closing it. She got back to her feet, tip-toeing to the door, exited.

"Ummm." The bland flavor-less oatmeal was heavenly. Rio sat at one of the commissary tables savoring every bite. When you were as hungry as she was, it didn't matter what the meal was, just that it was food. As quickly as she made her bowl of oatmeal, she devoured it at lightning speed, the bowl virtually empty as she set down her spoon. She licked the leavings inside the bowl. From the vociferous way she ate, someone might think that this was her first meal in years.

Rio set the bowl down in front of her. She had literally licked it clean. She unexpectedly burped, now she was ready to go back to bed. Rio rose to her feet, grabbing the bowl and spoon. She quietly washed the dishes in the sink, before putting them with the others to dry. The last thing she wanted was Marius and the others to know she was in here for rations without permission.

The commissary door opened as Rio entered the empty corridor. Did she dare go to her right? The back of the Red Rover, an area that she and her friends had not yet been given permission. Or did she go left, back to bed? Decisions, decisions.

Rio took a step right; her curiosity was getting the best of her. She took another step, before doing an immediate about face. Getting an extra bowl of cereal was one thing, but exploring other parts of the Red Rover without Marius' permission was a good way to have everyone angry with her. He probably would punish them all. Rio may have been hungry, but she was no dummy.

Rio tip toed to the habitation chamber entrance; she was almost home free. Just before reaching the door, she paused, hearing a noise. She remained perfectly still, listening to her surroundings, someone was awake. *Uh oh, what if it's Marius? How was she going to explain her reasoning for being awake at this hour?* She was still frazzled from her experience with him on their first day when he tasked her with waking everyone. Rio was shaken out of her madness by what sounded like someone crying.

She listened closely; the crying continued. Maybe it wasn't Marius after all. Across from their habitation chamber was the ship's locker room, where the neophytes showered, dressed and used the toilets. Rio moved to the other side of the corridor, listening further. It was definitely coming from inside the locker.

<>

Callista was sitting on a stall, the divider closed to give her privacy. Her cheeks were flush as tears streamed down her face. "Hello. Who's in here?" Rio called out. Callista immediately began wiping her tears away, remaining silent, maybe if she didn't say anything Rio would go away. "I know somebody's in here. What's going on?" Callista looked skyward, shaking her head.

Rio leaned up against the wall near the door, waiting for whoever it was to show themselves. She was not leaving. Callista exited the stall moments later as her eyes were red, she looked terrible. "Oh my God, Callista, what happened?" Callista stood there for a moment, shuddering. She looked at Rio.

"I'm worried about my Mom, Rio." Callista's voice cracked, the waterworks in her eyes turning back on. Rio approached her with her arms extended. She wanted to comfort her friend with a hug. Callista flinched, nearly pushing Rio away.

"It's okay, it's okay. I'm here." Rio was undeterred, pushing in tighter, not wanting to let go for any reason. Callista relented, resting her head on Rio's shoulder, beginning to sob.

The two girls were seated across from one another in the commissary. Callista could no longer go on like this, she had to tell somebody. "My mom has been sick for over a year now. One day, she said she felt lightheaded and then she fell. So I thought maybe she was just tired from, I don't know... so I helped her into bed. But after a few days, I realized she wasn't getting any better. She was always so tired and... I just, I just didn't know what to do."

"Callista, that's awful." Rio held her hand tightly. She didn't have any words.

Callista sniffled, wiping her eyes. This was the toughest thing she ever had to endure, but the only way for her to get catharsis was to tell somebody. "I told my Dad, who works on Prisca."

"Your dad works with my dad?"

"Not that I know of. Maybe there's another mining camp."

Rio nodded, that made sense. She shook her head. She was derailing their conversation. "I'm sorry, you were saying." Rio zipped her lips, wanting Callista to continue.

"Anyway, I told my Dad and he said, that I needed to keep my mouth shut, don't tell anybody anything. As far as they're concerned, Mom just chooses to sleep a lot."

Callista coughed. "He said, if anyone ever found out that she was sick, that they, they would just get rid of her, like they've had to do with the others who were too sick to help the community." Callista stammered as it was becoming evident that this story didn't end there. "So I did what he said and kept my mouth shut. The first couple of weekends he came home, everything was all right, but then like two months later... that's when it happened."

Rio looked perplexed. "That's when what happened?"

"My Dad started treating me like my Mom. He expected me to cook for him, clean up after him.... even..." Callista trailed off, she couldn't bring herself to even finish her sentence. She could never finish that sentence. Rio was stunned silent by all of this. No one would ever guess that Callista was going through this kind of anguish, she rarely shared her emotions beyond an eye-roll with anyone.

"He always told me how I was the prettiest girl on the Rover Base and that I looked just like Mom when she was my age." Callista actually smiled a bit, her emotions were still very much conflicted.

"He used to make me feel so special. Deep down, I knew it was wrong, but what could I do, he's my Dad?" Callista paused as she started crying once more. "Those weekends became the longest weekends of my life and I dreaded coming home whenever he was there."

Callista looked at Rio, somewhat lighting up. "That's why I was so happy when we got the news that we would be coming here. As far as I was concerned, the further away from him I could get, the better off I'd be. If only I were old enough to be on one of those Rover teams, I would've been gone so fast." Callista scoffed. "But, I'm not old enough and I'm just still worried about her. What if anybody ever found out? Would they just get rid of her like he says?"

Callista wiped away another tear. "It's just too bad this is all temporary. You guys are like the best family I've ever had since she got sick."

Rio sat there; her mind blown. She reached out, inviting Callista for another hug. That was the only comfort she could offer. Callista collapsed into her arms as Rio rubbed the back of her head.

Nothing she could possibly say would take away the pain that Callista had to endure but at least Rio was willing to be there for her in her time of need like the good friend that she was.

CHAPTER TEN

A HOUSE DIVIDED

Orion stared at his reflection in the locker mirror, feeling dejected. Two long metallic canisters sat on the floor beside his feet.

"I can't believe Marius has us doing this crap. Why doesn't he have the robots do it?" Callista called out, she was in one of the stalls, removing a canister. "Does he not realize how disgusting this is? Ugh, my nostrils. I feel like I'm gonna throw up." Callista stopped for a moment, it was too silent. "Orion, you still in here?"

"Yup." Orion was now leaning against the sink, using his forearm to cover his nose and mouth to protect him from the stench. He was enjoying this just as much as she was, although he'd rather not complain.

"Oh, well then say something. I thought you left me in here." Callista finally extracted the canister from its holder. She pulled her face back as the odor was unbearable. She covered her mouth as her neck pushed forward. Her puking seemed inevitable at this point. The stench was like feces mixed with rancid oatmeal and potato soup and now it was projecting everywhere.

"Nope. Just waiting for you to finish." Orion sighed, still covering his face. He was doing his best to avoid breathing in the fumes, but the longer she took, the longer they both would have to deal with it. Callista finally emerged from the stall, holding a canister, looking like a blowfish. She was determined not to throw up. Orion chuckled. He grabbed his two canisters, gesturing for Callista to lead the way. She hurried to the exit as he followed after her, trying to contain his laughter.

They carried the canisters just beyond the force-field border, which had been turned off for the day. "So do you seriously not think the robots could have done this? It's not like they need to breathe, am I right?" Callista was still agitated as she was nearly dragging her canister.

"I'm sure Marius asked us to do this for a reason. It's not like we're the only ones Callista."

"Well, this is my second time doing it. This is your first."

"That's because there are seven of us. It'll all even out in the end." Orion had a sheepish look about him; he wasn't actually sure if that were true or not. But he would have said anything at this point to stop her whining, so they could hurry up and finish.

The two teens came upon a hole latrine, setting the canisters down near the edge of it. Callista looked over the side, and wrinkled her nose. All of the waste and garbage throughout the years Marius had been conducting training exercises would be deposited in this hole. Centuries later, human beings still hadn't figured out a way to properly dispose of their trash that didn't involve just dumping it.

Callista turned to Orion. "Marius is sick. Why wouldn't he let us wear our helmets while we do this? I mean what's the point of having them, if we have to breathe this crap. I'm dying here."

She twisted off the cap of the canister, dumping the contents into the latrine. She recoiled as residue from the canister was slow to trickle out. Orion followed her example, trying his best to avoid the fumes. He was just as grossed out as she was. It was a dirty job and today they were the ones who had to do it.

The two neophytes headed back towards the Red Rover, carrying the canisters, when they noticed there was a commotion coming from the other side of it.

"Hey, something's going on. Come on." Callista took off running with the clunky canister as Orion attempted to keep up with her, not having as much success considering he had two canisters, that even when empty they weighed him down.

The two neophytes returned to see the rear ramp of the Red Rover open. The rest of their classmates were just beyond the force-field border standing in awe of two HoverSols roaming around the terrain in a circular pattern.

The HoverSols were sleek, aerodynamic silver and black chrome vehicles used for speedy ground travel while hovering above ground to avoid damage against the rough terrain. They could hover up to five feet off the ground and were also equipped with weapons on either side should they encounter danger or obstacles that needed to be eradicated.

The two HoverSols came to a stop, side by side. The butterfly doors opened in an upward trajectory as Ozone stepped out of the first vehicle. Dee-Dee exited the second a moment later.

Marius immediately addressed them. "Okay, I know what you're all thinking and it's not going to happen, not yet anyway. This exercise for you is strictly as passengers. So who would like to go first?"

Orion noticed just how excited his classmates were for the first time since they had been here. Heck, he was excited too.

"Please, I wanna go." Callista dropped her canister as she hurried to the front of the group. Her canister rolled as Andrew stopped it with his foot. The smell from it hitting him as he covered his nose. He kicked the offensive receptacle away. The least Callista could have done was put it back where she had gotten it from.

"Okay then. Go ahead." Marius pointed to June and Callista. The two girls hurried to the respective HoverSols. Callista got in with Ozone, while June was with Dee-Dee.

The butterfly doors closed as the seatbelts automatically strapped them in.

<>

Callista was in awe of the interior. "Whoa, this is crazy."

Ozone smiled. "But you haven't seen the best part yet." It flipped a couple of switches, illuminating the dashboard. The android took the wheel. The first HoverSol began to hover. Its booster rockets kicked in and away they went. The second one followed behind as the two vehicles increased their velocity, speeding through the terrain, easily maneuvering past the jagged rocks that stuck out.

Ozone remained its stoic self while Callista on the other hand was a hot mess. Her right hand clung to the ceiling, while the left was over her chest. The speed of the HoverSol was moving faster than she had ever traveled before. Ozone glanced at her. "Are you alright Callista?"

"Never better." Callista strained, refusing to change her position, especially if Ozone wasn't going to slow down.

The HoverSols continued their demonstration through the desert mountain region, taking divergent paths from one another as Ozone veered to the right, while Dee-Dee continued to go straight.

Ozone looked in its rearview to see that the second HoverSol had disappeared. "Hang on." Callista looked at the android with confusion, what did it think she was doing? Ozone stepped on the accelerator, the HoverSol was hitting speeds of up to 250 miles per hour.

"Ohhhhhhhhhhh." Callista cried out as they were going way too fast for her tastes. Ozone remained focused on the terrain in front of him as the pass was becoming narrower and narrower. The android activated the vehicle's weaponry, shooting from both sides of the HoverSol. Its ammo clipped the mountain range, busting up the rock.

The rock debris still hadn't created an opening large enough for them as the HoverSol continued to increase its speed. "What are you doing? We're never gonna fit." Callista screamed as the android paid her no mind. She turned back to the dash, saw them flying towards a tight squeeze "Oh my God…"

The HoverSol made a sharp maneuver right, the vehicle was now tilted at an angle with the passenger side upward. Callista was screaming for the heavens as the HoverSol slid through the space without a scratch. Ozone pulled back on the accelerator as the HoverSol was horizontal once more. Ozone took another glance at the weary neophyte. The android damn near gave her a heart attack. "See, I told you." Callista had her head back against the seat. After all that excitement she exhibited from first seeing the HoverSol, now she couldn't wait to get out. "We should probably go back now, so someone else can sit where you are." Callista nodded, this was one joyride she wouldn't soon forget.

The first HoverSol continued flying, before coming to an open area. Once there, Ozone turned the vehicle around to begin their travel back to the Red Rover. The android stepped on the gas once more as Callista began to see her life flash before her eyes.

"Ohhhhhhhh… not again."

<>

Orion held his batons tightly, his eyes focused and ready. He and his classmates were lined up once more across from Dee-Dee and Ozone with Marius off to the side watching. This time the neophytes weren't going to wait for Marius's instructions. They attacked, blitzing the two androids from the beginning. Jovan and Andrew led the way, but the results were the same as always. Dee-Dee and Ozone waited for them to attack, then over time would overpower them.

Be it a kick to the chest or a baton to the thigh, one by one, each of the teens were dropped by the androids as Marius shook his head in disappointment. They weren't just taking a beating; they also weren't working together. Their movements reflected no kind of strategy or synergy. If they were stopped once, they were more than likely to give up rather than regroup and attempt a different approach.

Rio and Jovan were the last to fall as Ozone stood over Rio, waiting for her to drop her baton. The android was about to strike.

"Enough."

Marius had ended the training session. Ozone and Dee-Dee instantly stopped, returning to a stationary position. The neophytes turned to see Marius walking back to the Red Rover without saying anything to them. They were taken aback; this was the first time he had ever left an exercise without offering his constructive criticism.

Orion sat in the commissary with a hologram of his family kitchen open in front of him.

"So… picking up any new tricks?" His mother had her head buried deep inside the family's refrigerator, her back to him. He could see bowls of unfinished potato soup sitting on every shelf in the refrigerator.

Ever since Delly first departed, she had continued making dinner for five, something his mother had been doing every day, at least since Pharaoh no longer needed to be breast-fed. This clearly hadn't stopped since he left. Maybe she did it to keep herself from having a nervous breakdown. There were dark circles under her eyes. Her constant need to worry was probably affecting her sleep even more than usual.

"Yeah, I'm learning stuff." Orion rolled his eyes; his mother was always so busy. As if she couldn't grab her dinner after they had spoken. Maybe she thought he missed her cooking or something. She finally closed the fridge, approaching the table with a cold bowl of potato soup for herself. She sat down.

"That's it? You're learning stuff. You mind sharing a little more details with your dear old mother? We barely speak enough as it is." She pulled the plastic covering off of the bowl. She grabbed a spoon, digging into the bowl.

"I don't know what you want me to say Mom. This is just really hard, that's all. Sorry, I don't have more to tell you." Orion sighed, slumping his shoulders. His mother tasted some of the soup, she sighed as well. She just looked at him for a moment, smiling. Orion could only look away as his conversations with his mother were only becoming harder the older he became. She didn't do anything wrong, he just never felt that comfortable talking to her.

"It's okay sweetie. I know you're stressed. Hopefully, you're out there showing everyone just how gifted we all know you are. I never had the opportunity to do anything like that when I was your age, so the way I see it, you're doing it for the both of us."

Orion shrugged. Just what he needed, more pressure to live up to. Surely, his mother had to notice his lack of enthusiasm at her encouragement. "Look, I know my words probably don't mean much to you right now, but what I do know is, you're getting through it and that's all that matters. In fact, I'm even having a nice bowl of potato soup just to celebrate this conversation." She laughed as Orion couldn't help but chuckle as well. She actually was able to get him to show some emotion that wasn't mopey, what a revelation.

"Yeah." Orion shook his head. He was surprised she had a sense of humor. This was rare. "Have you heard from

Delly?" His mother almost choked on her taste of soup. She wiped her mouth, pausing a moment. She smiled.

"Uh… yeah. Your sister's… she's doing great. Still out there exploring the universe like she's always wanted to do. From what your father tells me, everything is all going according to plan."

"Good. Well, the next time you speak to her, can you tell her I said hi and that I miss her?"

"Of course I will sweetie. We miss her too." His mother smiled once more. Orion knew how much it meant to her that he and Delly actually loved each other. Sure they fought a lot, but it was all out of love.

"Hey Orion, we gotta go. What are you doing?" Orion turned to see Jovan standing by the commissary door, peaking inside.

"I'll be right there. I'm talking to my Mom." Orion waved Jovan away. He turned back to the hologram. "Alright Mom, I gotta hang with the team, so I'll just… talk to you later."

"Alright sweetie, you take care of yourself out there. I love you" Orion clicked off the hologram as it faded away. He hurried to the exit. Their conversations were becoming shorter and shorter since he had left for Cnaeus. This was what happened when children grew up. Their peers became more of a priority than their parents.

Derrick was in the shower, his head lowered, eyes closed. The water cascaded down his chiseled shoulders and back, which were filled with scars. The road to becoming an officer on the Rover Base was filled with hardships, especially when you weren't born into a family that already had a member on the leadership council. His entire life he had to fight and claw to take his family to this level—and he was still the lowest ranking officer on the council.

Unlike his peers, Derrick was trained as a soldier. He also was only fifteen when he was sent, along with some others, on a similar expedition to the one that Delly was on. They traveled to an unknown star system that they now knew as Galicia. The ten-year journey took him from a boy to a man— and it changed him forever.

While he completely understood Delly's desire to see the stars and the universe beyond what was directly in front of her face, he also knew that just because a person hoped to discover something special, that didn't mean they would actually find anything. Derrick had seen the highs and lows of space travel and had become jaded as a result.

This was why he had fought so hard to become an officer on the Rover Base. He knew that without it he would be at the mercy of the leadership council and he never wanted to experience that feeling of helplessness again, especially if he ever had a family. Not a day went by that he didn't feel regret for not convincing Delly that joining the Rover teams was the wrong decision—even if it would have been a selfish decision on his part. He made the decision as a father supporting his daughter and not as an officer, which was why Delly was currently on her way to the great unknown. The guilt, brought on by a conflict of interest, was eating him up inside.

Derrick waved his hand across a sensor and the shower powered down. He opened the shower door. He stepped out, grabbing his towel to wipe his face. He dried his face to see Carolyn standing by the door.

"I just had to lie to our son."

"What are you talking about?" Derrick was still drying himself off not amused. This was an emotional trap set by his wife and one that he didn't appreciate.

"Orion asked me about Delly and I lied to him. Our son, Derrick, I lied to him." Carolyn was frustrated.

"Lemme guess, this is my fault." He was losing the stomach to argue with her. This was becoming a recurring theme in their household since Orion left. He wasn't happy either, but he couldn't understand why she couldn't just deal with it the same way he had been. He was sick and tired of having this conversation.

"No, it isn't your fault, but clearly you've heard something about her?" She was relentless. Derrick couldn't even have a moment of peace after taking a shower. He returned his attention to drying himself off, specifically his back. "Derrick, I'm talking to you."

The towel dropped to the floor; he was standing nude before his wife. Now she had his full attention. "Are you asking for Orion or for yourself?"

"She's my daughter, Derrick, I have a right to know where she is." Carolyn raised her voice; yelling was her only weapon at this point.

"I'm aware of that, but telling me that every single day doesn't change anything." Derrick put his hands out, he wasn't sure if he wanted to hug her or strangle her. This was turning into exactly what he was hoping to avoid, another argument. "If you must know, her team recently dropped a beacon. So as far as we know, everything's going according to plan. That's the best I got. Satisfied?"

"What I don't understand is why do I have to ask you? Why aren't you just telling me these things? Do you want me to be like this? Constantly worried. Am I not your wife?" Carolyn sighed, shaking her head, her disappointment impossible to hide. "I just hope to God you're right." She exited as Derrick rubbed his forehead. This whole situation was tearing his family apart and there was nowhere else for him to go. His only recourse was to deal with it.

Steam rose out of a bowl of oatmeal as Marius sat alone in the commissary. He took a spoonful and put it in his mouth. His mind was working overtime trying to figure out how to get through to the neophytes. From the moment they had arrived on Cnaeus he had worked them like mules, while giving them minimal sleep, daily chores and forcing them to battle Dee-Dee and Ozone at the conclusion of full-days of training.

That could be the reason why his instructions weren't being carried out to his satisfaction. He was overworking them, not taking into account that they were still children, even if he refused to ever let them use that as an excuse.

Marius shook his head, if this was being considered too hard for them, then clearly the blame needed to be placed on someone else, and that was General Aresco. He was the reason they were on Cnaeus in the first place. If the idea was to get one final group of adolescents to train here before leaving the solar system, it was doomed to fail from the start.

Young people were ready when they were ready, not at some arbitrary age set forth by the peanut gallery. When teaching a person to fish, they also needed to be taught everything that encapsulated it. They didn't just receive a hook, bait and tackle box and declare themselves fishermen. The process was way more elaborate than that. There were steps that must be taken first. Trying to take shortcuts would rarely help anyone achieve mastery of a new skill. Marius took another bite of breakfast. All this introspection was making his food cold.

The commissary door slid open a moment later as the neophytes entered in their spacesuits. He turned to them. From the looks on their faces, they seemed ready for another day. While he was sitting here wondering if any of his training was sinking in, the one thing he had to give them credit for was their stick-to-itiveness. Their ability to dust themselves off after getting seriously knocked around day-in and day-out was something to be proud of. He underestimated their toughness as they were literally becoming the axiom of "if at first you don't succeed, try, try again" right before his very eyes.

"Where are you guys off to today?" Marius smiled, taking another scoop of his oatmeal.

The neophytes sported confused expressions. "Don't we have training today, sir?"

Marius continued chewing. "Not as far as I know. Today's an off-day. Enjoy yourselves." The neophytes turned to each other, excited, this was the first day off they had since arriving on Cnaeus. They gleefully exited one after another. Rio being the last one, stopped at the entrance, turning back to their mentor.

"Thanks Dr. Marius, I mean sir." She sheepishly saluted as Marius returned her gesture. Rio exited as he resumed eating his breakfast. Giving them a day off was as much for his well-being as it was for theirs.

<>

Orion and the others were in the ship's corridor still riding the high off of Marius's benevolence when Jovan stopped, turning back to the group.

"So what should we do today?" A silence fell over everyone. It had been so long since they had what could be constituted as fun, they didn't really seem all too sure.

"What can we do? There's nothing to do on this planet other than play with rocks." June sarcastically remarked.

"We could always play hide and seek." Orion offered.

"Hide and seek, seriously?" Gordie scoffed. "We're not six years old Orion. Ugh, what I wouldn't give to have my video games or go swimming or better yet, sleep. Yes, that's what we should do." Gordie looked around at the others, no one seemed to be interested in doing that at all. After all, they had just woken up not too long ago, now they would be going right back to bed. That was a terrible idea.

"It's too bad he hasn't allowed us to use the guns yet. We could've gone shooting. I used to kick ass in the simulator at shooting." Said Callista.

"Shooting? That's it." Andrew's face lit up. "You guys got your batons, right?"

"Yeah, so?" answered Gordie.

"Okay, well, all we need is a good place to spar."

"I don't believe this. Marius gave us a day off and you wanna do more training? What the hell is wrong with you guys?" June rolled her eyes.

Andrew turned to her. "Well, I for one, am tired of getting my ass kicked by those robots. So I'd rather spend my free time figuring out a way to beat 'em."

"I like the sound of that." Rio co-signed.

"Yeah, me too." Orion agreed. He joined Rio, Jovan, Callista and Andrew. Gordie was conflicted, but he saw which way the wind was blowing so he decided to go with them as well. June was all alone as they waited for her to come along. She let out a deep, over the top sigh.

"Fine, I'm coming."

The others were giddy as June approached them. They were about to have some fun, working as a team. Rio attempted to put her arm around June, who pushed her away. She may have agreed to do this with them, but she sure didn't have to pretend she was going to enjoy it.

It was the middle of the day as Galicia burned bright, directly overhead. The neophytes were miles away from the Red Rover in a mountain pass. The velocity of the air was turning it into a wind tunnel as the girls kept fiddling with their hair to keep it out of their faces. The fact that they weren't wearing their helmets only exacerbated the situation. The neophyte's backpacks were on the ground as they had gathered in a circle.

"Alright guys, usually when we fight Dee-Dee and Ozone, we tend to attack at the same time, but we never have a plan."

"And you brought us all the way out here just to tell us that?" said a disinterested Gordie.

"No, I didn't. Jovan, you be Ozone, while Rio, you be Dee-Dee." Andrew pointed, having them stand where he was.

"Drew, why did you ask Rio to do it and not me?"

Andrew rolled his eyes. "Because she takes this a lot more seriously than you do and she's a better fighter than you. Duh." Everyone dispersed, getting ready to spar as June shook her head, she was not feeling this whatsoever.

Also, what had gotten into Andrew talking to her like that? She was so used to him just following along with whatever it was she wanted to do, but since they arrived on Cnaeus, he was becoming more independent and snippier. Andrew was finally developing outside of her shadow, which was something that clearly annoyed her.

Jovan and Rio stood side by side, each with a baton in both hands. The other five neophytes only had one baton in their strong hands, to better simulate the difficulties of fighting against Dee-Dee and Ozone, who were so much stronger than they were, even if it was apparent that the androids had held back quite a bit when in combat with the neophytes.

Gordie started the battle by attacking Rio first, but she easily deflected his attack, sweeping his leg using one of the batons. Gordie crashed to the ground, rolling over in pain. From there, Orion and Callista attacked Jovan. They were met with similar fates as he was able to easily defend against them.

Time and time again, the five neophytes attacked their two classmates, forcing them to defend. However, over the course of the battle, they began trying out new strategies, where after attacking one, they would quickly jump to the other, in hopes of catching them off guard.

The battle had lasted for hours as the neophytes continued to compete against one another. Their clothes were drenched in sweat, they looked exhausted, in definite need of a shower. However, if they were serious about winning, they had to push themselves to the limit.

Jovan and Orion were engaged in a one-on-one. Orion dodged his attacks, but ended up tripping over his own feet. Jovan was about to smash him with his baton, when out of nowhere appeared Callista, who slammed Jovan across his right wrist, causing him to drop a baton.

"Ahhh. Damnit." Jovan cried out in pain.

Jovan's first instinct was to protect his wrist, which gave Orion just enough time to hit his left hand, causing him to drop the second baton. Gordie looked like he was about to smash a defenseless Jovan with one good shot, which luckily Jovan noticed using his peripheral vision.

"Okay, okay, you got me. I give up. Jeez." Jovan recoiled, protecting his head as he hurried away from them.

Gordie approached Orion, extending his hand to help him back to his feet. "Thanks for the save."

"You kidding? I've been wanting to do that for a long time. He's lucky he gave up or I would've cracked him good." Gordie smirked as Orion couldn't help but crack a smile.

Orion took a look around at his classmates, everyone was running on fumes. So much for an easy day off. Felt like they worked harder today than any other day since they had first arrived on Cnaeus. Just the way Marius had always hoped. It seemed his methods were working, even if he wasn't present to see them.

CHAPTER ELEVEN

NO TURNING BACK

Matthys' shift supervisor watched as the Grey Rover engines roared and the shuttle lifted off. It blew dust in every direction as the mining crew took cover. The weekend was upon them as they were stocked with minerals and the lucky men whose turns had come to visit with their loved ones back on the Rover Base.

The dimensions of the camp had changed significantly in the months since the departure of the three Rovers. The cave the mining crew had been working in was now completely hollowed out, causing them to move further west inside the quarry to a new cave. The new site was closer to the Grey Rover landing zone. A "KEEP OUT" barricade had been erected at the old cave as there was no need for the crew to be inside of it for any reason now that they were finished.

The Grey Rover held to a level just above the mountains that surrounded the camp. The ship's auxiliary rockets activated, sending them off, headed for home after another week's hard work. With the ship gone, the sound of heavy drilling could be heard coming from inside the cave. For the miners who remained, their work day was far from over.

Several miners, along with their robot assistants, worked diligently busting iron ore in the new cave, as they were drilling in four separate places. At the east end of the cave, near the entrance, sat three broken drill bits from their machine. The rock in this cave was much stronger and older than the previous one.

"Keep going, we're making good progress." The drilling machine continued to push deeper and deeper into the wall as some of the miners moved away to avoid the flying rubble. Once it was safe, they began the process of clearing the iron ore, placing it in mining carts.

As they filled the carts, the trembling that they had experienced sporadically over the last couple of months was once again upon them. This earthquake was way more active and violent than the previous ones. The rumbling caused a couple of the mining carts to tip over as everyone scrambled to safety. The earthquake lasted a good minute, the longest minute of their lives, before abruptly ending. The miners breathed a sigh of relief, hoping the worse was behind them.

"That was a big one."

"Hell yeah, it was. Is everyone alright?" The shift supervisor looked around. He was doing a head count. Everyone was accounted for as they gave him a thumbs up indicating they were okay. "Alright guys, back to work. It's not like this is the first time we felt the ground move around us."

The miners and their robots resumed their duties. The robot miners lifted the upended carts, turning them right side up. As they did so, the trembling restarted. This time the quake was even more powerful, causing the cave itself to rupture. As debris fell, a burgeoning hole could be seen opening up below their feet. The robot miners fell in almost instantaneously, as although they were strong, they didn't have the best reflexes or agility for this kind of situation.

Pieces of iron ore fell from the ceiling on top of a miner, cracking his helmet, exposing him to the toxic fumes and lack of oxygen. He immediately tried to cover the area where his helmet had cracked with his hands but the oxygen was siphoning out of his suit at lightning speed. He keeled over, suffocating to death. The cave continued to shake as two of the miners plummeted to their doom. The supervisor was perched in an area up against a wall that hadn't fractured yet. He was trying to save his partner who was hanging on for dear life.

"Pull me up."

"I got you brother. Just hold on." The supervisor angled over to him, doing his best not to go out too far. One false move and they were both done for.

"Come on, please!" The fear in the miner's eyes was devastating. He strained to hold on. He was running out of time, unless the supervisor could get to him.

"Come on, we have to get outside."

Matthys led three members of his crew out of the commissary into the courtyard of the camp. Once outside, he turned back. The beams supporting the commissary were buckling under the pressure from the tremors. The effects of this earthquake were visible as far as the eye could see.

Many of the flood lights around the camp perimeter had crashed to the ground. One of the barracks had imploded, whoever was still inside, without their helmets and spacesuits, were not long for this world. Before they could make a move, the commissary collapsed behind them. They had made it out in the nick of time. Fear gripped the majority of the men. They were never prepared to deal with this type of natural disaster.

Matthys turned his attention to the cave, even amongst the chaos he could hear the screams coming from inside.

"We gotta save them." He took off running for the cave as the rest of his men followed his lead. One of them stepped toward it, but upon doing so, part of the ground gave way as he and another miner plummeted right through, disappearing from view.

Matthys entered the cave, soon discovering the last of his men hanging on by a thread as the hole had grown even larger. "Guys, we're here. Just stay with us."

Matthys was no coward. He heroically began making his move to save them, but the earthquake was showing no signs of letting up. More of the cave gave way, bringing him to his knees. A medium-sized rock broke off a wall, dropping on the other miner's head, knocking him unconscious.

Unfortunately for Matthys' supervisor and the other falling miner, their luck would run out as the area around them dissipated, taking them into the abyss as all they could do was scream until they could no longer be heard. Matthys attempted to get back to his feet, but now the entire cave was disintegrating. He was cut off from the cave entrance, with a chasm between them.

His only chance to make it out alive was to jump. Matthys breathed heavy as he was out of time and options. He took a flying leap over the chasm to the other side. He landed with only his upper torso against the cliff, with nothing for him to hold onto. He tried to get his footing against the splintering rock, but to no avail as it was breaking apart every time he dug in.

"Come on."

Matthys gritted his teeth as he tried mustering every bit of strength he had. The trembling finally stopped as a sense of relief came over his face. However, the tug of gravity was eventually too much on his arms as he fell to his demise. Matthys released an ear-curdling scream as he disappeared into the darkness.

<>

Another day of training awaited Orion and his classmates as they entered the side airlock in their spacesuits, sans their helmets. Callista approached the control panel. She pushed the button for the ramp which began to lower.

"I'm actually excited to get out there for a change. Dee-Dee and Ozone won't know what hit them."

"I'm pretty sure it won't be you Gordie, but it's nice to have dreams." June winked at him as everyone laughed. Gordie waved them off.

The ramp hit the ground as the neophytes exited. They were surprised to see Marius alone with a cart, covered by a sheet, in front of him. "Sir. Where are Dee-Dee and Ozone?" Orion asked.

"That's not your concern. We have more pressing matters to attend to." From the look in Marius's eyes, the neophytes realized this must be serious.

The seven neophytes were gathered around Marius as he held up two weapons. They were also holding one of each, although the noses of the larger one were pointed to the ground. They weren't yet strong enough to hold them with only one hand. This was why the weapons came with shoulder straps, so their weak hand could act as stabilizers.

The larger weapon, which would be their primary choice in combat, was a double pump shotgun that used ion energy bullets. Their energy clips could hold in excess of one thousand rounds of ammunition, so they were the perfect weapon to go into battle with should an incident arrive.

The secondary weapon or side arm, was a handheld weapon that was designed only to be used as a last resort or in tight spaces where the primary weapon's effectiveness could be nullified. This weapon carried significantly less rounds, about two hundred and fifty in total. This weapon affixed to their spacesuits at the hip via magnetics.

"In your hands, are your primary and secondary weapons. Every cadet must know how to function with and without them. However, before we begin, I want you all to remove your gloves."

The neophytes set their weapons down, began removing their gloves as Marius watched.

"Now, pick your weapons back up and hold them both out in front of you, like this."

Marius held his weapons out, elbows tight. The neophytes followed his lead, although all of them struggled with the primary weapon. It was so heavy. "Now clutch the trigger and hold it for as long as you can." The neophytes did as they were instructed. Five seconds later, they all screamed in pain, dropping their weapons simultaneously. Something had burned them.

"Ah, what was that?" Callista shook her hand repeatedly.

"That my dear... was a fingerprint reader. For the rest of eternity, no one will be able to use your weapons, but you. In a hostile environment, that little bit of information just may be the difference between life and death. Now... before you pick up your weapons, understand this, these are not toys, they can inflict serious damage if you're not careful, but they can also be used to protect you in a dangerous situation."

The neophytes were hanging on his every word. "I need maximum focus from all of you and I won't accept anything less or this will be the last time you'll use them. Am I clear?"

"Yes sir." The neophytes answered in unison. They understood the risks and the stakes.

Five bullseyes had been set up over two hundred feet away as the seven neophytes held their primary weapons behind a makeshift barricade. Their objective for this exercise was to hit each of the targets at least once before they were allowed to stop. The neophytes awaited Marius's instruction as they prepared themselves, locking in on the targets.

Marius blew a whistle as the exercise had begun. Energy bullets flew, the vast majority of them missing their targets completely. Orion, Jovan and Rio soon showed themselves to be the strongest shots of the group, while Andrew and Callista were right behind them. June and Gordie, unsurprisingly, were bringing up the rear. Once they completed that exercise, the barricade was pushed back an additional hundred feet, raising the difficulty. This particular one took the neophytes much longer to hit the targets as they had never been trained to shoot from such long distances.

Marius was now joined by Dee-Dee and Ozone. He constantly shook his head at the conclusion of each session. It was hard to tell if he thought they were doing well or not. He wasn't yelling at them, so that was something different.

The exercise switched from static bullseyes to moving targets as a plate flew into the air. Each of the neophytes shot at it, but none were able to make contact as the plate broke upon hitting the ground.

Marius gestured for them to keep shooting as more and more plates were shot into the air. Hours into this exercise, the neophytes began to concentrate, taming down their impatience, waiting for the perfect moment to shoot. The goal wasn't to have them shooting wildly. The goal was to improve their accuracy and only shoot when necessary.

Plates shattered in mid-air as the neophytes were now hitting them with far more accuracy, even June and Gordie. Orion seemed to have a natural ability to shoot as he never took a shot until he felt he had no choice. All of those years living with Delly and their father seemed to finally be paying off for him.

As darkness began to set in, Marius deployed upwards of forty plates all at once as the neophytes were thrust back into action. Shots rang out, blasting plates left and right. The neophytes were able to destroy them all with the exception of two plates, which landed many feet away, the faint sound of them shattering.

Marius looked at Dee-Dee and Ozone, nodded his head. He seemed impressed. He never anticipated them taking this quickly to live-shooting, although maybe he should have. They had been playing video games their entire lives, not to mention using them in the simulator.

<>

The neophytes were safely tucked away for the evening as Marius sat on the opened side ramp of the Red Rover. The force-field was deactivated. His journal was open as he looked up at the night sky. It was beautiful, illuminated by the stars both near and far. Constellations were developing from the galaxies still not yet explored by humanity.

While in previous centuries, humanity was only allowed to dream about what the stars were like, this current generation was actually experiencing firsthand the beauty and the tragedy of space travel.

What made cosmic exploration exciting in its infancy had morphed into a mundane reality as no one ever expected their journey to last this long. For most of the members of the Rover Base, cosmic fatigue had set in, which was exactly why these training missions were enacted once the youth had come of age. What better way to boost the morale of future generations than to train them to fight an enemy that may or may not exist? The unpredictable nature of the cosmos had literally kept this community from ripping itself apart.

Marius scribbled some notes, as he normally did at the conclusion of his day. He closed his journal. He rose to his feet, walking back up the ramp. Once inside, he keyed the control panel as the side ramp retracted back to the ship. The force-field reactivated, cloaking the Red Rover before the airlock had closed.

Marius poked his head inside as the blue-light of the force-field shined through the cockpit windshield. Dee-Dee and Ozone sat docile, in auxiliary mode. They were plugged into the ship's dashboard, re-charging their batteries. The androids were no different than the neophytes as they also needed rejuvenation every once in a while.

Marius entered the Red Rover's captain's quarters. Over the many years he had been ordered to train neophytes on this planet, this room had become somewhat of a sanctuary. Adorning the walls, were photographs of his previous teams who had successfully completed the program. Whether they became cadets in the future or not, he still loved all of his students equally. They were all valuable in some way to this community. Amongst the photos was a thirteen-year-old Delly and her group from five years ago.

To date, Marius had never had any of his neophyte teams fail to complete his training, an achievement in which he took great pride. While this current group seemed to need more of his task mastering than their predecessors, their growth was undeniable, although he would never tell them that. Kudos were to be earned, not given. They were still very immature and praise was the last thing they needed from him.

His stasis pod was unlike that of the neophytes as his was a vertical pod built into the inner wall of the Red Rover. A horizontal pod would never work in this type of room, not to mention Marius would never go for having the same kind of accommodations as the neophytes. He took a seat in his desk chair, which was bolted to the floor. While the chair itself was comfortable, the fact that he couldn't move in it, remained a consistent source of annoyance for him.

Marius removed his glasses, rubbing his eyes, it had been a long day. He turned to his computer, which was also bolted down. If faced with zero gravity, they could never take chances with their machinery. He clicked on the desktop keyboard, which was built into the furniture. Before he had the chance to do anything a video call request popped up on his screen. The request was from Captain Derrick Moore. Marius sucked his teeth.

Do I really want to have a conversation with a superior who also doubles as a parent to one of my neophytes? Nothing good will come of this.

Marius sighed, better to get it out the way now than later. He clicked the accept button as a hologram of Derrick appeared before him.

"Hey there." Derrick was sitting in what looked like the family kitchen.

"Captain. To what do I owe the pleasure?"

"Just wondering how's he doing?" Marius nodded, just as he suspected, this was not a courtesy call.

"He's improving. We just completed another day of advanced weaponry. He's got a good eye, like his dad."

"You mean like his sister."

"I was trying not to hurt your feelings."

"Well, you always were a kind soul." Derrick smiled, they've known each other a long time.

"I do my best."

Derrick's smile faded. "Thanks for looking out for my son, Donovan. I mean that. I can't think of a better person to take my boy to manhood than you. Other than myself of course." Derrick laughed.

"If the roles were reversed, I'm sure you'd do the same for me. It's a shame I never got married."

"You keep telling yourself that friend."

Marius smiled as Derrick did as well. There was clearly a mutual respect between the two men fostered over many years. "You take care of yourself, Donovan. And remember, I owe you a drink when you get back."

"Yes, you most certainly do." Marius ended the call, breathing a sigh of relief. His fears were unfounded. He leaned back in his chair, smiled. It was good to hear that he was appreciated after all.

There were many days where he felt like it was the complete opposite.

<>

June's stasis pod slid open as she rolled over on her side. She looked around to see if anyone else was up. She climbed out of the pod, using the ladder to come down to the floor. She checked the boys' pods, stopping once she reached Jovan's. She keyed his name in backwards, which released his pod as she stepped aside.

Jovan awoke, surprised to see a smiling June standing over him, he was still groggy as he looked like he was enjoying a good sleep.

"June, what are you doing?"

"Ready to race?" A mischievous look was in her eyes.

"What time is it?"

"Early enough. Look, you're always saying you're the best, so time to put your money where your mouth is boy." Jovan sat up in his pod, looking a little unsure. She was trying to get under his skin. While he didn't want to get in trouble, he also didn't want to give off the impression that he was all talk, so June had him in a bind.

"I don't know about this."

"Aww, you're afraid. Seems I misjudged you. For a second there, I thought I was talking to Orion. Maybe I should have woken Rio instead." June was relentless, poking at him. Jovan shook his head. If he refused to accept her challenge, she would just keep bringing it up every chance she got. So he might as well shut her up now, once and for all.

"Fine. Go get dressed." Jovan was firm as June unearthed a smile. Finally, someone who was not actually afraid to have a little fun with her.

The two neophytes entered the loading bay of the Red Rover in their spacesuits, helmets in hand. The loading bay was designed exactly like the one on the Rover Base, albeit a whole lot smaller.

The two HoverSols were parked against the wall furthest from the rear ramp of the ship. Also nearby was a transport vehicle called the WaftMar, which was a helicopter combined with submarine technology. This titanium ship had the ability to fly in the most adverse of conditions, but in a pinch could seal off its exterior so it could perform underwater explorations.

The WaftMar's design came about during conversations between base scientists wondering how would a Rover be able to get aquatic vehicles into water or water like conditions, without endangering itself? They wouldn't have the ability to load a ship on and off the Rovers, so they did the next best thing and that was fuse the two technologies together to make one awesome vehicle.

The two neophytes approached the HoverSols, passing the WaftMar. "Oh man, look Jovan. A Starforger." June pointed above her.

Both neophytes stood in awe at the sight of two Starforgers bracketed to the ceiling in an attempt to save space. These combat planes were the Rovers equivalent to a fighter jet, albeit these were designed specifically to operate in outer space. Their black exteriors for camouflage purposes, the Starforgers had yet to be used in combat till this very day, so no one actually knew if they would be useful in a battle. This was something the members of the Rover Base community gladly accepted however, as it just meant that they had never engaged in war.

June ran to a control panel just below the Starforgers. She clicked on a few buttons which lowered one of the fighters to descend to the floor via brackets. June began rubbing the exterior. "My Dad has a replica of this in his office. It's so beautiful." She was admiring it a little too much.

"June, maybe we should just go back to sleep." Jovan kept looking back to the loading bay entrance, realizing they were toast if Marius ever found out.

June turned back to him, "What's your deal? We haven't even gone out yet." Jovan shrugged, he just didn't want to get into trouble. "Okay, if you don't wanna do this, that's fine, but that means I win, which also means you lost... to a Girl." She knew just how much that would burn Jovan to hear her saying something like that. "So that's two things. You're a weenie and a girl is better than you."

"Fine. If you're really in that much of a hurry for me to embarrass you, so be it. Let's just get this over with." Jovan began walking to a HoverSol. June had officially made him angry enough to risk Marius's wrath. She pumped her fist before clicking the button to return the Starforger to its former position. She then hurried over to the control of the rear ramp, giddy as a schoolgirl.

The force-field de-activated as the rear ramp of the Red Rover lowered a moment later. June hurried back to her HoverSol, while Jovan was already inside his. He put his helmet on, turning on the HoverSol. He flipped all the primary switches as the seatbelt automatically secured around him.

June on the other hand, did everything he did, albeit she was not wearing her helmet yet. She reached for her helmet, which was in the passenger seat, affixed it. "Oh yeah. We'll see how cocky you are after tonight."

"You know I can hear you, right?"

"Why do you think I said it?"

The HoverSol doors lowered on both vehicles, locking them in. A moment later, the two vehicles hovered towards the exit. The HoverSols exited the Red Rover, passing the metallic rods which remained deactivated. The first HoverSol came to a stop as the second one continued hovering away.

"June, we should probably turn the force-field back on, don't you think? I mean just in case."

"Then do it. Later."

June guided her HoverSol away as Jovan watched her leave, sighing. He checked the dashboard interface, which lit up upon his touch. Although the machine was complex, its tools were quite simple to use.

171

A moment later, the rear ramp of the Red Rover began to close. Once it was closed the force-field reactivated a few seconds later.

"Jovan, what's taking so long? Where are you?"

Moments later, June spotted Jovan in her rearview. Finally, he stopped being afraid. She stepped on the accelerator. The race was on.

CHAPTER TWELVE

PLAYING THE FOOLHARDY

The two HoverSols effortlessly glided their way through the mountainous desert terrain. The Red Rover could no longer be seen in their rear-view mirrors. The mischievous neophytes had drifted a long way from the training grounds. The two vehicles weren't really racing as much as they were cruising, sight-seeing along the way. Cnaeus really was a peaceful planet, especially at night.

The HoverSols came upon a narrow pass as June remained out front of Jovan. About two hundred feet ahead of them was a cliff. The first HoverSol exited the pass as the second followed its lead. June continued flying, the view from inside the HoverSol was magnificent. The closer she got to the edge, the vehicle began sending out warning beeps that alerted her that she was running out of terrain.

The HoverSols theoretically could still operate above five feet off the surface, however the issue that would rear its ugly head had to do with the landing. Rover scientists had never perfected large scale landings, so driving one of the HoverSols off a cliff wouldn't be advisable even if they had no clue whether or not it would work. The risk was never worth it.

June heeded the warning, eventually engaging in a sharp turn of the vehicle. She came to a stop a few feet from the edge, lowering it to the ground. The second HoverSol landed right beside her. June shut down the vehicle, lifting the driver's side door. She removed her helmet, carrying it towards the cliff, in total awe by what lied ahead.

Just below the cliff was a mountain range, full of peaks and valleys, as far as her eyes could see. It was nighttime, a midnight blue, so the color of the daytime landscape wasn't obvious to her. All June knew was that it was absolutely breathtaking. She had never seen anything so beautiful in all her life, that wasn't on the computer screen or in a preserved photograph. This was what life was truly about, what they had been denied for far too long while living on the Rover Base.

It was ironic how something as simple as a desert landscape could mean so much to her. That sort of thing happened when you spent a lifetime floating around in space, with seemingly no destination in mind.

June breathed the air in. Even the smell was unfamiliar to her. It was neither pleasant nor unpleasant, just different. She smiled, the first time in a long time, she was genuinely happy. No snide comments or jokes about other people to make herself feel better. Just the fact that she was experiencing something abnormal than what she had grown accustomed to and that was enough to strip away the attitude. Now she understood why her father was so laissez faire about her coming to Cnaeus. He knew that she needed to see this for herself. It was the only way she could ever understand.

Jovan exited the second HoverSol. He was wondering what was taking her so long. At some point they needed to head back before Marius found out that they had gone. He approached her, still wearing his helmet.

"Are you ready to go back yet?"

"Why are you in such a hurry? All we've been doing since we got here is work, don't you like having fun?" June insisted, she had no interest in ending this moment prematurely.

"I do... but the whole point of us being here was to get us to work together. Not sight-see."

"And that's exactly what we're doing. Except it's just you and me." June approached Jovan rubbing her hand across his helmet.

"You should keep this helmet on forever. It's so much better than your face. A real improvement." June smiled as Jovan shook his head. If he thought June was beginning to evolve into a different person, sadly he was mistaken. She had no intention of changing anytime soon.

"God, you're so annoying. I don't know how Andrew puts up with it." Jovan watched as she sat on the edge of the cliff, her feet dangling over the side.

"Don't you mean how do I put up with him?" June turned her attention back to the peaks and valleys. Jovan removed his helmet, sitting down beside her. The two teens were silent for a moment as Jovan looked over at her. It was rare for anyone to see June this quiet. That could be due to the fact that she was never this mesmerized by anything before.

"Do you think they'll ever find a home?" June was motionless, not sure if she even heard his question. He was about to tap her on the shoulder.

"I sure hope so." June exhaled, still lost in nature's beauty. "It's not fair, you know?"

175

"What?"

"That this is the first time we've ever actually been outside. That we never got to experience the Earth. That we had to grow up on the Rover Base, because previous generations didn't know how good they had it." She turned to him. "That we may have to spend the rest of our lives living up there through no fault of our own. What did we ever do to deserve this? It's not fair."

Jovan soaked in her words, this was the first time he had ever seen June express any type of depth beyond the surface. Even she would admit that she was a shallow person. "So you don't think the Rovers are gonna find anything?" He was genuinely curious as to what her answer might be.

"I don't know. I hope so. But... even if they do find something, who knows when that'll be." June sighed. "Do you know my dad told me it took ten years for them to get here? They thought that this, whatever you call it, was gonna be perfect for us."

"Solar system." He softly murmured.

"What?"

"This is a solar system. Galicia. We revolve around it."

June looked at him for a moment, rolling her eyes. "Whatever. You know what I meant. All I know is, we still don't have a home. Those three ships, I hope they find something. If they do... that would be... amazing." June trailed off, the reality of what was going to happen to them once they left Cnaeus was staring her right in the face. On the Rover Base, things would simply go back to the way they were. What a cruel joke to be given a taste of freedom and

176

new sensations, only to be dragged right back into the mundane and the monotonous. It was not fair.

She took one last look at the peaks and valleys, smirking. She looked skyward, genuinely wondering at the possibilities that lurked within the billions of stars. She reached for her helmet, which was to her right. She put the helmet back on and secured it at her neck. "Alright, I've seen enough." June rose back to her feet as Jovan watched her for a moment. She smiled at him through her helmet. "Race you back to the Rover."

June hurried back to her HoverSol as Jovan stumbled getting back to his feet. "Seriously?" He hurried to his vehicle. June hopped inside hers first. She turned it on, as her harnesses secured her. She began hovering, before reversing field as she whipped the HoverSol around nearly hitting him as Jovan lunged out of the way. June was retracing their hovered steps back to the Red Rover.

Jovan rose back to his feet, got inside. Moments later, his HoverSol activated as he guided it into the mountain pass, hot in pursuit of June. The two HoverSols were flying through the terrain one after another. They were going much faster than during their initial trip. While June had a good head start on Jovan, his HoverSol was slowly making up ground on her.

Jovan had to be guiding the HoverSol as if he were a seasoned veteran. "Alright, you've had your fun June. Now it's time to show you who's really the man. Cause ready or not, here I come."

His HoverSol accelerated, significantly closing the gap as the two HoverSols were practically side by side.

June remained focused on the terrain in front of her as Jovan's HoverSol had totally caught up to her. Jovan was side by side as he looked over at her, trying to get her attention.

"Hey there."

June couldn't help but turn her head slightly, noticing Jovan smirking to her right. She quickly refocused her attention to the road. "Oh no you don't."

She stepped on the accelerator as her HoverSol surged forward. Jovan's HoverSol had edged out in front of her. His laughter could be heard as she should've known better than to poke the bear. It was only a matter of time before his skill was going to shine through.

Jovan's HoverSol was traveling much faster than hers, which would've meant certain victory for Jovan had they not entered such a narrow pass. The speed at which he was traveling didn't give him enough time to compensate for the lack of maneuverability around the jagged rocks all around.

His HoverSol clipped part of the rock wall sending the vehicle careening as it banged against the ground once, knocking it out of control. The HoverSol flipped over and over, dangerously whipping Jovan around. It finally slid to a stop against the mountain wall on the other side of the pass, upside down.

"Oh my God, Jovan!" June screamed.

She slowed her HoverSol. She tried undoing her seatbelt, but was unable to until she had completely turned off the vehicle. Once it shut down, she was no longer restrained. She opened the door, hopping out of the HoverSol. She tossed off her helmet, making a mad dash towards her fallen friend.

Jovan's HoverSol was a crumpled mess. June reached it only to discover that his door was bent up, allowing her to see inside. Jovan was unconscious, still strapped into his seat. "Jovan, can you hear me? Jovan." No response from him as June had begun to fear the worse.

"Help!" she screamed.

Her voice echoed all around her, but they were still so far from the Red Rover that there would be no help coming if all she did was yell. June was becoming frantic as she paced back and forth. She didn't know if she was coming or going. She stopped abruptly, pushing her hands in a downward motion, trying to calm herself. She breathed in and out. Her eyes teared up. This was all her fault. If only she had listened to Jovan, this never would've happened.

She wiped away tears, looking back to her HoverSol. She ran back to the vehicle, immediately trying to figure out how to use the dashboard interface. It was clear she hadn't been paying much attention during their previous exercises with Marius and the androids. After a few moments of confusion, she searched a compartment in front of the passenger seat, finding what she believed to be an operational manual. She frantically flipped through it, looking for the right section.

"Come on, come on, come on."

Marius had been sleeping peacefully when his pod door was opened. Dee-Dee stood before him with Ozone a few feet behind. Marius slowly opened his eyes to see the two androids looking at him. He was startled.

"You guys really have got to stop doing that. I mean it."

"Our apologies for disturbing you sir, but we just received a distress signal from one of our HoverSols." Dee-Dee said.

"Both of which are missing. Along with June and Jovan. We checked both areas." Ozone added.

"Oh my God." Marius was now beginning to understand the gravity of the situation. He wiped his eyes to wake himself up. He needed this like he needed a hole in the head. "Alright, so that probably means they're both out there." He stepped out of his pod as the androids stepped back. "We need to find them."

"Should we wake the others?" Dee-Dee asked.

"Negative. Let them sleep. We should be back before sunrise." Marius hurried to his closet as the two androids exited his quarters.

Marius entered the loading bay with Dee-Dee and Ozone trailing him. They moved straight to the WaftMar. He slid the cabin door open, turned back to them. "Dee-Dee, you fly."

"Yes sir." Dee-Dee nodded as all three entered the vessel. Dee-Dee moved into the pilot's seat while Ozone assumed the position as co-pilot. Marius sat in the cabin behind them, the seats were of the row variety.

The WaftMar blades spun. It slowly lifted off of the floor as Dee-Dee carefully maneuvered the transport towards the exit. The loading bay on the Red Rover wasn't large enough for a quick departure, so patience needed to be exercised.

The rear side ramp lowered as the force-field dissolved. The WaftMar flew out of the Red Rover, on its way to the distress signal. The force-field reactivated once they had left the confines of the ship's borders. Leaving the neophytes alone.

Dee-Dee took the WaftMar high above the mountainous desert region. From this height the view of Cnaeus was incredible. The planet was gorgeous, totally untouched by living things [plant life not included] as nature intended. It was too bad they didn't have much time to admire it. The neophytes were in trouble. Marius moved towards the back of the WaftMar, checking for their first aid equipment.

"How much longer?" he asked.

Dee-Dee checked their estimated time of arrival. "Approximately twenty minutes Sir."

"Okay. Pick up the pace please." Marius continued looking for the aid kit as Dee-Dee accelerated the WaftMar.

June sidled up next to the crashed HoverSol, crying. An unconscious Jovan was still strapped inside the mangled vehicle.

"I'm so sorry Jovan, I'm so sorry."

The tears continued to cascade down her cheeks, she couldn't stop them. Marius being mad at her was irrelevant at this stage, she just needed Jovan to be okay. She would never be able to live with herself if he didn't pull through.

"Arghhhh." A pained Jovan bellowed, slowly regaining consciousness. June perked up, turning back to the HoverSol door. She saw Jovan blinking, trying to figure out where he was exactly.

"Jovan, you're okay."

"Then why don't I feel like it?" He hadn't moved an inch. June sprang to her feet, attempting to pry open his driver's door. She tugged on it once, twice, but it was too crumpled and she was nowhere near strong enough to remove it, especially alone.

"Jovan, can you move?"

Jovan attempted to wiggle, even trying to turn his head slightly. A half-second into trying, he stopped. Even the slightest shift had him in agony. The pain was too intense for him to do anything but sit there.

"I can't. I can't feel my legs." Jovan's eyes widened, panic was setting in. "I can't feel my legs, June. I can't feel my legs."

"It's okay, it's okay, I'm with you. I called for help. They're gonna come get us, okay?" June was doing her best to keep him calm. While she did call for help, she never received word that anyone was coming to rescue them. She just wanted to make sure he was still with her. If he lost faith in a rescue, there was no telling what would happen next.

"Oh God, I can't feel my legs."

June was back leaning against the HoverSol. His moaning was killing her. She needed to do something to help him. If only she were strong enough to pry open the mangled door herself. However, even if she could, Jovan still couldn't feel his legs and she wasn't strong nor skilled enough as a medic to carry him without inflicting more pain upon him. She slumped her shoulders, the reality of their situation was causing her eyes to tear up once again. She wiped them away as the sound of the WaftMar propellers could be heard in the distance.

June sprang to her feet, looking skyward. "You hear that Jovan? They're here." She excitedly looked in the distance. The WaftMar emerged over the top of the mountain, gliding towards them as June waved her arms above her, trying to gain their attention. The transport settled over top, beginning its descent into the narrow pass.

<>

Normally, trying to land in this tight of an area wouldn't be ideal, but for an expert pilot like Dee-Dee, this was a piece of cake. The android maneuvered the WaftMar, its propellers clipping the mountain a bit as Marius flinched inside. No matter though as Dee-Dee set it down nice and easy.

Marius could see June running to the WaftMar as he slid open the cabin door. He exited the transport with the first aid kit. Dee-Dee and Ozone would exit after him. June held back tears upon seeing them.

"Jovan's badly hurt. This is all my fault."

"It's alright June. We're here now." Marius placed a hand on her shoulder to reassure her. He turned to Dee-Dee and Ozone. "We may need the gurney."

"Yes sir." Ozone hurried back inside the WaftMar to retrieve it. Marius and Dee-Dee moved towards the flipped over HoverSol. They moved alongside the vehicle as Marius set down the aid kit. He looked inside. "Jovan, can you hear me?"

"I can't feel my legs." Jovan wailed, the pain was obvious.

"Don't worry son, we're going to get you out. I promise." Marius spoke with a soothing tone to ease his young neophyte. He needed to keep Jovan coherent as he could go into shock at any moment, depending on how much physical trauma or internal bleeding he had sustained. Marius turned to Dee-Dee.

"Rip it off."

183

Dee-Dee nodded as Marius stepped aside. The android punched into the door, making sure its hand had gotten all the way through. Once it was, Dee-Dee pulled back on the door with all of its strength. Three seconds and off the door snapped as the HoverSol shook a bit which Jovan did not enjoy.

June stood nearby with her eyes wide. She must not have realized just how strong the androids were, which put in perspective how much damage Dee-Dee and Ozone could easily have done to the neophytes during their combat training. Dee-Dee tossed the door to the ground. The android then went back inside the vehicle, attempting to move Jovan.

"Ahhh…." Jovan cried out in pain.

"Dee-Dee stop. Don't touch him." The android complied as Marius turned back, looking for Ozone. "Where's that gurney Ozone?"

"Coming now sir." Ozone returned carrying a folded-up gurney. The android unfolded it, locking the gurney in several places. Once stretched out, it was able to support an adult sized human being, so Jovan would be a cinch.

Marius dropped down on one knee, popping open the first aid kit. He removed an upper portion of the kit, revealing vials of blue serum and some type of handheld device that had a compartment to store the serum. Marius grabbed one of the vials, securing it to the device. He waited for a click, rose back to his feet.

Marius approached Jovan, leaning inside the vehicle, searching for Jovan's left hand, which wasn't easily found amongst the wreckage. The HoverSol had crumpled around his body. He tried to remove Jovan's glove, but Jovan winced every time he did. Marius sighed, this serum was supposed to alleviate his pain, but he couldn't do that unless he could inject it into Jovan's bloodstream first.

Marius put the device back on the aid kit. He began to carefully remove Jovan's glove. His pace was turtle-like, but in this case slow and steady would definitely win the race. He removed Jovan's glove with minimal discomfort to the teenager. He grabbed the device, immediately searching for an accessible blood vein around Jovan's wrist. He turned Jovan's hand over as the neophyte cried out. Marius injected the serum into his bloodstream anyway. He had no time to waste.

"Oww. Why'd you do that sir?" Jovan seemed genuinely dismayed that Marius had hurt him.

The initial shock of the serum hitting his bloodstream was powerful. Before Marius could answer him, Jovan's head slumped forward, he was out cold. Marius checked his left wrist, making sure that Jovan still had a pulse. He did. He removed the serum from the device, putting the vial and the device back inside the kit as June looked at Jovan.

"What'd you do to him?" June was still very much afraid for her injured classmate.

Marius closed the aid kit. "I gave him a sedative. With the amount of pain that he was about to endure, we couldn't afford for him to go into cardiac arrest."

Marius turned to Dee-Dee. "You can get him out now. But please be gentle."

Marius stepped away with the kit as Dee-Dee ripped Jovan's seatbelt away. The android held him in place, before carefully removing his broken body from the wreckage. Dee-

Dee set him down flat on the gurney, placing his arms at his side. He looked peaceful, if it weren't for his mangled suit, it would be easy to think that he had been sleeping all this time.

The two androids looked to Marius awaiting his instruction. "Alright, now we need to flip it."

"Sir?"

"Well we can't just leave it out here. So I need you two to flip it." Dee-Dee and Ozone complied, first cautiously moving Jovan safely away from the wreckage. They came back to the wrecked HoverSol. Ozone was in front, while Dee-Dee took the rear. They flipped it right side up as the vehicle made a thud, its broken parts rattling in the process.

Ozone hooked cables from the front of the mangled HoverSol to the back of the functional one. Dee-Dee was in the driver's seat. The broken door was folded up, sitting in the passenger seat beside it. The mangled HoverSol activated, somehow it still hovered. Dee-Dee exited the vehicle, approaching Marius and Ozone.

"Take these two back to the Rover. Put him in the infirmary and do a full scan of his injuries. Check for internal bleeding, blood levels, bacteria. We want to make sure there isn't a chance of septic shock."

"Yes sir."

"You're not coming with us, Dr. Marius?"

"Someone's gotta drive these back, I'm afraid. And just for the record, I'm very disappointed, in the both of you. But we'll discuss that later."

June nodded. There was no way she was going to be able to talk her way out of this punishment, whatever it may be. Her father being a major meant nothing to Marius in this moment. She had crossed the line and would not be able to blame it on youthful immaturity.

Marius walked to the HoverSol as Dee-Dee and Ozone lifted the gurney, taking Jovan back to the WaftMar. June slowly followed behind them. The two androids carefully loaded Jovan into the WaftMar, strapping him down in the back of the transport, so he didn't jostle on the journey back to the Red Rover. June got inside next as the androids slid the cabin door closed.

The WaftMar's propellers began spinning as Marius watched. The transport lifted into the air. This time Dee-Dee was being extra careful, not nicking the mountain pass even a smidge with the WaftMar blades. Once they had made it safely out of the pass, Marius got back inside the working HoverSol. He turned it back on as it lifted five feet off the ground with the broken one still tethered to it.

Marius could see Galicia appearing just over the horizon. This was the first time he hadn't been able to appreciate its beauty. He was too busy worrying about Jovan to care. He closed the driver's door. Now it was time to head back to the Red Rover. The HoverSol disappeared into the mountain pass as the sun continued to rise. This was a night to forget.

CHAPTER THIRTEEN

BROKEN... BUT NOT BEATEN

The infirmary door slid open as Marius entered. *Beep. Beep. Beep. Beep.* Three consistent blips traveled across a medical monitor, which was currently measuring Jovan's vital statistics. His blood levels, heart rate, oxygen flow and intracranial pressure were all ebbing below the normal rate for a person his age. Jovan's eyes were closed. He was resting comfortably on a medical table, although from looking at him, it would be hard to deduce that.

The upper torso on his spacesuit had been sliced open as tubes connected him to the monitor. A breathing apparatus had been secured over his mouth to help with oxygen flow. Tubes ran to his stomach, providing him with vitamins and antibiotics to fight bacteria while he remained in this weakened state. Dee-Dee and Ozone were with him, performing a full examination of his body.

Seeing him in this state was devastating. Marius had hoped Jovan might at least be awake by now. It had been several hours since he administered the serum and it usually didn't take this long to wear off.

"How is he?"

"Not good sir." Ozone turned to him. "He's suffered several injuries, including trauma to the spine, three broken bones in his lower back, as well as fractures to both legs. We're running a second scan to confirm as well as testing for internal bleeding, per your instruction."

Marius shook his head, wiping tears from his eyes. The beeps from the medical monitor were driving him crazy. He wondered how could something like this have happened. In all his years of teaching, he had never once experienced a situation of this kind. For the first time, Marius seemed legitimately unsure of what to do next. This event had shaken him to his core.

He turned his attention back to the two androids caring for Jovan, taking a cursory glance around the room. He spied an empty chair with his name on it. He walked to it, sat down. He wanted to be here for the moment when Jovan awakened.

Rio entered the corridor from the locker, followed by her classmates' sans June and Jovan. They were pumped for another day of training. They were heading for the commissary, breakfast awaited. Their youthful exuberance hadn't yet been extinguished by Marius's gruff exterior. They were actually growing closer to one another while learning new things about themselves, physically, mentally and emotionally.

"God, I'm so hungry I could eat a big bowl of potato soup."

"I could've sworn you told us that you hate potato soup?"

"Nope, I never said I hated it. I just said it isn't my favorite. Maybe you were confused since the words sound alike." Orion chuckled.

The others laughed as well as Callista frowned. "But they don't sound anything alike Orion. What you said makes no sense?"

"Maybe. But who are you, the sense police?"

The others laughed again as Callista's eyes widened. She looked as if someone had just let one rip right in front of her nose without saying excuse me. Orion was not known for being funny and this situation wasn't any different, yet for some reason they were all laughing, even Gordie. Orion was more corny or clueless than anything. She shrugged it off and resumed walking towards the commissary door.

It slid open, revealing June, who was seated alone with a blanket covering her. Her face in her hands, she was hiding her distress. A bowl of oatmeal and a cup of tea also sat in front of her, untouched.

"There you are." June turned to see the rest of her friends. "I was wondering where you were. Have you seen Jovan?"

June dropped her head in shame as the door closed behind them. She instantly began to cry. Everyone paused a moment, unsure of how such an innocent question could turn on the waterworks.

"June, what's wrong? What happened?" Rio approached June as the others sat on the second table nearby.

June wiped away her tears. *Did she dare tell them the truth? If so, how would they judge her?* Rio sat down beside her, draping an arm over her.

"Hey, it's okay. We're all here. Right guys?" Rio looked to the others for support.

"Yeah. Of course. Did something happen to Jovan?" Callista added.

June exhaled. If she didn't tell them what happened, then Marius was most certainly going to, so there would be no wiggling her way out of this one. She was going to have to face their criticisms head on. June swallowed, searching for the right words.

"Jovan... had an accident."

"An accident? Like he fell?" Rio asked.

"No, umm, we were riding in the HoverSols last night and he crashed."

"What? You guys went out last night? Did Marius let you go?" Gordie jumped in feet-first. It wasn't clear if he was more jealous or inquisitive.

June shook her head, indicating no. "I... I dared Jovan to race me in the HoverSols, because I, I just wanted to have some fun. That's all." The room fell silent as they were all stunned by June's admission. "On the way back here, we were going too fast and... he crashed... badly."

"Well, is he okay?" Orion asked. The way June was speaking. They were all beginning to wonder if Jovan was even still alive.

"I don't know. I hope so." June's eyes were tearing up again. "The robots were looking after him, but that's all I know." Her head dropped, she resumed crying as Rio attempted to comfort her.

"How could you be so stupid, June? Your dad's gonna have a fit." Andrew was pacing back and forth, stewing. This

191

was the last straw, finally her antics had caused some serious damage that she couldn't just fake apologize for and move on. There were real-world consequences here. "See… this has always been your problem. You just think you can do whatever the hell you want, no matter who it hurts. Just because of who your dad is? So how are you gonna explain this to him? That's what I wanna know."

"Okay Andrew, she's clearly sorry."

"No, screw that. Don't defend her. This isn't cool. Now Marius is probably going to punish all of us. And I'm sick and tired of taking the blame for her. It's been happening to me since I lost my parents. You don't think I've had it hard?"

Callista clammed up as the last thing she wanted to do was go tit-for-tat in the oppression Olympics. She put her hands up as she and Rio made eye contact, yet remained quiet.

Andrew went on. "The fact is, everything is handed to you and yet, you still complain. Grow up already. Cause even if they won't admit it, I'm not the only one who's sick of it. Damn." June could see from the look on Andrew's face that he had bottled up those emotions for far too long. He probably had wanted to chastise her in that manner for quite some time.

Silence enveloped the room again as no one really knew how to react to his diatribe. Andrew was the one who had to deal with June every day for the last decade or so. He stood in a corner, trying to calm down.

The commissary door slid open as Marius entered the room.

"Sir."

<>

"Is Jovan alright?" Callista asked.

"Can we see him?" Gordie was right behind her.

Marius put a hand in the air, indicating for them to be quiet. He was seconds away from ranting and raving himself, however, this moment didn't feel like the appropriate time to chastise them, especially considering how could he possibly punish everyone for the folly of the few? While his thought process had always been that they won together and they lost together, blaming the neophytes who were obeying his orders would have been the wrong decision.

"Jovan is resting at the moment." Marius paused, he needed to choose his words carefully. "Unfortunately, his injuries are severe and if he wants to make a swift recovery, then he's going to need treatment... on the Rover Base. They have the facilities to help expedite the healing process that we do not, here on the ship."

The neophytes slumped their shoulders. Reading between the lines, it was apparent what Marius was saying. "It was my recommendation that we cut your training short and end the mission right now."

Andrew sucked his teeth. June had just ruined everything for the neophytes. All of their hard work over the last year was for nothing.

"However, after speaking with Jovan, he implored me not to do that, taking full responsibility for the accident. So..." Marius turned to June. "You're off the hook June." June continued to keep her head down in shame, although one would think she was secretly breathing a sigh of relief.

"As such, I will begin making preparations for your final exercise. Which will be a team field assignment. Consider today another day off…"

Orion smiled. The last few moments had definitely conjured up a whirlwind of emotions for everyone. Who could have guessed that Marius would go easy on them for a change?

"After you have cleaned this room, the habitation chamber, the locker and your cabins. Twice. Then I expect you to do four hundred push-ups, clean those rooms again, then another four hundred. After that, you're free to have some time for yourselves. Is that understood?"

"Yes sir." The neophytes responded as the mood had radically changed. Marius departed as Andrew sneered at June, who kept her head down, hoping to avoid the incoming wrath from her classmates. Her selfish desire for fun was literally causing them all to suffer, none worse than Jovan.

Jovan continued to rest in the infirmary. His face contorted slightly, feeling some discomfort in his lower body. The discomfort caused him to slowly open his eyes. There was a grey tube feeding pain relievers into his right arm, otherwise he'd be in agony right now. He gingerly turned his head to see his six classmates together, just waiting for him to wake up.

He slightly smiled, "Hey. What are you guys doing here?"

"Marius gave us the day off. After we're finished being enslaved of course."

Orion shot Gordie a look. Although Gordie had a right to be upset that they had so many chores, that didn't have to be the first thing said to Jovan, especially while he was in this condition. Even if they were upset with Jovan for what Marius decided was their punishment, the timing was not great.

"We really should go back to the Rover Base, Jovan." Callista said. "At least that way they can fix you up."

"But how would you finish the training?"

"We'd fail, but we could always train in the next star system." Andrew answered.

"The most important thing is getting you better." Rio added.

Everyone was in agreement here. No one wanted to see him like this. Jovan repeatedly shook his head no. He hated that plan with every fiber of his being.

"Guys, I'm okay, really."

"You don't look okay." Said Orion. Seeing all of those tubes attached to his body was a real eye opener for them.

"Please. Please. You guys need to finish this. I'm already dreading what I'm gonna tell my dad about what happened, the least you can do is give me a couple of days to figure it out."

Jovan pleaded as he began to cry. The realization of the consequences for his foolish decision was too much to think about. "This is probably going to keep me out of the cadet program. Who knows how long it will take for me to recover? If I can't walk, they're never gonna let me be a soldier. All that work till this point for nothing. I keep wishing this was a bad dream."

The group looked at one another. They were heartsick for Jovan. He was hurting physically, mentally and emotionally. They all wanted him to see him get the medical attention he needed but they would be lying if they didn't admit that they also wanted to complete their training and prove Marius wrong.

They had no way of knowing what would happen upon arriving in a new solar system. Who knew how long it would take the leadership to put together a new training camp or if they would be disqualified due to what happened already? This experience for them would have all been for nothing other than seeing their friend get severely injured, with a strong possibility that it was permanent.

Jovan had given them a lot to think about.

Marius sat under a light in his quarters, turned away from the desk. In his hands was a paperback as he skimmed several pages. He stopped on a page. He was reading this one much more carefully, his fingertips following the words as he read. The words "training" and "neophytes" came up several times as he went. He flipped the page; the next one was blank.

He opened a compartment in his desk, turning the latch. Inside were pencils. At least a half dozen packs of them. He reached inside, pulling one out. This pencil was the smallest one of them all, having been worn down very close to a nub. He pulled out a twentieth century child's eraser to sharpen the pencil. The shavings landed on the floor as Marius looked at them for a moment.

When the Rover Base departed the Earth, one of the more important items stored on board were pencils and journal notebooks. Without knowing exactly how long humanity's journey would take, the powers that be intelligently presumed that they would one, not have immediate access to paper, considering the trees on the Rover Base were for vegetation and oxygen, and two, for the well-being of the passengers, they would need something to document their life experiences while in space. A form of emotional cleansing for everyone if necessary.

It had been ingrained in Marius since he was a child that he should never let his emotions overwhelm him of analytical thought. Logic and reason must always rule the day. Whenever he felt the need to overreact, his parents instructed him to write down his feelings and study them, understand what they meant and how he could use them constructively. Not having children of his own, Marius had often sought to pass along his wisdom through subtleties. From the moment he first began working with adolescents, he learned that they didn't all absorb information in the same way or at the same rate.

Marius dug his well-worn pencil into the journal half-way down the page. He wrote asterisks to differentiate from his previous entry. He captioned his entry. "Day 87." Marius thought for a second. *Had it really been almost three months?* He underlined the caption. He was about to add more when he heard a knock on his door.

Marius immediately closed the book, with the pencil inside. "Yes. What is it?"

His chamber door slid open as his six healthy neophytes stood just outside his door. They entered, Rio first with Orion bringing up the rear. "We have a request sir." Rio looked back to her classmates, who gave her approving nods.

Marius adjusted his posture in the chair, his expression stoic. "I'm listening."

The wind blew dirt everywhere as it was an overcast day on Cnaeus. Orion and his five remaining classmates were lined up across the training field in their spacesuits, holding batons in both hands. Marius was in his usual position beside Dee-Dee and Ozone on the opposite side.

"So this is what you wanted. You're a man down, who is technically your best athlete. I'm giving you one last chance to decline." The group stood firm, saying nothing, but ready for a fight. "Very well."

Marius turned away from the neophytes, lowering his head, so they couldn't read his lips. "Do not go easy on them. That's an order."

Dee-Dee and Ozone remained focused on the neophytes, slightly nodding their heads. They understood his directives. Marius stepped off the field. The androids stood waiting for the neophytes to attack, but this time they did the opposite and waited as well. The six of them never once taking their eyes off Dee-Dee and Ozone.

"Remember what Shaw taught us. Even on defense, we need to stay on the offensive and vice versa." Andrew said.

The neophytes remained still as Marius observed what was happening. He whistled. The two androids turned to him as he gestured for them to go to work.

Dee-Dee and Ozone extended their batons. They approached the neophytes in an aggressive manner. Just before reaching them, the neophytes scattered. Their new style of attack causing confusion on the part of Dee-Dee and Ozone. The teens ran by several times, avoiding being hit, while swiping low, this was their attempt to put both androids on the defensive due to their unpredictable style.

Up until now, Dee-Dee and Ozone had found it easy to defeat the neophytes due to their impatience and unsophistication in their fighting style. However, this time their attacks indicated an actual plan was being carried out. One after another, the neophytes attacked Ozone, but remained on the defensive when faced with Dee-Dee. With Ozone having to defend so many attacks, it couldn't keep track of all six of them as their agility and smaller size was becoming an advantage.

Dee-Dee attempted to keep the neophytes at bay, but whenever it did, they were prepared for it, blocking the android's attacks and then quickly getting out of its way as not to be overpowered. Andrew and Callista knocked a baton out of Ozone's left hand. The android tried to defend against them with just one, but without the other, all it could do was remain on the defensive.

With Gordie, June and Orion defending against Dee-Dee, out of nowhere came Rio with her leaping double sided attack from Ozone's right hand. She slammed down on the android's wrist, causing Ozone to drop the second baton. It was eliminated.

Dee-Dee was now all by her lonesome as Ozone left the field in defeat. The android held its position, but the neophytes screamed out, all six attacking Dee-Dee once as Marius was taken aback by their newfound success in combat.

What in the world has gotten into them?

Dee-Dee did its best to repel them, but now it was twelve batons flying at the android as it only had the two to protect itself. The android swung wildly, the neophytes had officially rattled it. It was only a matter of time now before they would overwhelm Dee-Dee as well.

Dee-Dee dodged an attack from Orion, causing it to lose its balance. One of the batons fell out of its hand as it tried to break its fall. Before Dee-Dee could get upright to retrieve the lost baton, all six teens pounced, hacking away at the android until it finally dropped the second one.

The sound of the baton hitting the training circle felt like a sonic boom, as the six neophytes paused, stunned that they had actually defeated the two androids. Whether it was improving skill, supreme adrenaline or just dumb luck, they accomplished something they didn't initially believe they were capable of and they did it while a man down. This was a prime example of what they could achieve when they worked together. Smiles were all around as they looked at one another, soaking in this moment, relishing an actual victory here on Cnaeus.

Marius smirked. To call this unexpected would be putting it mildly, especially after he instructed Dee-Dee and Ozone not to hold back. That his neophytes were able to not only hold their own, but win, said an awful lot about their ability to overcome adversity. He needed to stop underestimating them. Maybe they were ready for their next challenge after all.

The steering mechanism rattled in the hands of Webb as the Grey Rover traveled through the turbulent clouds of Prisca. Etsitty and Janis braced themselves. Every time they traveled through here, it was like the first time all over again. The Grey

Rover surged out from below the clouds as darkness was upon them.

The flood lights hit the blackened landscape as they were in route to the mining camp. Janis checked his monitor. While he normally would see two blips on his screen, he was only seeing one at the moment. "That's odd."

"What is?"

"I'm not picking up the mining camp on my radar."

"Since when did you need the radar to tell you how far it is from where we are?"

"Well, what's it for, if not to use? I'm pretty sure you guys don't bring me along for my devilish charm and boyish looks."

"No of course not. We bring you along for your weak bladder and inane blather." Etsitty laughed.

Webb reached out his right fist as they exchanged fist bumps. Janis shrugged off their enjoyment at his expense.

The Grey Rover continued on its journey as Webb's eyes widened. Something had caught his attention on the surface below. "Oh my God."

"What?"

"Look." Webb pointed as Etsitty faced forward, stunned by what he saw outside.

The mining camp below was in shambles, almost as if there had been an attack of some kind. Almost all of the perimeter lights were destroyed. The barracks, along with the commissary tent had all imploded. The grounds had holes all over the place, although they were not easily visible in this type of darkness, even with the lights from the Grey Rover.

"I thought this planet was uninhabited." Etsitty asked.

"It is." Said Webb.

"Should we wake the others? I mean they know this place better than we do."

"I don't think so." Webb turned back to Janis. "We better call the Rover Base."

"I'm on it." Janis immediately began working his console to connect the ship to the Rover Base.

<>

The landing zone showed signs of decay as well, it was anyone's guess how much weight it could support. The Grey Rover settled over it, hovering as its booster rockets activated. It remained a good four feet off the ground.

The side ramp lowered as Etsitty and Janis, now completely suited up, carrying weapons, appeared. They activated the flashlights on their helmets, surveying the area around the Grey Rover.

"Do you see anything?" Webb echoed in their helmets from their com-links.

"Negative, it's a wasteland. What are you hearing from the Rover Base?" Etsitty answered.

"They say to investigate the ground and report."

Etsitty and Janis turned to one another. "I was afraid he was going to say that." Janis said as the two men carefully hopped down off the ramp, which was not completely touching the ground since the Rover was still hovering. As they landed, they could feel the ground shifting beneath them.

"Did you feel that?" Etsitty turned to see Janis nodding at him. The two men continued to approach the carnage as they noticed large cracks in the ground ahead of them.

"Hold it." Janis reached his hand out in front of Etsitty.

He draped his weapon over his shoulder, carefully walking to a loose piece of ore that was smaller than a human hand, but still heavy enough that you needed two hands to hold it. He lifted the piece of ore, tossing it out in front of them as hard and as far as he could. The ore skipped across the ground, but as it did, parts of the ground gave way. It was clear that there was no longer a solid foundation below the surface of the camp.

"Grey Rover, are you seeing this?" Etsitty asked.

Webb was standing in front of his chair, viewing through the dash windshield. From where he stood, the area around the mine was basically hanging on by a thread.

"I am. Get your asses back in here now."

Janis and Etsitty ran back to the ramp, kicking up dirt in the process. The ground was very shaky under every step they took. Janis reached the ramp first, climbing on, before reaching back to help Etsitty. The two men hurried up the ramp as it began to retract and close.

Once the ramp had closed, the Grey Rover booster rockets re-activated. The ship was lifting off as the ground beneath it also started to erode from the ship's power. The secondary boosters activated as the Grey Rover flew away from the site. One last look at the mining camp revealed that it had now decayed to the point where it was unusable.

"Can anyone tell me how we're supposed to explain what we just saw out there?" Janis asked.

Webb and Etsitty remained silent as they guided the ship back towards the turbulent clouds above them. There would be no easy answers to that question.

CHAPTER FOURTEEN

AN EXODUS COMMENCES

"E.T.A. in less than fifteen minutes." Janis said, his hands shaking nervously.

The Rover Base could be seen through the dash windshield of the Grey Rover. Webb had the spaceship flying at a speed he had never flown it before. His hands were shaking, his nerves frayed, the image of the mining camp's obliteration forever burned into his memory. All those men lost, some of whom he considered dear friends. The real tragedy even beyond their demise, being that they would never receive a proper burial.

Etsitty looked at him, his eyes immediately gravitating to Webb's hands. The shakiness was worrisome. "You might wanna slow down there, bud. We're almost to the Rover Base. Maybe even use the auto-pilot."

Webb turned to him. His glance met with a concerned look from his long-time partner. "I mean unless you want us to crash, of course." Etsitty half-smiled. His was an honest statement wrapped up in a plea.

At this leg of the journey, the Grey Rover needed to glide through space rather than fly. Webb began checking his instruments, pulling back on the throttle, not giving Etsitty much thought.

<>

The Loading Bay alarm sounded as the few maintenance workers still inside, immediately found the exits. They knew the drill. Once those doors opened, there would be nowhere for them to go except into space.

The Grey Rover could see the doors opening before them as Webb wasn't even taking the time to whip the shuttle around as he would normally do so. He was flying the shuttle directly in, nose first.

Shimizu could be seen watching the Grey Rover enter the base from the upper control room, the same place he watched the Red Rover depart. He sported a determined look, grinding his teeth. The wheels were turning in his head as something was afoot. He balled up his fists, walked to the exit. The Grey Rover's rockets had been deactivated for landing. The magnetic field inside the Loading Bay would guide them in safely.

The ship passed a solid white line on the floor which ran across the room. Once it did, brackets engaged from the floor and the ceiling to secure the Grey Rover. The cockpit was jostled a bit by the brackets as all three men breathed a sigh of a relief. They were finally home safe. The Loading Bay doors started to close.

<>

Webb turned to see Etsitty and Janis removing their harnesses. "You can wake them up now. I'll leave it up to you if you wanna break the news or not."

Janis stood, hesitant. It never dawned on him that he might be responsible for telling the miners still in stasis that the mining camp was destroyed. Janis scratched his head. He waited for both his colleagues to exit first, rather than say something he would one-day regret.

With the Loading Bay doors now closed, the side ramp of the Grey Rover lowered. It reached the ground as the side air lock opened. Webb, Etsitty and Janis were joined by fifteen members of the mining crew.

They walked down the ramp where they were welcomed by Shimizu and eight base officers carrying weapons similar to the ones the neophytes were using on Cnaeus, except these were much more powerful. Only the elite of the Rover community were allowed to access them.

Pulse action assault rifles, which were capable of shooting in upwards of five rounds in less than three seconds. The pulse had an expanding fusion bullet that upon hitting its target, exploded. Even though there hadn't been an enemy to fight in generations, somehow, someway, the weapons technology had continued to evolve into being more precise and dangerous than ever.

Shimizu waited with baited breath as Webb led everyone who was on the Grey Rover towards them. "Major Shimizu. Sir." He saluted as Shimizu returned his gesture.

"Is this everyone?"

"Yes sir. We weren't able to locate any survivors at the mining camp. Everyone on board came with us from the Rover Base."

Shimizu rubbed his chin. "Okay. Thank you very much Lieutenant. It's been a harrowing day for you and your team,

I'm sure. In the meantime, I would ask that you gentlemen join our officers for a debriefing."

Some of the miners around Webb looked at one another, wondering what was going on. From their faces it was evident that they were still in the dark. "There's going to be a lot of chatter about what you've just witnessed and we want to make sure that you all are aware of what can and cannot be said at this highly sensitive time."

Shimizu turned, gesturing to a side door where two additional base officers awaited, although they were weaponless. "If you'll just see those two officers at the door, they'll get you all taken care of." The men still seemed unsure. "Go on." Shimizu's tone was disarming, because he said it with a smile. It was difficult to tell if he was up to something.

The Grey Rover crew and the remaining members of the mining company headed towards the two officers.

Shimizu watched the men exit one by one just to be sure nothing unexpected happened. Once they had disappeared, he received a nod from one of his officers before heading in the opposite direction to a similar door. Now that they had been secured, he was needed elsewhere.

Shimizu rode a chrome elevator to the highest level of the Rover Base. His face was apathetic as he sighed. What he had to do moments earlier in the Loading Bay was beyond comprehension. The vast majority of those men were his.

His knowledge of mining was one of the main reasons he was able to secure his position within the Rover Base hierarchy. However, this was what being a member of the leadership council demanded. A willingness to make the tough decisions even when they hit closest to home.

The elevator came to a stop. Shimizu waved his right hand across a sensor below the level buttons. The sensor read his fingerprint, opening the elevator doors. If the sensor couldn't identify him, these doors would never open. This level was off-limits unless a member had proper security clearance. Shimizu stepped off the elevator, a long corridor awaited him to the war room, where two more base officers stood guard.

Shimizu approached them, his expression never changing. The pace of his steps neither quick nor slow. Just regular, today was just another day for him.

<>

Aresco looked around the conference table at his leadership council. "Thank you all for coming on such short notice. You're all probably wondering why you're here. We just received word that one of our mining sites on Prisca has been destroyed." Murmuring began among the other members of the council, this was a shock indeed.

"We believe the cause to be rolling earthquakes more than likely." Aresco glanced at Thayer briefly who wore a look of indifference. This was exactly what she said would happen.

"And the other site? Have we nothing to be worried about with that one?" Hurley inquired.

"Not that we know of." Shimizu leaned forward. "The earthquakes appeared to have only affected the one site. There have been no reported earthquakes at the other site. And we've asked."

"Which is exactly why, I am bringing to a vote that we begin our exodus protocols." Aresco cleared his throat. "It appears that our current star system can no longer support us and as such, the time has come for us to find a new one."

"General, with all due respect, for such an undertaking, do we have any idea where the Rover Base would even go? We still haven't a clue if our rovers have settled into any of those systems safely, let alone found a suitable planet. Or one with the natural resources that we need." Shimizu was demonstrative in his disagreement.

Aresco had grown to expect Shimizu to comply with any order he put forth, like he had done with the Grey Rover moments earlier. While he understood that his defiance mostly had to do with his worriment regarding his children, Aresco could not let such distractions affect his leadership. He had to account for everyone, not just those in this room.

"I'm aware of that Major. As such, we're all going to have to act on a little bit of faith here. Here are the facts. All three beacons are working. Which means that the rovers are still out there, in route to the other systems. So we shouldn't be making proclamations to the contrary. That's counter-productive."

"Precisely." Thayer interjected while looking directly at Aresco. It was clear that she was getting some pleasure in seeing his leadership questioned.

"What about the Red Rover? They're still on Cnaeus." Captain Moore asked.

"Derrick and I have children there, in case you all have forgotten." Shimizu agreed.

"No one has forgotten anything. I've been in regular communication with Marius, since this all began. The plan is, we'll pick them up on our way out. However, our first priority has to be preparing the Rover Base for departure. Without it, we have nothing." Aresco was growing tired of the constant back and forth as he gestured demonstratively. He looked around the table. From the look on everyone's faces, he wasn't sure exactly which way the wind was blowing.

"So... are we all in agreement?" Hands slowly rose. First two, then a few more, then everyone else, with the exception of Captain Moore and Shimizu. Their concern for the Red Rover had superseded everything else for them. As concerned fathers, no one would expect anything different.

The other members continued to keep their hands raised as Shimizu began to feel the pressure. This was the first time he had ever been on the opposite side of a decision made by Aresco. The Loading Bay incident was a prime example of that. Once a boot-licker, always a boot-licker. Shimizu would eventually raise his hand, which surprised Captain Moore.

"Ian." Captain Moore looked disheartened, almost resigning himself to the fact that he had no allies in this conversation. It was either go with the tide or drown fighting against it.

"Captain Moore." Aresco said his name in a way that sent shivers down his spine. His position in the leadership was tenuous at best. There was nothing stopping them from stripping him of his rank, which ultimately would affect his family for the worse. All eyes were on Captain Moore. The council never made major decisions such as this one without it being unanimous. He reluctantly raised his hand, it was official.

"Alright people. We all know what must be done. Let's get to work." Aresco's eyes never wavered from Captain

Moore. He had a way of showing just how he was able to stay in control for as long as he had. He was a political animal. When he was focused on something, the smartest idea was to stay out of his crosshairs. Unless they enjoyed being crushed.

<>

Carolyn sat at the side of Pharaoh's pod. His angelic face having just fallen asleep after another one of her sweet renditions of "Hush Little Baby." At least some things still hadn't changed in this family. She rose to her feet, closing his pod. She set the timer on his pod for 7:25am, just another one of her routines. She walked to the exit, shutting off the lights before leaving.

She crossed to the kitchen as the front door slammed. Derrick was home. He made a beeline for the bedroom. "Derrick? Is that you?" Carolyn called out, receiving nothing but silence in response.

She entered the family room, looking around, still no sign of her husband. She entered the bedroom to see Derrick gathering all of their belongings. "What are you doing?"

He ignored her as she moved further into the room. "Derrick, I'm talking to you." Derrick stopped, turning to her.

"We have to get out of here." The look in his eyes telling her that this was no joke. He was dead serious right now.

"Derrick, what are you talking about?" Carolyn was perplexed. "Where is this all coming from? An hour ago, you told me you have a meeting, now you tell me we have to go? What just happened?"

"Carolyn, we are running out of time." He tossed some clothes onto the floor. Carolyn was uneasy. His behavior was out of character and beginning to scare her.

"Derrick, I'll ask you again. What's going on?" She approached him, a softer tone, tender. She was not trying to pick a fight. She just wanted him to be straight with her for once. He stopped running around like a whirling dervish, allowing his wife to hold him.

"This doesn't leave this room. Do you understand me?" Carolyn nodded, of course she would never betray his trust.

"Aresco just enacted the exodus protocols. The Rover Base is leaving this star system."

"Isn't that a good thing?"

"It is if we knew where we were headed. But we don't. The other Rovers have barely breached those other star systems and the truth is, we don't have a clue what they're gonna find out there."

Derrick paused, he was saying too much, but not exactly explaining to her what really had him so spooked. "One of the mining camps was destroyed by an earthquake. Everyone who worked there, has been completely wiped out." Derrick snapped his fingers.

"Oh my God." Carolyn covered her mouth in horror.

"Thayer thinks it's because of the sun and judging by our actions over the last year, not to mention her track record, I'm inclined to believe she might be on to something. I'm just worried about you and the kids. Something keeps telling me that we need to go. I don't care if we have to steal a Starforger, but we gotta get out of here." Derrick exhaled. At last, he was finally able to lay it all out there for his wife.

Carolyn soaked in his words. No wonder he preferred not sharing information with her. A prime example of why ignorance was bliss. Her silence was concerning, but she was trying to find the right words for him. Derrick looked as if he was waiting for her to give him the greenlight so they could leave, even if she knew the idea sounded ridiculous.

"Derrick, you just said it. Without the Rover Base, where could we possibly go? These other star systems, one of which our daughter is heading to, are millions and millions of miles away. If we left in a Starforger, we'd be dead in a week's time." Carolyn shook her head. His whole plan was a pipe dream. Somehow within this conversation, they had switched roles. She was the rational one, while he was being ruled by his emotions. "All we can do is hope for the best and prepare for the worst."

Derrick rubbed his forehead, the realization that he was absolutely powerless in this situation was devastating. Carolyn was right. There weren't any moves for him to make that would change their fortunes. They just needed to hope that time was on their side and that the exodus protocols weren't executed too late.

<>

A violent electrical storm system with high winds had developed over the mountain desert region. Lightning struck the force-field antenna of the Red Rover several times, but the ship remained protected.

"Sir, my apologies if I am speaking out of turn, but I am not sure this is the best decision to have them out in the field today." Marius was getting dressed while his two android assistants awaited instruction.

"On the contrary, Dee-Dee, this is exactly the perfect storm, no pun intended. The neophytes need to be able to perform in less-than-ideal conditions. This is like manna from

213

heaven." Marius turned to them. "Besides, it wasn't my choice to make. The Rover Base has initiated its exodus protocols, which means for us, it's now or never. So this is happening, understood?"

"Yes sir." Marius shooed them to leave as the two androids turned to exit his quarters allowing him to dress in peace.

<>

Orion could hear the storm all around them. He and his classmates were in the locker room, getting outfitted in preparation for their final exercise. This was the moment they had all been waiting for since they first arrived. That it was finally here was a surreal feeling for them. After losing Jovan to such a horrific injury, the fact that they made it this far was incredible.

"I wonder what the grouch has planned for us this time." Gordie chuckled while putting on his boots.

"Who knows, but one thing's for certain, it's not gonna be easy, especially after we beat his precious toys." Andrew said.

"Amen." Orion's helmet rested on the bench in front of him as he checked his sidearm, it was firmly secured. His backpack was on as he draped his primary weapon over his shoulder via the shoulder strap.

"Alright guys. Weapons check. Everyone got what they need?" Rio asked.

"Yup. Time to prove the old man wrong." Gordie rose to his feet, sporting a look of determination. The others nodded in agreement, while holding up their helmets. They confidently exited the locker room one after another

The corridor entrance to the loading bay slid open as the six neophytes entered led by Rio. As the group pass the mangled HoverSol, all of them, with the exception of June, stared at it. This was their first time seeing just how bad Jovan's crash really was. It depressed their enthusiasm a bit, a sober reminder that things could have easily been much, much worse for him.

Once passed the HoverSols, they noticed Marius, Dee-Dee, Ozone and a wheelchair bound Jovan. Just like that, their energy levels spiked as they all raced to greet him. Their movements clunky and disjointed as they still weren't totally comfortable when running in full gear.

"Jovan, are you coming with us?"

"I wish. But this'll do, at least until we get back to the base."

"In the meantime, everyone needs to get on the WaftMar. We're taking a little field trip." Marius pointed to the futuristic helicopter. The group of six turned back to Jovan. He exchanged fist bumps with all the boys, while Rio and Callista gave him delicate hugs. They each got on the WaftMar right after. June hugged him last, gently at first, but the fact he was smiling only made her squeeze him tighter. She released her hug, giving him a kiss on the cheek.

Jovan rubbed his cheek. "What was that for?"

June smiled. "Just my way of saying sorry. Also, you probably would've won. We both know that." She hurried onto the WaftMar joining the others as Jovan continued rubbing his cheek. While the kiss definitely didn't make up for his injuries, at least he's finally getting something nice for being hurt.

Marius sat in the cockpit of the WaftMar as the neophytes found their seats in the cabin. While getting situated, Gordie noticed two generic looking blueish androids, known as duplicates, seated in the last row. Unlike Dee-Dee and Ozone who had well defined facial and physical features, these duplicates looked exactly the same. They were asexual in creation. Gordie took a seat in the row ahead of them as Orion joined him.

"Hey." Gordie nudged Orion as he was still trying to get comfortable and into his harness.

"What?"

"How much you wanna bet those two things are a part of our training?" Gordie pointed to the duplicates behind them. Orion took a look before turning back to his seat buddy.

"Why do we have to bet anything?"

"Because, if you don't agree with me, we have a bet."

"But I don't disagree with you Gordie."

"Oh just forget it. Never mind." Gordie shook his head. He strapped himself in as Orion took one more look at the duplicates. There had to be a good reason why these androids were on board.

The lightning storm system continued to lay siege on the Red Rover and its surrounding areas as the force-field deactivated. The ramp to the rear loading bay lowered. The WaftMar propellers began to spin as it lifted slightly off the ground. It moved out of its docking space, slowly flying off the ship as Jovan, Dee-Dee and Ozone watched.

The loading bay doors began to close a few moments later as Dee-Dee and Ozone led Jovan back towards the cabin. Just before the ramp closed the blue light from the force-field shined into the bay, re-activating for the Red Rover's protection.

The WaftMar began its travel to the final mission in the worst conditions they had experienced since they arrived on Cnaeus. Although there was no rain in these clouds, there was turbulence all the same.

Dee-Dee entered the cockpit first as Ozone wheeled Jovan in next. His eyes widened as this was the first time he had ever been in this section of a Rover. His brother had never shown him the interior like he was willing to do for Delly.

"Whoa, this is sick. Do you guys fly the ship too?"

The two androids looked at one another for a moment. It was easy to forget that Jovan was unconscious during his airlift back to the Red Rover. He also never saw them fly the ship from the Rover Base as most of his time was spent in a stasis pod.

"We do Jovan. It's easier because we don't need to sleep."

Ozone wheeled Jovan over to the navigation station. "We can track their movements from here. If you're interested in helping us?" The android leaned over him.

"You bet your robot asses I am." Jovan immediately clasped his hands over his mouth, he had let his excitement get the best of him. Dee-Dee and Ozone looked at him as Jovan removed his hands, his demeanor more subdued. "Sorry. I mean yes. I would like that very much."

The two androids smiled, it was good to see Jovan still full of energy, his injury notwithstanding.

CHAPTER FIFTEEN

THE LONG WAY DOWN

Orion stared out his window as the WaftMar continued its journey over the mountainous desert terrain. The electrical storm had only worsened as Marius diligently worked to keep the transport steady. While he was probably a competent pilot, he definitely wasn't inspiring much confidence while handling the reins on this particular day. With every violent bump from the atmosphere they endured, a small part of Orion wondered if they would've been better served just waiting for the storm to pass.

The turbulence inside the cabin was getting worse, non-stop shaking. All of them beginning to wonder if this would be the last ride they ever took. Rio glanced over at Callista beside her. Her eyes were closed, her hands clutching her harnesses as tight as she could. Her helmet was tucked between her thighs, under her elbows to keep it from bouncing around. Rio's helmet was lodged beneath her legs, she totally got it.

"You don't look like you're having too much fun there, Callista."

"Oh yeah? What gave it away?" Callista rolled her eyes.

After enduring multiple lightning strikes that were near misses, the WaftMar eventually departed the storm system, the sky was clear in front of them but Galicia was burning brighter than they had ever seen before. Marius shielded his eyes, as he was forced to temporarily move the WaftMar into a downward dive to escape Galicia's glare. Even the neophytes had to shield their eyes, the radiance was that powerful.

Awaiting them was a dual mountain pass that somehow had a huge, snowy wooded valley embedded between them. The neophytes looked out their windows, marveling at the hidden forest below.

"Look, there it is. I knew it wasn't just a simulation."

Orion lit up, if ever there was a mission he was ready for, it would be this one. He had something to prove, not only to everyone who had ever doubted him, but especially to himself.

Hidden within the mountain, one would never believe it to be possible to land here, it was so remote. The WaftMar came over top of a landing zone that was distinguished by its Rover Base emblem. It began to slowly descend, touching down very smoothly. Marius had done this many times before. The engine shut off as the propellers stopped spinning.

Marius removed his harnesses, stretching in his seat. That was a long and bumpy ride. "Alright neophytes, time to see what you're really made of." The WaftMar cabin door slid open as the neophytes were the first to get out with all of their gear as Marius remained inside.

<>

"What's he doing?" Gordie was the only member of the group to look back at the WaftMar as the rest were way more interested in the valley below. "Uh, guys. I think you better look at this."

The neophytes turned their attention back to the WaftMar to see that Marius had exited with the two duplicate androids. Now that they were standing before them, these androids were actually a tad larger than Dee-Dee and Ozone, both in height and girth. They were also totally devoid of personality.

"Now is the moment of truth. The moment where we separate the neophytes from the cadets." The six teenagers stood at attention, their focus directly on Marius. Whatever he was throwing at them, they were ready. "Unlike your previous exercises, failure of this one, means you'll never be eligible for a Rover team for the rest of your natural lives. And unfortunately, there are no exceptions."

Orion looked around at his classmates. From the looks in their eyes, it was clear that this was a wrinkle they never anticipated. The pressure had just been turned up several notches. Now it was becoming clear why there were always so few in their Rover community who were allowed to carry weapons. To do so was considered more of a privilege than a right.

"However, for you to successfully complete this exercise, only one of you has to advance."

"What's the assignment, sir?" Callista asked.

"I'm about to show you." Marius turned to the two duplicates. "I'm sure you all have probably been wondering who these two are. They're duplicate androids, given the same capabilities of Dee-Dee and Ozone."

Orion sighed, remembering firsthand what fighting those two over the last couple of months had felt like. Although they finally were able to defeat them, the kids took their fair share of lumps in the process.

"Your mission is a simple one. Track them and defeat them. They are fully armed, same as you, although their weapons are more akin to that of a stun gun. You get shot, you're out. They get shot, they're out. The last member of either group standing, is the winner. When one of you is eliminated, your ability to communicate with your team also ends, so you would be unable to let anyone know that you're no longer a part of this exercise."

Marius smiled. "So… are we ready?"

"Yes sir!" The neophytes stood tall and proud.

"Very well." Marius turned his attention to the androids once more. "Duplicates, we're live." The two androids saluted, before turning to the forest. The first android transformed into a Battle-cat-like animal, while the second transformed into an Eagle Hawk.

The neophytes were stunned. Just when they thought they had gotten a handle on this test, here came a new wrinkle. The Eagle Hawk flew into the forest, soaring high above the trees, while the Battle-cat hopped down the side of the mountain, running down the cliff into the forest as if it were running on flat land. Gravity apparently wasn't that big of a deal to an animatronic fighting machine.

"Oh my God. We're really supposed to defeat that?" Andrew gulped.

"Neophytes." The group of six turned back to Marius. "A final reminder, but definitely the most important one of all.

You're using deadly weapons in a hostile situation and environment. That means no friendly fire. Watch where, what and who you're shooting at."

Marius paused a moment. He needed them to understand just how important this message really was. He couldn't afford to return to the Rover Base with another injured student. One could be construed as a mistake, but two would more than likely be considered a trend and career ender, definitely casting his future amongst the community into doubt. He loved teaching too much to not take every precaution to ensure their safety at this stage. His ass was on the line.

"Use your heads. Be safe out there. And remember. You're in this together."

The six neophytes continued to stand confidently, the stakes for them had never been higher than they were right now. This was their moment, so they needed to make it count. Marius walked back to the WaftMar.

<>

The six teens secured their helmets before turning their attention to the cliff ahead of them. They looked down on the wooded valley below.

"That's a long way down." Callista shook her head.

"There's a mountain path over there, but that seems like it would take forever. We're pretty high up." Andrew said.

"It would, wouldn't it?" Rio's eyes lit up as she removed her weapon before taking off her backpack. She dropped to her knees, opening the backpack while the others looked on in confusion.

"What are you doing Rio?" June asked.

"What's it look like?" Rio continued rummaging through her backpack as June threw her hands up. She never answered the question. A moment later, Rio pulled out her grappling hook, setting it beside her weapon. She closed her backpack. "We can use this." She pointed at the grappling hook, while still on her knees.

"Use it for what?" Gordie asked.

Rio left the grappling hook on the ground, as she rose back to her feet. She put her backpack on, draping her weapon over her shoulder. Her mates were still clueless where she was going with all this. Rio slid the grappling hook onto her left arm.

"I'm about to show you." Rio winked, turning back to the forest. She took aim, shooting the grappling hook out. The hook flew over many of the trees in a straight line until hitting a tree about thirty feet away. The hook's prongs fanned out, securing itself to the bark.

Rio tugged on the line hard a couple of times to make sure there was no slack. If there were any, that would mean the hook wasn't secure and thus wouldn't be able to support any weight. Rio gestured for them to give her some space as she took a few steps back, the grappling hook line extending as she moved. She noticed Marius watching with his arms folded, leaning up against the WaftMar. This was her chance to show out and she wasn't going to disappoint.

"Rio, please tell me you're not about to do what I think you are?" Gordie pleaded.

Rio took off running for the cliff. She closed her eyes, taking a flying leap off of it, the grappling hook line tightened as she swung through the forest like she had done this a million times before. As she swung, there were numerous trees around her, forcing her to contort her body to avoid hitting any of them. While her move was daring, make no mistake this was very dangerous.

The others stood completely in awe by what she had just done. All except for Gordie anyway. "If she thinks I'm doing that, she's lost her damn mind." He turned to the others. "Am I right?"

Much to his chagrin, the others were already in the process of removing their weapons and backpacks, so they could get their grappling hooks and follow her lead. "Aww man." Gordie sighed, slumping his shoulders. Looks like they made his decision for him. After all, they were in this together.

<>

Rio was still swinging, nearly to the ground as she deftly maneuvered around a tree using her boots to bounce away from it. Just before touching down, she pushed the button on her grappling hook band, which caused the hook to release its grip on the tree bark.

Rio landed on the ground smooth as could be, almost as if she were casually walking into the front door of her home. Not bad for a first-timer. The grappling hook line recoiled back to her. She averted her eyes as the speed in which the line retreated was swift. It came all the way back, making a soft clicking noise as Rio looked at her arm. The grappling hook was right back where it belonged. She smiled. "Now that was cool. Really glad it worked too." She exhaled, hoping she never had to do that again.

Rio was about to remove her backpack once more when she heard the sounds of the others using their grappling hooks to join her. She looked skyward to see five grappling hook lines above. She moved to a secluded area still in the vicinity just to make sure none of them landed on her.

<>

Marius was now in the cockpit of the WaftMar. He watched as one by one, the neophytes leapt from the cliff swinging into the forest. Gordie was the last to go as Marius smirked.

If nothing else, he understood that using their grappling hooks in that manner was something they would have never been capable of doing when they first arrived. Their ability to adapt to new environments had probably been the biggest pleasant surprise for him since leaving the Rover Base. Once they gained familiarity with their surroundings, it didn't take them long for their nervous energy to dissipate and get to the task at hand.

Marius activated the WaftMar's onboard navigation system, allowing him to track the movements of his neophytes as well as the duplicates. Six flashing red dots appeared on his screen while two flashing blue dots were closing in on them from different positions in the forest. "Alright neophytes. Time to show me what you're made of."

Marius put on his headset. He flicked a couple of switches on the WaftMar console. "Duplicates, proceed to phase two."

<>

In the forest, with a sight line aimed directly at the bottom of the mountain path the neophytes spied earlier, awaited one of the duplicates, now in android form. From the duplicate's position, the neophytes would have been ambushed before they could even enter.

The other duplicate, sill in Eagle Hawk form, was perched in one of the trees, hidden from sight. The tops of the trees around it would typically be near white, due to the frost. However, Galicia's energy was causing the frost to melt, making everything slick.

The Eagle Hawk transformed back into an android. It began climbing down the tree, hoping to blend into the environment to catch the neophytes from above. As it climbed down, one of the slick branches snapped under the weight of the android. The android fell, grabbing at any and all branches. It caught a branch about six feet below, its free hand punching into the nearest tree, to pull itself back up.

<>

Rio could hear the noise of the falling duplicate above. She spied the trees that extended deeper into the forest, but couldn't see anything other than more trees and snow. Her interest was piqued. She knew the duplicates were out there, even if she couldn't see them.

The others recoiled their grappling hooks landing safely. All of them, except for Gordie, who was bringing up the rear. He released his grappling hook seconds too late as his momentum was out of control.

"Ahhhh." He screamed as he landed face first in the snow. His hook recoiled as he laid there motionless. "Ah, why is this so painful?"

Callista dropped her weapon and backpack, rushing to his aid. "Gordie, are you alright?" She turned him over as Gordie looked up at her through his helmet.

"I don't know Callista. Maybe you should kiss me and find out." Gordie smiled as she pushed him away.

"Eh. He's fine." Callista rose to her feet. Gordie reached his hand out, looking for a little help, but she went to retrieve her things. She was through paying him attention. Gordie eventually realized no one was going to help him up, so he did it himself.

"Come on guys, time to dig in here. We can't afford to fail this mission. Those duplicates are still out there, waiting for us. So we need to be ready." Orion tossed his backpack over his shoulder. Once secured, he brought his primary weapon into ready position as he looked around at the others. Everyone was doing the same, with Gordie playing catch up.

"So where should we go first?" June asked. Without Jovan around, there was an undeniable void in their leadership. Usually, he was the one who took charge in these situations. Now he was many miles away unable to help.

"I heard something in the trees. We should probably go this way." Rio pointing further ahead of them into the forest, veering to the right. "I'm guessing that's where we'll find them."

"Works for me. Let's do this." Orion stepped forward, headed in that direction as the others looked at one another. The game was on.

<>

The six neophytes carefully moved into cover formation, two by two by two. Orion was out front with June beside him, Callista and Andrew in the middle with Rio and Gordie bringing up the rear. In this formation, Callista and Andrew were responsible for their left and right sides respectively. This formation allowed them to cover six distinct areas and avoid friendly fire as Marius had instructed.

The forest was silent, which was par for the course on Cnaeus. However, seeing how one of their simulations was an exact replica of this location, everyone was also confronting old memories.

To raise the difficulty factor, Marius had always inserted dangerous wildlife into their simulations, so they would have awareness when facing an enemy that was prepping for a strike. In this particular exercise, however, their mechanized opposition had zero intention of making it that easy.

"It's so quiet out here." Andrew kept his weapon in ready position as he carefully stepped over a few broken branches in their path.

"That's what I'm afraid of." Callista turned to him, the two making brief eye contact. Moments later, the roar of the electrical storm system they had flew through earlier could be heard. It was loud enough to startle everyone.

"Is that better for you two?" Gordie said as Andrew and Callista exchanged smirking glances as the group continued to move deeper in their search of the duplicates.

The neophytes remained tight in their formation as they heard multiple noises, in front of them veering to the left and directly behind them. "What was that?" Callista asked.

"Everyone hold." Andrew whispered. The neophytes all stopped, checking their areas to make sure there was no activity. At first glance, it seemed as if nothing was out of the ordinary. However, before they had a moment to move another step, several electric charges fired out in their directions. "Get down."

The charges were being shot from positions both in front of and behind the formation as the neophytes dispersed into three groups of two, in an attempt to avoid being eliminated. Clearly, Marius's duplicates were not interested in handing them a victory, they were going to have to earn it.

Andrew and Callista shot into the wilderness behind them, but all they were able to hit with their weapons were the trees. They still had zero idea where their enemy was. The duplicates continued shooting at them from their hidden positions as both neophytes were forced to maneuver back to the ground. Some of the charges were coming from above them.

"Everyone spread out. We've got no chance if we stay in one place." Andrew said.

"I'm with ya Drew." Andrew gestured to Callista. She needed to move on his mark. He crouched, shooting into the trees closest to the area where some of the charges originated. The duplicate hidden amongst the foliage ducked to avoid being hit by his return fire. It hopped away using nearby branches to regroup for a counter-attack.

Andrew shot several more times, before placing his weapon back over his shoulder. He reached out with his free hand to help Callista back to her feet. While doing so, an electric charge hit him square in the back, which dropped him to his hands and knees. "Andrew!"

From the duplicate's eyes, it could see that Andrew was eliminated from the exercise. "One down." Andrew, Callista and the others could hear Marius's almost gleeful voice in their helmets. They weren't amused.

Andrew was still feeling the effects of the duplicate's charge. He could barely move. The impact of this attack seemed a lot stronger than an ordinary stun gun. Marius had undersold the pain he was feeling. Callista wanted to help him, but that would only put a bigger target on her back. She wasted no time getting back to her feet, took off running. The duplicate noticed, began shooting, before chasing her.

With the effects of the charge beginning to wear off, Andrew slapped some of the snow away in frustration. He attempted to get back to his feet, but his legs were a bit wobbly. He used a nearby tree to get upright. He began trekking back to the WaftMar, his day was done.

<>

Rio was running out front with Gordie struggling to keep up with her. She was determined to win this exercise for the group. "Rio. For god sakes, stop." Gordie stopped running. Rio stopped as well, turning back to see him resting against a tree. He looked as if he was going to pass out. She sighed, approached him, while keeping an eye out via her peripheral vision. She always kept her weapon in ready position.

"We have to keep moving." Rio tapped his helmet with hers, lifting his, so they were looking eye to eye.

"Nothing's chasing us."

"You don't know that Gordie."

"But I can't just run forever like you... we should stay and fight." Rio reared her head back, he did have a point. They couldn't just keep running. Eventually, there would be nowhere left to run. What they needed was a plan. She scanned their surroundings, something having caught her eye.

"Catch your breath. I'll be right back." Rio shouldered her weapon, began running away from him.

"So, you're just gonna leave me?" Gordie slightly lifted his hands up in disgust. Sure he hadn't been the ideal buddy in this buddy system, but that didn't mean she should leave him to fend for himself.

"I'll be right back, I promise. In the meantime, stay outta sight." Gordie watched as Rio disappeared into the forest.

Gordie waved in disgust. "Great. When the going gets tough, it's every Kishore for himself. It's like I'm right back home." Gordie sighed, began breathing deeply, in and out, unaware that one of the duplicates had been quietly stalking them.

Rio was still running as she dipped beneath a broken tree to hide behind. She put down her weapon and fiddled with her helmet settings. She activated her infrared sensors. Rio looked back in the direction she came from, scanning the forest. She could see June and Orion running at a diagonal direction seventy feet from her position, while Gordie remained posted up against the tree right where she left him. "Oh shoot, of course."

"Guys listen to me. I just turned on my infrared. I can see some of you. Which means if I can, so can the robots." Gordie lifted his head in fear, that's about the last thing he wanted to hear. "Either find something to hide under or cover yourself with snow. That way they can't easily detect you."

Gordie immediately pushed his weapon out. He looked around, still no sign of the duplicates. Undeterred, he took it upon himself to randomly begin shooting into the forest. The duplicates were not going to get the drop on him. Orion and June were forced to take cover from Gordie's friendly fire as Rio could see their movements from the infrared.

"Watch where you're shooting! You almost hit us."

Gordie was not coping well as he lowered his weapon, heeding Orion's warning. Gordie looked around once more for the duplicates, but there was nothing out there except for snow and trees. Some snow landed on Gordie's helmet as he shook his head. He looked above to see the duplicate directly over him with its weapon pointed. "Son of a…"

The duplicate released a charge as the impact dropped Gordie flat on his back. "Ahhh. Looks like I'm out." The android jumped down as Gordie watched it casually stroll away while he was still twitching from its charge. Of course it would only be him who allowed a duplicate to just roll up and give him the combat version of a tap on the shoulder, eliminating him. "I really hate this game."

<>

"Two down. Four to go."

Marius watched as Gordie's dot solidified on his screen. The duplicates had barely gotten started and his pupils were already a third of the way to having failed. He shook his head, no matter how much they protested, with each passing moment they were proving him right. They weren't built for this. At least not yet.

He turned his attention back to the navigation screen to see one of the flashing red dots moving in a direction leading back towards the WaftMar while a blue dot was hot on its tail.

<>

Callista ran as fast as she could, dipping behind a tree. She looked back in several directions, before bending over to catch her breath. These androids were way more aggressive than Dee-Dee and Ozone ever were.

She heard rustling nearby as she tensed up. She looked out, not seeing any signs of her robotic nemeses. She noticed an embankment nearby that might make for a decent hiding place. She dropped down and rolled over to it, so the duplicate couldn't track her footsteps. Upon reaching the embankment, she began packing as much snow over top of her as she could, until you couldn't see her legs and most of her torso. She saved her helmet for last. "I sure hope Rio was right." Callista laid flat on her back having totally disappeared under the snow.

Minutes later, one of the duplicates arrived in the vicinity, trudging through the terrain looking around for her. The android scanned the area but Callista was nowhere to be seen. The duplicate continued in its search, pausing several times in hopes that she would foolishly make the first move. Even without the heat signatures, the duplicates were very adept at using sound to guide them as well.

Callista remained perfectly still. She had no intention of moving until she absolutely had a clear shot at the duplicate. From her position, she could hear it, but she still couldn't see it. The duplicate passed, now several feet away from her as Callista continued to lie and wait. From her position, if it turned right now, it would be game over.

However, luck was on her side as the duplicate continued to search elsewhere while still remaining in her line of sight. She carefully moved her fingers under the snow over her trigger. Callista swallowed. "It's now or never."

She sat up, the exact same way she had every morning since she and her classmates first arrived on Cnaeus. The muscle memory from using her abdominals to lift herself out of those stasis pods daily somehow was aiding her in this moment. The duplicate heard her movement, but it was too late as Callista had gotten the drop on it.

She let off several rounds, hitting it multiple times in the chest. However, right before the duplicate received her first shot, it released an electric charge of its own. Callista sat immobile as the return fire was coming straight at her.

"Uh oh." A direct hit as she twitched in the snow for a few seconds.

The duplicate fell to the ground, deactivating itself. Callista had defeated it. "Oh my God." Callista let out a deep, frustrated sigh as her head went backwards. She was now looking to the sky. "Seriously girl, what are you doing out here?" Callista took a few moments to get her bearings.

At least she gave as good as she got.

Jovan monitored the action from the mission via the Red Rover on-screen navigation. He pumped his fist. "Yeah, we just got one of 'em. Way to go guys. Just one left."

Although he was miles away, he had never felt closer to his classmates than he did now. He pumped his fist a second time, wincing as the pain shot up and down his back. He was still on the mend and needed to be careful about making sudden movements. He noticed Dee-Dee and Ozone watching him. "I'm okay."

The two androids looked away from him as he grimaced once more. Getting used to his new physical reality was going to be a much longer process than he had anticipated.

CHAPTER SIXTEEN

DESTRUCTION IS OUR DESTINY

Aresco stood stiff as a board in front of his grand view of the universe. He was in a state of disbelief as he watched the surface of Galicia bubbling like a cauldron under a flame. Although the Rover Base was millions of miles away from it, he could still see the volcanic activity taking place all over the hyper-star. It was that powerful. The eruptions resulted in deafening booms as Galicia's particles exploded onto the surface, only to be sucked in and regurgitated back out through more explosions.

"Just give us a little more time."

Aresco shook his head, almost pleading with the invisible forces of mother nature. Galicia's current composition was reminiscent to that of an enlarged heart that was beating way too rapidly. Something strange was going on inside it, yet it was impossible to figure out what exactly. Neither Thayer nor any of her subordinates were able to get close enough to figure out what elements the star was made of.

The Rover Base was ahead of schedule, nearing the atmosphere of Sonain and its five moons. From the moment Aresco made his decision to leave, he wrestled with the question of if he had taken too long to make a decision.

After all, this was the first time in almost twenty-five years that the Rover Base had traveled this great a distance in such a short period of time. Due to its massive size, the Rover Base had always been limited in how fast it could travel, especially when juxtaposed to that of the Rovers. At their current pace, they would reach Cnaeus to pick up the Red Rover sometime within the next day or two and would be nearing the outskirts of the solar system within a month. He would be lauded as a hero, securing his legacy.

While uncertainty undoubtedly lied ahead for the Rover Base for the first time in a generation, for Aresco and his community, many of whom having experienced the last exodus a generation ago, this was an inevitable part of their existence, at least until they were able to find a suitable planet to colonize.

Aresco clicked his remote, closing the blinders to his quarters. He tossed it away, as it bounced against his couch nearby. If there was no way for him to mute the horrible sounds coming from Galicia, he wasn't going to give himself nightmares watching it either.

He returned to his desk, plopping down in his plush chair. He exhaled, putting his head in both hands. A moment of peace was impossible with Galicia being this noisy. He let out a frustrated sigh, pushed his chair in. He waved his hand past his computer screen as the monitor lit up.

On the screen was his virtual simulator, tracking the voyages of his three Rovers. Even with Galicia ringing in his ear drums, he remained focused on that screen. The simulator displayed the route of the Rovers beginning from the Rover Base to the triangular beacons they dropped a half-million miles away, before veering off in three separate directions to explore the Marilia, Ogun and Heru star systems. The simulator also offered a projection as to their current whereabouts in those respective systems.

What his exploration teams would find in them was anyone's guess, but just knowing that there were three separate possibilities for humanity to move forward was enough to keep him sane.

Another boom went off. This one strong enough to shake the Rover Base itself as Aresco nearly fell out of his chair. His good vibes had totally evaporated. Galicia being that powerful was terrifying. He rose to his feet, walking to his couch in search of his remote once more. He grabbed it and turned back to his blinds. He paused.

"Shit." This was the first time he realized that Galicia's illumination was so bright that it was actually coming through his blinds. The realization crumpled him to his couch, if he was looking for a sign, he just received one that he didn't want.

The irony being that Galicia's solar power had played a pivotal role in allowing the Rover Base to remain operational for a generation. And yet because of their complacency, it was possible that the hyper star would also be the same entity that would be their undoing.

<>

Derrick huddled with Carolyn and Pharaoh on the sofa in their family room. Pharaoh had tears in his eyes as his mother covered his ears. The booms from Galicia were so loud they felt evil. Their youngest child, their precious little boy was terrified. In fact, they all were.

Derrick continued to hold his family tight, not letting go for even a second. Not until normalcy had returned. His mind raced, wondering about Delly and Orion. Today was Orion's big test, but he had no way of contacting them unless Marius attempted to first, so he was totally in the dark. Carolyn was no better. There was no peace in knowing that her family was fragmented during these tumultuous times.

The booms continued, louder and stronger, shaking their home. How could sound be powerful enough to shake anything as large as the Rover Base?

Pharaoh was full on crying now, "Make it stop, Mommy."

Carolyn rubbed his head, trying to ease his fears, but nothing appeared to be working. She turned to Derrick for comfort, the terror in her eyes was devastating. They weren't going to make it at this rate. Derrick kissed her on her forehead, pulling her in tighter. He had no words that could assuage her fears, so all they could do now was hope for the best.

"I love you guys."

Carolyn turned to her husband. Tears beginning to form in her eyes. "I love you too, Derrick." She leaned in, kissing him. A long, passionate one. Possibly the very last one they would ever have. And just like that... silence. A moment in time, that they didn't want to lose, even if they secretly knew that the end was nigh.

<>

The Black Rover was docked on a landing zone within the second Prisca mining camp. The flood lights around the quarry remained the only source of light due to the planet's heavy cloud cover. The dimensions of this quarry were an

238

exact replica of the first, at least before the tremors came and the planet swallowed the company whole, ending their existence.

The rear ramp of the ship was lowered as the miners and their robot assistance loaded the ship with cart after cart of mined ore. They had less than a week to go before they were gone for good, so there had been no weekend trips home for this bunch, especially since the destruction of the first camp. Just pure work, mining that ore to power their home base.

Nelson Guimaraes, a hardened, despicable man with soulless eyes and an enlarged stomach, came barreling down the ramp. He passed the other carts being pushed up by the robots as another boom from Galicia caught his attention. He looked skyward, whatever was happening above the darkness, he and the others had no way of knowing. Some of the other miners stopped working as they exited the caves. The booms had gotten so loud that they had even drowned out the sound of the drills even when inside the caves.

"What in the world?"

Nelson noticed the ground under his feet beginning to fracture. He turned to the Black Rover. The ground underneath it was also giving way as the entire camp was falling apart, but not in the same way as the first camp. Energy began to shoot through the clouds, landing on the ground like fireballs as everyone scattered. One of the fireballs landed directly on a miner, who screamed bloody murder. What a terrible way to go.

The pilots of the Black Rover hurried up the loading bay ramp in hopes of getting the shuttle back into the air. But before they could even get through the loading bay, the ground beneath it totally gave way as the Black Rover sank into a giant sink hole. The ship banged against the interior of the planet, the loading bay ramp breaking off in the process. The fall into the planet, caused the ship to explode as Nelson and the remaining survivors attempted to run back to one of the barracks for shelter, but it was too late, no place was safe. They were now trapped on Prisca.

The winds were howling, heat was rising and the ground was withering beneath their feet. Nelson dropped to his knees. *What can I do other than repent my sins and hope that one day my wife and daughter would forgive me for becoming the terrible man this world had turned me into?* He un-secured his helmet, the quickest and least painful way to go would probably be asphyxiation at this point.

"I'm sorry Fern. I'm sorry Callista, my baby girl. I'm so sorry. I wish I was better. I wish I was..."

He removed his helmet, instantly grabbing his neck as the air was siphoned out of his body. He keeled over as the chaos still continued on around him, his eyes open, but no longer amongst the living.

Thayer stood perched at the observation deck watching the cosmic event with an eclectic mix of wonder, frustration and rage. She lowered her head, banging it against the glass. If only Aresco hadn't been such a stubborn old fool and listened to her. He doomed them all. Her eyes began to water, the inevitable was truly upon them. A hand reached out, touching her shoulder in an effort to comfort her. Thayer turned to see a smiling Toni beside her. She immediately collapsed into her colleague's arms.

"We were too late."

"I know. But we tried our best." Toni gently stroked the back of her head.

Their embrace was short-lived, however, as the most thunderous boom of them all was seen and heard culminating with the supernova of Galicia. This cataclysmic explosion sent an apocalyptic expanse of heat, pressure and energy out in every direction of the solar system. This was the cosmic form of a tsunami, with the exception that there was nowhere to run and there was no such thing as higher ground.

The smaller planets closest to Galicia were almost instantaneously consumed by its energy. That same energy busting the rocky interiors of the planets, in some cases disintegrating them fully. Galicia was on the warpath as Prisca was up next in the supernova's line of sight. The planet was enveloped as the pressure was so great, that it was ripped apart, right down its center core, creating two symmetrical halves. Its atmosphere had been annihilated, turning the planet into two gigantic floating pieces of dead space rock. The reach of the supernova had extended far enough that the Rover Base wasn't safe at all, even at its current position.

With the power from Galicia on a collision course with the Rover Base, Thayer pushed Toni away. She reached for her armband. She had one last call to make. She was calling Aresco. His face sheepishly appearing on her band a few seconds later.

"I'm not watching, if you were wondering."

"Well, isn't that convenient. When the going gets tough, the tough finds some place to hide. Just remember, whatever happens, this was your doing. Not mine."

Thayer turned her arm towards the oncoming cosmic matter. She couldn't give him the satisfaction of being able to avoid what he had doomed them to.

"Ananke…"

Thayer clicked off her armband. She turned back to Toni, resumed her embrace as they watched as the supernova continued devouring everything in its path. It was apparent that the Rover Base didn't stand a chance. Both women stood with tears in their eyes.

<>

The supernova engulfed the Rover Base, no parts of this massive structure would be spared. The temperature and intensity crumpling the titanium alloy exterior as if it were a piece of toilet paper. Panic ensued as some of the people on the observation deck ran looking for a place to hide, but the fire rose around them causing them to spontaneously combust.

Others had boarded the Purple Rover in an attempt at a last-minute escape, but as the Loading Bay doors opened, more flames and energy were let in. The booster rockets at the bottom of the space station exploded, setting off a chain reaction of explosions on board as the Rover Base Alpha was completely destroyed.

The supernova continued unabated as it passed Sonain and its five moons. The planet's moons began to swirl, its two smallest ones colliding with each other. The gravitational field of these celestial bodies had been thrown into bedlam as nothing made sense anymore. What was once a peaceful star system had been turned into a cosmic warzone.

Cnaeus was the next planetary body in its path as the supernova was met by the planet's protective asteroid ring. The asteroids on the outermost portion of the ring were immediately absorbed and disintegrated by the supernova. However, a strange occurrence happened as the red rock particles from the asteroids began to change the composition of the supernova. It was still trying to consume Cnaeus but this asteroid ring was stronger and deeper than anticipated acting as a great wall repelling its advances. The destruction of this planet would not be as easy nor as quick as the other planets were.

<>

The sky over Cnaeus had been altered to a bright orange and red glow, the asteroids providing the latter coloring. Typically, Sonain and its moons could be seen from the sky, but they were nowhere to be found. Even with the terrible electrical storm raging above the dual mountain pass, the energy being sent out from the supernova was so immense that cloud cover was no match for it.

Callista carefully moved through the forest, staying tight to the trees, afraid to look up as the lightning had added a new dangerous wrinkle to this training mission. Near the edge of the forest, she saw Andrew and Gordie staring up at the sky in awe, frozen in place. *Had they lost their minds? They were totally unprotected should lightning strike.* She hurried towards them.

"What are you guys doing?" Neither one paid her any attention as she went against her better judgment and looked skyward as well. "Whoa." Callista was taken aback, same as them.

243

Before them were the remnants of the Galicia supernova, which had created one of the most beautiful and terrifying horizons they had ever witnessed. A horizon that felt like the heavens had been opened, except nothing about the color of the sky looked heavenly. If anything it looked terrifying. Even with the current chaotic planetary weather overhead, the supernova's effect superseded it. The three neophytes found themselves riveted in the moment.

"What is that?" Callista asked.

"I don't know. Are we in danger?" Gordie was scared as the other two looked at him, uneasy at the thought. For the first time in their young lives, that was a question they had to ask themselves.

<>

Deeper in the forest, nearing the second mountain range, Orion was leading June, still fleeing the remaining duplicate in the exercise. June began to lag behind him as Orion noticed, turning back to her. "We have to keep going. Come on." He wrapped his arm around her, he had no intention of leaving her behind. June nodded, now was the time for her to dig deep. She picked up the pace as the two continued running. If they lost this exercise, it definitely wasn't going to be because of her. She had to atone for Jovan's injury somehow.

Orion led June to a hidden location, so they could re-group. "Need you to hang tight, I'm just gonna check on Rio."

"Wait." Before he could take a single step away, June grabbed his arm, tugging him back towards her. Orion turned,

244

he understood she was a little rattled, but they still had to account for everybody.

June pointed to her eyes, then elsewhere in the forest. Orion understood as he ducked down. There was something running perpendicular to their position. She put her weapon in the ready position, pulling the trigger several times as whatever was there was forced to take cover. June barely missed it.

"Heilige kak! Hold your fire."

"Rio? Is that you?" June and Orion skittishly looked at one another. They were both prepared for trouble if this was a trick by the duplicate.

"Yes, it's me. Don't shoot." Rio remained hidden, holding up her weapon which was the same as theirs so they could see that it must be her. They rested their weapons and hurried over to Rio's position.

"Sorry Rio. I thought you were one of those robots."

"Well obviously I'm not." Rio got back to her feet as June and Orion joined her.

"Where are the others?" Orion asked.

"Gordie and Andrew are out, I don't know where Callista is. She might be out too." Rio answered.

"So we're all that's left?" June sighed, this was exactly the scenario they were hoping to avoid. The duplicates had forced them to disband and then began picking them off one by one.

"Attention neophytes." The three teens snapped to attention as Marius's voice rang in their ears. "I need you all to stop what you're doing and come back to the WaftMar, immediately."

"What happened? Did we lose?"

"That wasn't a request neophyte. That's an order. Hurry."
There was a worry in Marius' tone. This had to be something else.

"You heard the man. Let's go." The three neophytes began trudging their way back the way they came, not completely sure why the exercise was called off, but they were not in a position to argue with Marius, nor did they want to be.

<>

The fallout from Galicia's supernova was being felt in every direction. It was as if the solar system itself was caving in, having lost its center of gravity. These huge planets that hadn't yet been consumed by its energy were spiraling out of control.

Cnaeus' asteroid ring had done yeoman's work thus far protecting the planet from the supernova. However, with the gravitational center of the solar system no longer there, the asteroids closest to the planet began to fall back inside it towards the surface, creating a meteor shower.

Marius stood just outside the WaftMar cabin. He was looking skyward at the atmosphere itself. Lightning struck several times all around the area but he could care less. He had bigger problems on the horizon. "Holy mother of God." If this was what he was seeing on Cnaeus, lord only knew what was happening up in space.

"Dr. Marius. Come in. Sir, do you read me? Dr. Marius." Marius snapped out of his haze as Dee-Dee was calling into the WaftMar. He re-entered the ship, hurrying to the cockpit. He put his headset back on.

"I'm here Dee-Dee."

"Sir, we are receiving an overwhelming amount of energy flooding into the atmosphere. And it does not appear to be slowing down."

"Have you contacted the Rover Base?"

"We've tried, but have not received a response thus far."

"Alright. Well keep trying. I've called off the mission."

"Yes sir." Marius shook his head, in his heart of hearts, he knew something was wrong, only he wasn't exactly sure what. Still, his responsibility remained the neophytes and until they were safely back on board the Red Rover, he couldn't begin to worry about whatever was happening thousands of miles above them.

<>

Meteors of varying sizes fell from the sky worsening the conditions around the Red Rover. "Red Rover, come in. Do you copy?"

"We read you sir." The two androids seated at the controls, while Jovan remained positioned at the navigation station still frustrated from Marius calling off the mission before they had a chance to finish. Their instruments were reading a ton of activity coming from above. Luckily for them they were still being protected by the force-field.

"Something's wrong. The neophytes are still out there. I need the Red Rover to come to our position immediately."

"Affirmative. We're on our way."

"What's going on?" Jovan was genuinely concerned. This was an unfamiliar position for him to be in. A state of complete helplessness. It was eating him up inside that he couldn't be out there with his mates.

Dee-Dee turned to Ozone. "We need to secure him before we take off." Ozone rose to its feet, approached Jovan, who looked up at the android.

"Can't you tell me what's happening?"

"We need to get you strapped in Jovan. We don't have much time." Jovan slumped his shoulders, allowing the android to secure his chair to the ship's floor, before moving onto his harnesses at the navigation station.

The Red Rover's engines powered up as the force-field deactivated. The lower booster rockets initiated, slowly rising off the ground as the ship struggled to lift off, blowing dirt in every direction. Many of the metallic rods fell out of place as the ground shifted due to the ship's movement. The Red Rover continued to climb. Once it reached a suitable altitude free of the mountains, its primary rockets activated, shooting the ship out into the sky in route to retrieve the others.

The falling meteors had begun to descend all over the landscape. Some of the bigger ones had broken apart in Cnaeus' atmosphere. One in particular landed in the exact location of their training camp for these last few months. The meteor crushed everything in its path, leaving nothing but a crater. Even if the Red Rover had its force-field active, there was no telling if it would have been powerful enough to protect the ship from the velocity of such an onslaught. Their departure came at not a moment too soon.

<>

Marius could see Gordie, Callista and Andrew from the WaftMar cockpit as they exited the mountain pass, entering the landing zone. Running with their weapons, suits and gear on their backs was definitely taking its toll. They looked exhausted.

The WaftMar was still several yards away. Even with the lightning striking all around, his neophytes were undeterred. The finish line was in sight as they mustered up every bit of strength they had to make it back. The cabin door slid open as the three neophytes hopped inside. Marius looked back at them from the cockpit.

"Where are the others?"

"They're still in the forest." Andrew answered.

Marius watched as Andrew, Callista and Gordie removed their helmets. They definitely had no intention of going back outside. He turned back to the cockpit console. "No, no, no." Marius quietly banged his forehead so the neophytes couldn't see nor hear him. This situation was only getting worse with each passing moment.

He took a deep breath, re-composing himself. If he couldn't keep it together, then what chance did they have? "Okay, okay, get strapped in. We have to wait." The neophytes followed his instructions as Marius was about to do the same.

A long, loud whistling was heard as Marius looked skyward, his vision above somewhat obstructed from being in the cockpit. The three neophytes wondered what that could be as well as they immediately crowded around the cabin windows. Marius looked out his cockpit window to see a smaller meteoroid hurtling straight for the second mountain range on the opposite side of the valley.

"Oh No!" Marius gasped as the rock soared overhead casting a brief, yet frightening shadow over the forest. Rio,

Orion and June were still down there and he had no way to rescue them.

CHAPTER SEVENTEEN

THE RIPPLE EFFECT

The meteor screamed over top of the wooded valley, a collision with the second mountain was imminent. Orion looked skyward as the clatter above him, June and Rio was too boisterous to ignore. The meteor smashed the mountain creating a deafening crash. The force of impact so powerful that the neophytes were tossed like ragdolls to the ground. The collision sent a shockwave across the valley that must have been felt even as far as the WaftMar on the next mountain.

June stumbled, before looking around for Orion and Rio, who also seemed to be disoriented from the crash. "What the hell was that?" A fear permeated her eyes. This had gone way beyond what Marius had in mind for them as a final exercise.

Orion was the first to get back to his feet, draping his weapon over his shoulder. "I don't think we wanna know. Come on guys, get up, we gotta keep moving." He extended both hands to them as Rio grabbed his left, while June grabbed his right. Orion reared back, pulling both girls to their feet. The three neophytes immediately checking one another to make sure nobody was injured. Rio and June would follow his lead, draping their weapons over their shoulders. They resumed their journey back to the WaftMar, picking up the pace. Time was of the essence.

The fallout from the meteor crash had begun as the mountain itself was fissuring. The ground closest to it had also started to give way. Slowly but surely the wooded valley was eroding along with the damaged rock, sinking further into the interior of the planet. Unlike the simulator, there would be no crystal blue lake below to break their falls. No, in real life, there was only a hollow interior to an unexplored abyss that awaited.

Marius sat in the cockpit rubbing his chin as another conundrum had begun to rear its ugly head. The longer the WaftMar remained on the landing zone, the more vulnerable they were to the same fate that befell the second mountain. He owed it to the three neophytes in back, not to mention the three still on the ground to come up with an alternative that didn't revolve around them being sitting ducks.

Marius activated the ship's console. The circumstances around him having made his decision was a no-brainer. "Are you all strapped in yet?" Marius continued checking the instruments to make sure they were ready for take-off.

"I thought you said we aren't leaving them?" Andrew responded.

If Marius were willing to leave, then they would know that the danger was much worse than he had been letting on. That scenario would be anything but reassuring. Marius turned back to his three neophytes. This was a moment where they needed to see his sincerity and that he was just as determined as they were to see their mates back safely.

"We aren't. Just hold on." Marius unearthed a comforting smile before making eye contact with each of them. He had never let them down before and he hadn't planned on starting now. Marius turned his attention back to the console. His words were all he had to give them right now, so they were just going to have to take them at face value.

The WaftMar propellers began to spin as the three neophytes put their helmets back on. The ship lifted off, the electrical storm had made it so that Marius couldn't fly too fast for fear that the energy it was using would attract the lightning, so the movements of the WaftMar needed to be deliberate.

Lightning struck thrice, barely missing the WaftMar on one of those occasions. The neophytes cringed from how close it was to them. Nothing they had done up to now could have ever prepared them for what they were currently enduring. This was new for all of them, even Marius.

Orion, June and Rio remained determined in their desire to escape the disintegrating forest. The neophytes didn't dare look back for fear that it would only slow them down.

Luckily for them, Marius had called off the exercise just early enough to keep them safely away from ground zero of the devastation. Had they been any closer, it might have been game over. At their current pace, it wouldn't be long until they reached the WaftMar.

There were still falling rocks from the crumbling mountain behind them, although thankfully none were as large as the meteor that crashed moments ago. Some of the trees closest to the mountain had been uprooted as they slammed into others that were still upright, creating even more rubble.

Above the trees, still below the mountain peak, the sound of the WaftMar circling the area could barely be heard amongst the bedlam. There was also no way to see the neophytes on the ground. "Orion, June, Rio, can you hear me?"

"We hear you, Dr. Marius." Rio came to a stop as the other two followed her lead. She looked back at them, just to be sure they were still together.

Marius breathed a sigh of relief in their ears. "I'm going to get you out, but I need you all to get to higher ground first. There's no place for us to land."

The three neophytes remained still, having just received new orders. "Higher ground? What higher ground? The mountain's still that way." June pointed. Surely, she couldn't be the only one thinking that Marius's plan was ridiculous. Orion looked skyward, there were nothing but tall trees as far as the eye could see.

"We gotta climb." Orion said.

"Are you crazy? We'll never make it." June crossed her arms, almost pouting, she was on the verge of becoming hysterical. This had gone on long enough. If only she were at home right now, safely tucked away in her bed with her precious pillows. Anything would be better than this. Their lives being in danger was never supposed to be a part of the mission. Orion reached out, putting both hands on her shoulders. This was his attempt to comfort her, the same way he remembered Delly with Pharaoh when they parted ways those many months before.

"June, this is what we've been training for, we can do it. We just gotta do it together." June looked away, but Orion stood firm. She turned to him, looking deep into his eyes. Somehow, he wasn't afraid. Orion actually believed what he was telling her. "Right?"

"Right." Rio placed a hand on June's left shoulder as well.

June nodded, not that she had much of a choice. If they thought she could do it, then maybe she should stop doubting herself and give it a shot. Rio approached a nearby tree, digging her boot into the bark first. She attempted to climb as Orion and June gave her some assistance, pushing under her backside. She reached the closest branch to them, using her upper body strength to lift herself.

"Looks like all those push-ups Marius had you doing are finally coming in handy."

Rio looked down at Orion, unamused. "Just for that, I'm helping June first." Orion shrugged as Rio extended her hand to June. With a boost from Orion, in no time at all, the two girls were side by side. Now it was Orion's turn.

Just as Orion was about to dig his boot into the bark several electric charges were shot in their direction. Orion fell back to the ground, ducking for cover as the two girls held tightly to the tree. The second duplicate was shooting at them from a hidden perch somewhere in the forest.

"Dr. Marius, we have a problem?" Rio called out.

"We're almost there, just hold on."

Rio continued. "But the robot is shooting at us."

The duplicate continued shooting as June and Rio remained stuck in their current locations, clinging to the other side of the tree. They were unable to climb higher nor find a different place to move.

Orion shook off his fall, his eyes tracking Rio and June. He turned his attention to the trees where the electric charges were being fired from, even if he couldn't see the duplicate itself. He quietly removed his weapon from his shoulder, bringing it into ready position. He steadied his shot, locking into an area, letting off several rounds.

The fusion blasts from Orion's weapon destroyed several branches, just missing the duplicate, while forcing it out of hiding and into the open. Orion shot several more times as the duplicate ducked behind a larger tree. Shrapnel from the bark flew as Orion continued shooting. The duplicate remained hidden, patiently waiting for an opening. Orion paused, thinking he may had gotten it, but his hesitation only served to give the duplicate an opportunity to return fire. Orion leapt back into the snow to avoid being shot.

"Keep going guys. I'm right behind you."

Orion took three short breaths, hopping to his feet. He took off running, shooting blindly in the direction of the duplicate to give himself some cover fire. His adrenaline had kicked into overdrive. The duplicate waited for Orion to stop shooting, before giving chase. He wanted the android's attention, well now he had it.

June watched as the duplicate passed underneath them in its pursuit of Orion. With both Orion and the android disappearing from view, she paused. June received a tap on her helmet as she turned to Rio.

"Come on June, up we go."

June watched Rio resume her climb as June had no choice but to follow her lead. If they were going to get to the top, they still had a long way to go. This tree was enormous.

<>

The robot. What robot could she be... oh, there was still a second duplicate out there that hadn't been accounted for.

Marius keyed a few controls, changing the screen back to their training mission. The duplicate was close to all three neophytes. Marius attempted to shut the duplicate down as another bolt of lightning struck, this time landing a direct hit on the WaftMar.

The neophytes inside the cabin screamed as the WaftMar dropped several feet. With the ship going haywire from the surge in energy, Marius fought with everything he had to regain control of the reins, giving his all to swing the ship around, keeping it upright and steady. Once stable, he attempted to shut the duplicate down again, but the console sparked, there was a malfunction. He wouldn't be able to deactivate it from up here.

The WaftMar resumed closing in on Rio and June's position, however, due to the threatening weather, along with the falling meteors, their location was a disaster waiting to happen. Marius was doing yeoman's work to keep the WaftMar steady. "Okay guys, I've got an idea. I need you to get your grappling hooks out."

"Sir?" Andrew responded as he and Callista exchanged looks.

"Just do it. And stay strapped in, do you understand me?"

"Yes sir." The neophytes deftly removed their backpacks, while remaining strapped into their seats. Marius checked his navigation screen once more. He could see the two girls still climbing the tree via their signatures.

"Damnit, there's only two of them." The plan he was cooking up would've allowed them to grab all three. "Alright guys, change of plans. I can only see two of them, so I need you to listen to me very carefully. I'm about to open the door and when I do, I need you to shoot your grappling hooks into the tallest tree closest to us."

Andrew and Callista remained focused and ready while Gordie's eyes had never been wider. His hands were trembling. This was definitely the moment where he wished he had taken their rock climbing exercises a little more seriously. His body language wanted zero part in having to do this.

"Once that's done, you need to wrap your end to the base of your seat, so you create tension and don't lose control. Got it?" Marius slightly turned back, "If you don't do it exactly as I said, you could rip your arm off."

Callista and Andrew gulped. The last thing they needed to hear was that their potential rescue of their mates could end in them losing a limb, even if it was imperative that they knew the risks. Gordie leaned forward behind them. "He's talking to you guys."

Andrew and Callista turned back to Gordie, before looking at each other, shaking their heads. "Oh Gordie." Thankfully, they were up to the task otherwise their friends would be in big trouble.

The WaftMar leveled out as Marius struggled to keep it in a holding pattern amid the worsening conditions. The cabin door slid open as the high winds immediately slammed them, destabilizing the cabin. Luckily for the neophytes they were still wearing their helmets or it would have made it very difficult for them to breathe.

"Are we ready?" Marius took short breaths as he didn't have a helmet. Andrew and Callista looked out. They could see June and Rio still climbing the tree from their position. Beads of sweat were coming down Marius's face as the WaftMar controls were hanging tough. "Do you see them or not?"

Andrew turned back to Callista, sharing reassuring nods. "We see them sir."

"Well then what are you waiting for? Do it!"

Callista and Andrew held their left arms forward, their grappling hook arm bands securely fastened. Callista pushed her button first as Andrew followed her lead a moment later. The grappling hooks screamed out of the WaftMar cabin, traveling through the inclement weather passing several trees, before hitting different parts of the same tree, expanding and latching solidly onto it.

Andrew and Callista carefully removed their arm bands, not wanting to hit the return button, which would make this plan null and void. They wrapped their ends of the grappling hook around the bottom of the seats as Marius had instructed.

The grappling hook lines were several feet above Rio and June. "What the hell was that?" The jostling from the hooks almost caused June to lose her balance. She held tightly to the tree. She looked down, then immediately back up. Falling at this height was not an option.

Rio looked skyward. She could see the two grappling hooks embedded in the upper portion of the tree. "Above us. Come on, we're almost there." Rio resumed climbing as June struggled to keep up with her.

Rio reached the lower hook, tugging on it, making sure it was secure. Rio then continued to climb for the higher one as June watched her. "Rio, what are you doing?" Rio stopped her ascent, looking down on her.

"You grab this one. I'll get the other. Come on. You can do it." Rio gave her a reassuring nod. She refused to move until June did. June eventually reached a branch which was just below the lower grappling hook. She climbed up a little more, reaching out to grab the end of the hook. She began tugging on it, up and down, until it broke loose from the tree.

"I got it. Now what am I supposed to do with this?"

"Tie it around you June."

"Oh yeah, duh." June tied the end of the grappling hook around her waist. She then minimized the hook, before tucking it under her armpit. "Okay, I'm secure."

"What about you Rio?" Marius' voice rang in her helmet.

"Almost there." Rio closed in on the higher hook, but unfortunately at this height, there wasn't a branch for her to use as leverage, so she was going to have to jump for it. If she were to guess wrong, it would literally be all she wrote. Rio took a moment to compose herself, she knew she could do this. She imagined how Zenobia would handle this situation. A true leader didn't have time for fear. They only had time to act.

Rio opened her eyes, jumped for the hook line. She held on tightly as if she were a trapeze artist.

"Rio!" June watched with big eyes. Up close, that was a scary sight to behold.

"I'm okay." Rio remained focused on the hook line. Somehow, someway she was going to have to get this line wrapped around her body. She would never be able to hold on long enough to get to safety.

"Hold on." June continued watching as Rio struggled. All she could do was hope Rio could find the strength to figure her way out of this predicament.

Rio began swinging dangerously on the line, mustering up all the strength she had, maneuvering her legs back towards the tree bark. Her boots landed against it, her body was now parallel to the hook line. However, she now had the leverage she needed to lift herself over the line. She scaled the line closer to the tree, bending her knees to give her the extra power she needed to lift her left forearm over the hook line. Once her left was up, her right would be a piece of cake. Rio then wrapped both of her arms around the line as best she could.

"Rio, are you secure?" Marius's lips had turned white around the edges from the moisture and air pressure. He was growing ever impatient that he still couldn't give the order.

"As secure as I'm ever gonna be."

Marius nodded, her answer was good enough for him. "Okay guys, pull 'em in."

Andrew and Callista reached below them, pushing the return buttons on their grappling hooks. The hook lines recoiled as June and Rio were sucked back to the WaftMar, kicking and screaming, holding on for dear life as they crashed back inside the cabin.

The two girls rammed into Callista and Andrew respectively, having flipped seat partners from their ride here. Gordie leaned forward, seeing all four of his friends, writhing in pain from their collision. "We got 'em sir!"

With the two girls safely onboard, Marius closed the WaftMar door, finally stabilizing the cabin. "Red Rover, come in. Where the devil are you?" Marius tapped his headset microphone, a mix of anger and concern in his voice. It had been some time since he had heard from them and he wasn't sure how much longer he could continue to keep the WaftMar airborne.

"We're closing in on your position sir. Please standby." Marius shook his head. If they made it out of this one alive, it would be a miracle.

Orion continued running through the forest, which began to look a shell of its former self due to the ruined mountain. The duplicate continued to give chase shooting at him as Orion was unable to retaliate without nearly getting hit himself. He dodged the shots, eventually taking cover behind a snow embankment.

Orion was breathing heavy. "What the hell am I doing? Why am I running from it?"

In all the confusion, he, along with everyone else, had forgotten that the duplicates could only shoot a charge that temporarily stunned them. Their weapons were always different from the neophytes. The exercise had already been called off, so he was running away for nothing. Orion closed his eyes, exhaled. He had no legitimate reason to be afraid now. He stepped out from behind the tree. "Here I am. Come and get me." He spread his arms, goading the android into a showdown.

The duplicate emerged from the shadows as Orion tossed his primary weapon to the ground. He was now unarmed. The duplicate continued approaching as Orion had his left hand dropped near his side-arm. As the duplicate raised its arms to shoot him, Orion quickly drew his sidearm, dodging the duplicates shot. He returned fire to the duplicate, connecting twice with the android's chest.

The duplicate fell into the snow as Orion put the side-arm to his mouth, blew over top of it. "Like taking candy from Pharaoh." Orion put his side-arm back beside his hip, the magnet taking over from there. He retrieved his primary weapon, draping it back over his shoulder, when he heard more rumbling.

He looked skyward as another meteor was coming in hard, hot and fast. This one was about the size of a boulder, however, the speed in which it impacted the woods totally devastated the landscape. More trees were upended. Danger was all around. The force blew Orion forward as he slammed helmet first into a tree, which cracked the shield protecting his face. He crumpled to the ground in agony.

Orion remained on the ground, writhing in pain. He rolled onto his chest, popping his helmet off, before batting it away. Getting thrown into a tree like that probably gave him a concussion. He was bleeding from his nose and his forehead as he touched it. He brought his hand down so he could see. He was not used to seeing himself bleed.

Orion wiped the blood in the snow around him, turning it pink. He struggled to get back to his feet. He checked for his sidearm, his backpack and his primary weapon. He looked in one direction, the forest was in ruins. He turned in the opposite direction, a lot of it was still intact or so it seemed. That must be the direction he needed to travel.

<>

"Orion can you hear me? Orion?!" Marius looked out his windshield to see some of the damage caused by the boulder-sized meteor. He promised Derrick he would take care of his son and they were not leaving him behind.

Orion's helmet remained in the snow, his blood stains inside of it as Orion had left it behind. "Orion, can you hear me? Orion?"

"Do you see him?" Rio entered the cockpit, leaning over Marius's shoulder. He was too worried about Orion to scold her into getting back in her seat.

"I can't see anything. It's a mess down there."

"Maybe I can help." Rio removed her helmet as she hopped into the co-pilot's seat. Rio strapped herself in as Marius watched. He had always been impressed by her take charge attitude, but even he would have never expected this at her current age.

"What do I do now sir?"

Marius pointed to the navigation screen and the buttons that controlled it. "Check for his heat signature. See if you can locate him."

"Yes sir."

Marius took a brief glance behind him at the other four neophytes. "The rest of you, all strapped in?"

"We are sir." Callista answered.

"Okay, here we go." Marius pulled back on the reins. The WaftMar was now beginning its search for Orion. They needed to figure out another way to rescue him.

The WaftMar flew over the trees as Marius struggled to avoid the lightning and falling meteors. He had the ship hovering at a forty-five-degree angle pointed skyward, so he could at least see what was coming at them from above. "Do you see him Rio?" Rio's eyes were glued to the navigation screen in front of her.

"I think so." The bead on Orion was faint, but there definitely was something below from the flash on her screen. "According to this, we should be almost right over top of him."

Unfortunately for them, Orion's helmet, which was how Marius had been able to track the neophytes all along, remained in the same place Orion had left it. "Orion, can you hear me? We're right above you. Orion?" Rio turned to Marius. "He's not responding Sir. What does that mean?"

"It means, either he's not wearing his helmet or… worse." Rio dropped her head, nothing in her fiber could bring her to believe that Orion wasn't still with them. He risked his life for her and June. They had to find him.

"Dr. Marius, do you copy?" Marius snapped to attention, a familiar voice in his headset.

"We hear you Dee-Dee. I sure hope you're close." Marius and Rio exchanged hopeful looks at one another.

From just over yonder through the electrical storm, the Red Rover finally appeared, cloaking the WaftMar from above. Marius and Rio immediately noticed the darkness that engulfed them. They were no longer alone and now had some heavy-duty protection. "What's happening sir?"

"The cavalry's arrived." Marius smiled. At last, a stroke of good fortune for him and the neophytes. Boy, did they ever need it. He lowered the nose of the WaftMar, keeping it steady. With the Red Rover obscuring them, he no longer had to worry about something damaging them from above, at least temporarily. "Dee-Dee, open the rear loading bay. We're coming in."

"Yes sir."

Rio reached out to Marius's right arm. "But what about Orion? We can't just leave him."

Marius winked at her. "I hadn't planned on it. Trust me."

The Red Rover remained steady in the air as the autopilot was now engaged. Next the loading bay doors began to open. Marius maneuvered the WaftMar into a U-turn, flying out from underneath the Red Rover. The WaftMar climbed until it became parallel with the Red Rover's position, making a second U-turn as it flew back towards the ship.

The WaftMar entered the loading bay, flying in much faster than it usually would under normal circumstances. Its blade clipping against the Red Rover upon entry, which jerked them back and forth as Marius attempted to maintain control, decelerate and land safely.

The neophytes braced themselves for a bumpy landing as the WaftMar spun around several times before powering off, touching down with a thud.

CHAPTER EIGHTEEN

NEOPHYTES NO LONGER

The WaftMar powered down as Marius leaned way back in his seat, a futile attempt to return his adrenaline and blood pressure to normal levels. He had never been in a situation like that before, that was frightening.

A moment later, he vomited to his left, the projectile landing just behind his left boot in the cockpit. Rio, still seated beside him, received a bird's eye view of his gastric incident, causing her to recoil, before quickly departing. The other neophytes still in the cabin, looked at one another, smiling. At last, it would seem that the worse was finally behind them.

Marius wiped his mouth with the backside of his hand, flicking the saliva residue away. His eyes widened in terror, in his haste to save everyone else, he had almost forgotten that Orion was still out there.

"Alright, we're inside. Close up the loading bay." Marius firmly held the microphone affixed to his headset. His body jerked once more. However, this time Marius covered his mouth, swallowing the unrest that was trying to escape. One upchuck that day was most certainly enough.

"Doing that now sir." The loading bay ramp began to close as the meteor shower could still be seen. It looked like it was raining rocks outside. How Dee-Dee had been able to pilot such a large vessel like the Red Rover without being severely impacted by the bedlam all around them was nothing short of a miracle.

"Ozone!"

"I'm here Dr. Marius."

"I need you to meet me at the side airlock. Immediately."

"On my way."

Marius unbuckled his straps. He rose to his feet, turning back to the neophytes. "Alright guys, I need you to get to the main cabin and strap in."

"Yes sir." The neophytes unbuckled their harnesses.

The Loading Bay doors were finally closed as the WaftMar's cabin door slid open. The neophytes hopped out first, hurrying towards the front of the ship. An interior door slid open as they entered the corridor running as fast as they could towards the cabin. Marius lagged behind them, he was no match for their thirteen-year-old legs, especially in his current condition.

Coming upon the air lock, the teens continued running, passing Ozone, who awaited Marius's directives. Marius entered a moment later, clearly out of breath. It had been many years since he had to run like that. His hands dropped to his knees as his back was almost completely horizontal.

"You needed me sir?"

Marius raised his left hand. What he needed was a moment, maybe two or even three. "Yes… Orion's still out there and I'll be damned if we're going to leave him behind. I need you to bring him back."

"Yes sir." The android moved to the airlock control panel to begin activating it.

The side ramp of the Red Rover began to open as the swirling air devoured the area, forcing Marius to hold on for dear life. Ozone, unaffected by the inclement conditions, gathered itself before taking a flying leap off the ship, transforming into an Eagle Hawk. The android's wings extended out. It departed as if it were shot from a cannon in search of Orion.

Marius watched as Ozone flew away. "Just hold on kid, we're coming to get you."

Orion trudged through the snow, without his helmet. His arms crossed around him, rubbing up and down, the weather was beginning to have an effect on him. His nose and ears were becoming redder by the minute. While the sky above had become brighter from Galicia's supernova, it was still freezing cold on the surface of the planet. Fatigue was setting in. Hours had passed since he departed from the Red Rover for this exercise.

Orion lost his balance, falling to the ground once again, perplexed by the deteriorating conditions around him. What he originally believed was the correct direction was leading him right back to the danger he had worked so hard to escape. He was cold, tired, hungry and had no idea what to expect next. He eventually noticed what looked like a cliff about fifteen feet ahead of him.

He slowly regained his footing, approaching the cliff. He reached the edge, taking a gander below, it was exactly like his missions in the simulator, albeit there was no lake. Just a large hole filled with the debris caused by the fallen asteroids. Orion shook his head; he wasn't totally sure what to make of all this. He was alone. He looked around, then above. The falling cosmic matter was as beautiful as it was terrifying. He needed to figure out his next move and fast.

High above the trees, scanning the terrain using its heat signature in search of Orion, was Ozone. In an environment like this, Orion shouldn't be that difficult to detect considering there was no life on Cnaeus.

"Did you find him?"

"I think I'm closing in on his position sir."

"Well then grab him and get your asses back here. Pronto." Marius continued holding on for dear life just inside of the airlock as the Red Rover was now flying in a circular pattern above the area. Remaining in one place was just asking for it to become damaged beyond repair, which would prove disastrous for everyone onboard.

<>

Orion had taken a defensive position between the trees as Ozone closed in on the remaining neophyte's location, unaware at the danger lurking. He instinctively held his weapon close as he closed his eyes.

In that instant, it was like Orion was transported back to the simulator where he first encountered the ravenous snow leopards just as they were ready to finish him off. Orion reached for his waist, this time his side-arm was still with him. He was tired of running and he was no longer afraid, which was probably the concussion talking for him.

270

"Orion don't shoot." Orion snapped out of his haze, his weapon drawn. Ozone, still in its bird-like form, attempted to swoop in closer to him. "Orion. It's me, Ozone. I'm getting you out of here."

"Ozone?" Orion's eyebrow rose in suspicion. He had never seen Ozone outside of its android form. And the last time he saw an Eagle Hawk, it was one of the duplicates, so this had to be the other one trying to win the mission. Orion raised his weapon, steadying his shot. "Nice try."

He began shooting at Ozone, who abruptly changed direction, seeking cover. Orion had shown tremendous improvement with his shooting accuracy, nearly clipping Ozone several times before the android was forced to take evasive action and regroup.

"What's happening out there?" Marius asked.

"Sir, he's shooting at me."

"I don't believe this." Marius face palmed. The level of danger around them was worsening by the minute. If he didn't act fast, they were all going to die. "Ozone, listen to me. Do whatever it takes to incapacitate him. We're running out of time."

Ozone looped around, the situation had become the literal definition of do or die. It spotted Orion from a distance, not realizing that Orion was already a step ahead of it. Orion resumed his attack as Ozone attempted to maneuver around him, while the conditions continued to worsen around them. It dodged the fusion blasts as best it could, but Orion managed to ding one of its wings just enough, forcing Ozone to bank left to avoid getting shot more or crashing into a tree. If the android was to crash, they'd both be doomed.

"Yeah, uhhh, I gotcha your ass." Orion threw his hands up in triumph, mission accomplished or so he hoped.

Ozone made one final swoop around, sneaking up behind Orion, who realized what was happening a few seconds too late. Before Orion could gather himself into another shot, a fishing net was deployed from Ozone's under carriage. Orion attempted to turn and run, but just as he was about to do so the netting enveloped him, subduing him with an electric charge.

Orion screamed out more in frustration than agony as the charge rendered him unconscious, collapsing to the ground.

Ozone swooped in, grabbing the netting with its talons. It began carrying Orion out of the forest dodging the falling rock fragments on the way back to the Red Rover.

<>

"Target acquired sir."

"Great job soldier. We're waiting for you." Marius smiled, removing his headset. He breathed a huge sigh of relief. He took an oath to protect these young people and would have never forgiven himself if he violated that oath.

Marius could see Ozone approaching in the distance. He waved the android to hurry up. Orion remained unconscious in the netting. Ozone entered the airlock moving way too fast as Orion's attack on it had caused several of its balance mechanisms to malfunction. Ozone crashed into the wall, dropping Orion in the process. Once they were safely inside, Marius keyed the airlock control panel causing it to close, stabilizing the area around them from the elements outside.

Ozone transformed back into its standard android form as Marius hurried towards Orion. He ripped the netting apart, began gently smacking Orion to wake him. "Orion. Orion, can you hear me?"

Orion looked dazed, the electric charge temporarily sapping him of his strength. "Dr. Marius? Did we win?" Orion's eyes barely opened.

Marius smiled, letting out a slight chuckle. "Yeah, you did great kid."

"Dr. Marius, Dee-Dee is calling you to the cockpit." Marius gently lowered Orion, before rising to his feet and turning his attention to Ozone.

"Get Orion strapped in, then join us in the cockpit."

Ozone nodded. "Yes sir." Marius took off towards the front of the ship as Ozone slowly helped Orion back to his feet.

Dee-Dee and Jovan remained in the cockpit as Marius entered. "What's going on? Why are we still sitting here?" He immediately made a beeline for his android pilot.

"Sir, we still have not received word from the Rover Base Alpha. It's as if they were unable to communicate with us."

"Jesus." Marius and Jovan exchanged eye contact. For the good of any mission, Marius had to always remain cool, calm and collected, even in the face of extreme conditions. If he didn't keep it together, how could they be expected to?

"And that's not all... the asteroid ring that protects the planet, is collapsing back towards the surface."

"Yeah, I kinda figured that one out on my own. Time to get us out of here, Dee-Dee. Full throttle." Marius climbed back into the captain's seat.

"Yes sir." Dee-Dee flipped several switches. The time to bid Cnaeus adieu had finally arrived as the android confidently steered the ship.

The booster rockets of the Red Rover activated. It stopped hovering, beginning to fly away. Before they could depart the planet, however, they would first need to build enough momentum. The Rover departed the area between the two mountains. Moments after it did, a huge meteor would come screaming by, a thunderous boom as it landed against the wooded valley, completely destroying it forever.

The ferocity of the impact sent the area whistling in every direction. The Red Rover was jostled as well as Dee-Dee did its best to maintain control. The neophytes could also feel the impact from outside in the cabin. Would they ever be free from this mayhem? The Red Rover continued to increase in speed, dodging the falling asteroids. Dee-Dee pulled back on the reins causing the ship to begin its ascent.

Through the dashboard windshield it looked as if they were flying right into the heart of a stone-related hell. Dee-Dee flipped a few more switches, activating the Red Rover's defense mechanisms.

"I don't believe it." Marius whispered. Aside from the falling meteors, what remained of Sonain and its many moons seemed to be dangerously close to Cnaeus, as if they were invading its orbit. Worlds were colliding. The Red Rover dodged the meteors as if this were a video game. As larger meteors impeded their path, Dee-Dee fired projectile rockets which broke them up, clearing the skies.

Cnaeus' gravitational field was all out of whack now as the cabin pressure was rising to levels beyond the Rover's technological capabilities. The neophytes could barely move a muscle as their arms and legs became contorted. From the looks on their faces, this experience was quite uncomfortable.

With Orion safely strapped into a seat, Ozone began moving toward the front of the cabin. The pressure against the android was so severe that it could barely move. Ozone gripped the two seats in front of it, but gravity continued pulling against it the more vertical the Red Rover became. Eventually, the pressure was too much for even Ozone to overcome as sparks began to fly, a malfunction forthcoming.

To save itself from a total shutdown, Ozone released its grip of the chairs, hurtling backwards, crashing into the wall with a loud thud, damaging the back wall. The pressure in the cabin was so intense, the neophytes could barely move their heads even the slightest bit to check on Ozone.

Jovan's eyes were filled with tears as he winced. Without his helmet, he felt the full brunt of the atmospheric pressure pushing his skin back into his bones. Marius was no different as Dee-Dee continued to do its best to fly the Red Rover out of harm's way.

"Ahhh, what's happening?" Jovan was practically smiling as the pressure was so severe that he couldn't even keep his mouth closed.

"It's the gravitational field. Its intensity is unlike anything I've ever dealt with."

"Give it everything you've got Dee-Dee, whatever it takes. You can do it." Marius had become delirious from the pain.

His arms and legs were now limp. This was enough to make a person feel like they were having a stroke.

"Yes sir." Dee-Dee fought the gravity with its right hand, placing it over a secondary throttle lever. Dee-Dee continued to reach for it, its hand sparking as the pressure was destroying it. It grabbed the lever, using all of its strength to pull back on it, which sent a bellow throughout the Red Rover, the ship was finally at full power.

Every booster and afterburner on the Red Rover activated as the ship maneuvered past the few remaining rocks, breaching the upper atmosphere of Cnaeus causing the pressure to finally subside. The Red Rover entered the devastated solar system surrounded by decaying planets, distant light particles and fragments from Galicia.

Marius shielded his eyes as space was brighter than he ever could have imagined it to be. This couldn't be right. The asteroid ring that had been protecting Cnaeus, for billions of years more than likely, was almost totally gone. The planets closest to Galicia, had either been decimated or destroyed.

Jovan was seeing the exact same thing as Marius, but his first thoughts had nothing to do with the planets. "Dr. Marius." Jovan turned to him. "Where's the Rover Base?"

For the first time ever, Marius seemed to be totally speechless. He was fearing the worse but the last thing he wanted to do was share that with him or the other neophytes. Marius pulled out the keyboard attached to his chair, typing in a code which shaded all of the windows in the main cabin. If the worse had happened, better to only have to lie to Jovan than all of them at once.

Fragments of the Rover Base Alpha could be seen floating around. It was patently obvious that there were no survivors onboard.

<>

Peace and tranquility had somewhat returned as the light from the solar system continued to wane. The Red Rover was floating through the silent darkness, unsure of where they would end up next.

Orion looked around at everyone sitting behind him. They were all quiet, still pretty shaken up by the events of today. Not even Gordie could muster up a single joke. The reality that they almost perished on Cnaeus was not lost on them. June covered her face, hiding tears no doubt. She was not the only one doing that. That was the scariest situation they've ever had to endure. May it never happen again.

Moments later, Jovan rolled in as Marius was right behind him. The others perked up upon seeing them, quietly awaiting instruction from Marius. After what they had just gone through, surely he would have something positive they could hold onto.

Marius cleared his throat. His demeanor was somber. "First of all, let me state for the record that I am incredibly proud of you all." He made it a point to make eye contact with everyone. "What you've accomplished over this last month or so has been nothing short of remarkable. Your growth, undeniable."

Callista's eyes wandered to Jovan's face, he was struggling to hold back tears as well. "Something's wrong? What aren't you telling us sir?" Marius paused, fishing for the right words.

"The Rover Base is gone."

"Gone. What do you mean gone? It can't be gone." The anxiousness in the room grew as June abruptly stood. Surely Jovan was mistaken.

"How can this be?" Rio shook her head back and forth, not wanting to believe. Her entire family with the exception of her father were still on board the Rover Base. She would never accept that they had just abandoned her. That just wasn't the type of family she came from. Their station may have been of the lower variety, but they were a close-knit group from observing them over the years.

The neophytes were literally two seconds from bombarding Marius with a million and one questions. He raised his arms in an attempt to pacify them. "Guys listen up. At the moment, the Rover Base is not currently showing up on our radar."

"So what are you saying? That they left the solar system without us? How could they do that? Why would they leave without us?" Gordie asked. He was becoming frantic.

"What about my family? Are you saying I'm never gonna see them again?" Orion's eyes welled up with tears. To think that his mother, father and Pharaoh could be gone. This couldn't possibly be real life.

"Unfortunately, I can't answer that." Marius's words had done nothing to assuage their concerns. Callista covered her mouth. Her lips were quivering as she began making sad noises. She was mere seconds from full on crying.

"Oh my God." Rio put both hands to her head, none of this was making any sense. Up until now she had shown tremendous poise but even she had her limits. After all, they were still only thirteen nor were they ready to believe that they were all that's left of their space community.

"I'm sorry guys, I truly am. Until we have more information, I am as much in the dark as you are. That being said, we have to keep our heads, do you understand?" Marius was trying his best to keep everyone in line. It was not working as their minds continued to gravitate towards the worst-case scenario. There would be no "Yes sirs" coming his way until he could provide them with answers.

"So are we all that's left Dr. Marius?" Andrew asked.

Marius didn't respond, this was overwhelming even to him. He looked at Andrew. If any of them knew what it was like to lose loved ones prematurely and without warning, it would be him. Thankfully, Marius had never been in a situation like this before and it showed. He was never prepared to have to relay this kind of news to teenagers, even if he totally understood their anger and confusion. It would be very easy to accept hopelessness, if he wasn't the one they looked to for leadership.

What was to become of them without the Rover Base? Not only would I be responsible for taking care of myself, but I had seven young people, one of whom was severely injured, to look after as well. If the Rover Base was really gone, I would be their parents now.

Marius rubbed the back of his head, his courage was in doubt. He remained unsure if it would be best to just tell them the truth or at least what he believed to be the truth. After all they couldn't be children forever, at some point they were going to have to grow up and see the downsides of their existence.

From the very first time they met, he explained to them that the wonders of the universe were often counterbalanced by the dangers. If they didn't believe him then, surely they would see what he was talking about now.

"Dr. Marius."

Marius and the neophytes looked to the rear of the cabin where Ozone remained. The android was still embedded against the back wall suffered during the Red Rover's furious escape from Cnaeus' atmosphere.

"Dee-Dee is communicating that she is picking up a signal from a beacon at the far reaches of the solar system. One of ours."

Marius's shoulders rose. "The Rover Base?"

"She hasn't indicated with one-hundred percent certainty, but she is charting a course to the beacon as we speak."

"Maybe that's them. They're probably waiting for us." Orion smiled widely as he slapped the headrest of his seat in celebration.

Marius noticed the faces of his neophytes lighting up at the possibility that it was the Rover Base. It was remarkable how quickly their moods could see-saw from distressed to exuberant. He realized that this may be the only way he could keep them from losing all hope. He understood if he were to let them succumb to those dark thoughts, in that very dark place, that he would be sealing their fate. No mission could work without hope and faith, especially for the neophytes. They had to believe in themselves, but most importantly, they had to believe in each other.

"Exactly! That's exactly what they're doing. And we're not going to just float around here wondering when they're going to come back and get us. We're going to go out and find them, because that's what we do." Marius made it a point to make eye contact with each of his students. "Isn't that right?"

"Yes sir." The neophytes' confidence had stabilized. He was fortunate that not only were their attention spans short, but also that, deep down, they never wanted to believe that all of their loved ones were gone. That wouldn't be a future worth living in.

"Alright then. It appears that we've just been given our first mission, cadets. From this point forward, you are neophytes no longer. The time has come for you to put the skills you've been honing these past couple of months to good use." Marius unearthed a smile. He was speaking to himself just as much as he was speaking to them. "You all have been chomping at the bit for new experiences free from the Rover Base. Well here it is. This is your moment. Seize it."

The now-cadets, with the exception of Jovan, who still didn't seem to be completely buying this stroke of good news, looked at one another, their confidence swelling. Jovan remained stoic, sitting in silence as Marius had given his comrades another mission they could believe in. After all they had endured together thus far, their lives had been irrevocably changed forever.

<>

Marius sat quietly in the cockpit of the Red Rover, his left hand massaging his chin. He had assuaged the fears of his students, but the question remained just how long would he be able to keep it that way? The journey for them was only just beginning.

Dee-Dee was at the controls; its right hand was badly in need of repair. The same could be said for Ozone, regrettably. The ship was now set on a course to find a beacon, not totally sure what they would discover once they reached it. If they ever reached it.

In that moment, Marius was reminded of the three beacons sent out a half-million miles away from their position by the Blue, Green and Yellow Rovers. Ultimately, it would be through the successes of those Rovers that his group would survive. After all, they were still just kids, regardless of if he no longer considered them to be his neophytes.

The Red Rover traveled farther and farther away from the epicenter of the cosmic destruction in what was formerly known as the Galicia star system. With each passing moment the remnants of Galicia diminished, this was what a dead solar system looked like. The remaining planets that were untouched by the supernova had darkened. Now orphaned, they too would soon become shells of their former selves, perhaps annexed by another star system yet to materialize in another million years.

Marius let out a deep sigh, a smile inexplicably emerging from his lips. Even after facing such a hellacious ordeal, there was still hope. They were not alone. Primarily because they had each other.

Deep in his core, Marius had to believe that their best was yet to come; if for no other reason than they had proved to him, not to mention themselves… that they were survivors.

THE END

C.E. WHITAKER III

A writer/director/producer living in Los Angeles, C.E. was born and raised in Hollis, Queens (NYC). He attended Bradley University in Peoria, Illinois, graduating with a BA in Radio/TV Production. In 2016, C.E. was selected as a finalist in the Warner Bros Emerging Film Director's Workshop. In recent years, he has optioned a sports feature as well as a political drama pilot. He has also written, directed and produced two (2) short films.

In 2019, he worked in London on the Guy Ritchie-directed feature, *THE GENTLEMEN*, for Miramax/STX, starring Colin Farrell, Matthew McConaughey, Charlie Hunnam & Hugh Grant and the Sir Kenneth Branagh-directed fantasy adventure, *ARTEMIS FOWL*; 2018, saw him work on the Jessica Chastain led-feature, *EVE*, directed by Tate Taylor in Boston; 2017 was busier with the Dan Gilroy-directed film *ROMAN J. ISRAEL, ESQ.,* starring Denzel Washington & Carmen Ejogo; the Chicago-based feature, *WIDOWS*, directed by Steven McQueen starring Viola Davis, Liam Neeson, Michelle Rodriguez, Elizabeth Debicki, Cynthia Erivo, Robert Duvall, Brian Tyree Henry & Daniel Kaluuya; and the live-action re-imagining of Disney's *DUMBO* directed by Tim Burton, starring Danny DeVito, Michael Keaton & Eva Green in London.

When he was a senior in college, C.E. had the pleasure of meeting the late Ray Bradbury, who told him that C.E. reminded him of a young Orson Welles. There is a possibility that Ray was simply being nice, but he did autograph C.E.'s copy of the Martian Chronicles, stating the following: *"to Charles, S.O.B., love Ray."* The context of this coming from a story told by Ray to C.E. and his classmates about meeting the legendary W.C. Fields for the very first time. Fields said, *"son, if you wanna make it in this town, you need to be a real son of a bitch."*

Follow him on Instagram: @mrwhitaker3

Made in the USA
Middletown, DE
19 April 2022

64433638R00172